I0594411

# ENEMY ALLY

## An Echo's Way Adventure

by
Mike Waller

Rampart Publishing

MIKE WALLER

# Copyright

This book utilizes American English spelling.

First edition
Published by Rampart Publishing 2019
ISBN: 9780648275572

Cover Design: 100 Covers

# Contents

## The 'ECHO'S WAY' Adventures

The Echo's Way stories relate the adventures of Cinta (Echo) Bourke, a remarkable young woman who finds herself embroiled against her will in the harsh reality of a war between the Federation of Humanity and a powerful alien neighbor, the Tolleani.

Each Book is a separate adventure, rather than part of a continuing, single story, and can be read as a stand-alone story in the life of our heroine.

**Enemy Ally** is the third adventure in Echo Bourke's journey, and tells the story of her first mission as a member of the Federation Special Missions Group. On a hostile moon, she has to rescue a group of scientists, but soon finds herself fighting for her own life. Upon her success rest the lives of thousands of federation citizens, and an entire alien species.

# Chapter One

A PALE GLOW FROM the planet's single, giant moon filtered through the dense trees to the nearby animal path, giving just sufficient illumination to ease the otherwise total black of the forest night.

The lack of light did not bother Echo. With night-vision goggles, she could see the surrounding ground easily as she lay prone in the tangled undergrowth, cushioned by vegetation that surrounded and concealed her.

Faint noises!

Muffled rustles reached her ears from the darkness, betraying the passage of small creatures moving through the night on their never-ending quest for the next meal. Echo ignored them; nothing here could bite through the resilient fabric of her sortie suit, and besides, things that were more important concerned her now.

She reached up and fine-tuned the goggles to bring the nearby bush track into sharper focus. Just ahead, a pale-green line marked the path through the ghostly vegetation. Any minute, her enemy would pass that way.

Only two passable routes existed between Echo's camp and her opponent's base. Seven kilometers apart, the sites were separated by boggy marshlands and dense tangles of choking undergrowth, the ideal arena for tonight's mission.

An animal trail was the easier way, the alternative being a rough goat-track around the rugged cliffs lining the canyon. The trail was also quicker, following the bank of a stream that meandered over the flat valley floor. Echo's plan of action relied on one certainty: Lieutenant Jackson Cooney, the enemy commander, would choose the easy route and attack her by coming this way in force. He was in for a surprise.

The mission had time constraints, and he was as aware of them as she was. The cliff passage took longer, and this business had to be settled before the first rise of this world's sun.

Echo understood her opponent well. She expected he would not only come this way, but also would move with stealth and deliberation despite the time limitations. A creature of habit, he rarely rushed anything. Tonight, his predictable behavior would be his undoing.

Echo and her companions had sprinted through the night to conceal themselves at a point two-thirds of the distance between the camps. Cooney and his men would, she hoped, pass by without detecting them hidden in the undergrowth. It was a play-off as to who would succeed tonight, but she chose to gamble knowing her opponent would not. She was confident of success.

Head turned to one side, Echo pressed her lips tightly together and willed her body to keep as still as possible. She glanced towards the dark figure lying prone in the undergrowth two meters away. Only two of her team accompanied her—the best two. The others remained behind, well hidden and ready for any attack on her camp. At what would appear to be a poorly defended site, a trap awaited.

Located in a small clearing on the southern side of the valley, her center of operations comprised little more than a few dome-tents surrounding a pole on which flew the blue pennant of her command. Below it, concealed behind a barrier of piled equipment, two soldiers crouched at the ready, back-to-back and each keeping a wary eye.

Those men would never be able to resist an attack by a larger group, and therein lay the trap. Echo's squad consisted of ten, including her, her two sharpshooter companions, and the two guarding the flag. The remaining five hid in the trees surrounding her camp, positioned to be above and behind any approaching enemy force.

Cooney's biggest failings were his predictability, his unwillingness to take risks and his complete self-assurance that he was always right. Completely lacking in imagination, he did things by the book always. How he attained his rank puzzled Echo, but she knew birth and privilege had been a factor, rather than ability. She expected him to try to surround his target, and that would be his undoing. Once there, he would find himself under attack from both front and rear.

With luck it would not come to that. If Echo reached her goal first and dispatched his guards, she could conclude the mission before he reached her base. Her break-neck sprint through the night placed her much closer to his camp than to hers. Once he passed she would move on, and her team would arrive while he was still en-route. The risk was worth taking, and Echo knew Cooney would not expect it. It paid to know your enemy.

As she waited in the darkness, she allowed her mind to reflect. A few years ago this would have been the last place she would have expected to find herself. She was now twenty-four years old. Seven eventful years had passed since the day the Tolleani invaded her planet Corros and destroyed everything she held dear, including her family, friends and the home in which she grew up. Her world crumbled then, and she spent four years surviving alone, the final year with a Tollean research base occupying the mine site near her old town.

Then Ben Teague arrived. Sent to determine whether the forces of the Federation could retake the planet, his ship was brought down by the aliens. He escaped and stumbled into her forest refuge. Together they found a way to flee the planet, but not before destroying the enemy base and stealing the research of the scientists who worked there.

Soon after, Ben received a promotion to captain, a new command and a re-deployment. Only weeks into his first mission he went missing in action after an attack by pirates, and thus began the long chain of events that led Echo to this moment.

She had decided to join the Fleet academy to become a flight officer after completing six months of intensive study. In times of war things happened quickly, and after basic training she was waiting for assignment to a ship as a junior navigator when something unexpected changed her course.

Her commanding officer proposed an alternative option, to take a tour with a special force tasked with the purpose of high-level infiltration and rescue. Every member of the division was a volunteer, many of them officers. It was a hard and dangerous assignment, but Echo's commander thought her ideally suited.

Before entering Fleet Echo had earned two Civil Cross awards, one for her activities on Corros and the other for rescuing Ben and helping the inhabitants of Kerac 5 overthrow a pirate family that held the small mining colony in virtual slavery, the same pirates who had captured Ben's ship months earlier.

Thanks to those affairs, Echo possessed greater skills in ground warfare than did the average raw recruit, and to her commander a spell in the Special Forces seemed appropriate. The division was a part of Fleet, with squads in each operational task force. Most of her service time would still be spent in space, but she would have a chance to show her ground skills as well. She accepted the proposal without hesitation.

Something else influenced her choice: the knowledge that danger gave her a thrill of elation felt at no other time. On several occasions, both on her home world and on Kerac 5, she had experienced a rush of adrenaline—a racing heartbeat, a sense of awakening and awareness, and a spreading warmth throughout her body—that she had grown to love. She was an adrenaline junky, and the threat of immediate peril added something extra to her life, something she craved.

Only Ben balked at the decision. After surviving Kerac 5, he returned to the front line of the ongoing war between the Federation and the Tollean Empire, while she attended the Academy. At first he had opposed her choice, but capitulated because of a promise that he would never stand in her way no matter what path she chose. They had seen little of each other since, and she had no idea where their relationship stood. She dreaded how it would feel if he was no longer there for her.

Echo returned her attention to the moment and checked her companions were still in position, well hidden from the track. In the dim moonlight and this dense undergrowth it was difficult to spot anyone in a matt-black sortie-suit. She lay still, listening to the sound of her own breathing, waiting for the first warning of an approach.

As the moon slid behind the clouds, the forest turned darker and became almost silent. Only the soft chatter of nocturnal wildlife disturbed the otherwise absolute quiet.

Minutes after Echo and her team concealed themselves, the faint sound of footfalls reached their ears. Whispers grew to the gentle crunch of multiple feet moving through the night. Echo lay motionless; she lifted her night-vision goggles enough to see boots as they tramped past her position.

Holding her breath, she counted off as they passed by. There were six soldiers in the group, more than expected. The enemy squad, like her own, consisted of ten in total, so four remained at their camp—four obstacles between her and her target.

For a few moments longer she waited as the footfalls faded in the direction of her camp. Her home team would have the advantage; seven against six were acceptable odds. For her, three against four was less so, but she had dealt with worse. With a wave of her hand to her companions she moved away, two shadowy, silent figures following behind.

The moon reappeared. Two kilometers remained to reach the enemy camp, and Echo picked up speed as the bush gave way to clearer grassland. In the distance black shadows marked another patch of forest, on the far side of which a rocky buttress, mottled a ghostly gray in the moonlight, stood out from the cliffs lining the basin's northern boundary. Her objective sat below the outcrop, an old, crumbled, drilling depot now little more than a derelict, concrete ruin.

Two hundred meters from the target, Echo stopped and waited for her companions to gather around. Crouched in the dense undergrowth, she raised her head and focused her night-vision on the scene ahead.

The ruined building sat hard against the buttress, the rock wall forming the rear of the ancient structure. At the front of the flat roof a flagpole carrying the red pennant of the opposing force stretched up for three meters. Around the bottom of the pole, sandbags formed a forward-facing barrier. Echo saw a movement; at least one soldier was there, in a high position from which he or she could see any approaching threat.

The other guards would be at ground level, well hidden and ready to take down anyone who attempted an attack from the front. Their barriers would be no hindrance to heavy weaponry, but were more than adequate against the light laser rifles carried by Echo and her team.

The site was approachable from several directions, and the defense covered all options. Approach from the rear appeared impossible because of the sheer rock face, and Cooney had likely assumed his enemy had no choice but to come from the front. Echo was never so accepting. She studied the layout, searching for a flaw in his defense.

On one side, high grass provided cover along the foot of the cliffs to where a cleft split the rock. Deep enough to hide a climber, the split extended up to the highest point on the buttress. Echo waved her team closer.

"Katch," she said, addressing one of her companions in a low whisper. "Move around to the western side and get up that big tree over there. Sarra, you do the same in those trees on the other side. Try to get a clear line of sight to the camp; you need to have a clean shot when the guards on the ground show themselves.

"I'm going for the buttress. I'll fire on them from behind and force them to adjust position. When they do they'll show themselves, and you take them out while I deal with the one under the flagpole. Go!"

As the others moved away to their appointed tasks, Echo crept into the trees seeking to reach the rocks without being seen. Then she turned west and began the long crawl towards the buttress.

Voices drifted up from the base of the blockhouse, sounds of conversation and subdued laughter. The guards were not expecting an attack so early; it looked as if Echo's headlong rush across the valley might pay off.

Once through the tall grass she eased into the rock-crevice and began the climb. The gap was less than a meter across at the base and narrowed higher up—perfect for climbing. Ten minutes later she reached the top and scrambled out to a narrow ledge.

The position was exposed; even with her head down Echo ran a risk of being shot if spotted. Luck stayed with her as the moon once again vanished; a solid shroud swallowed the star-speckled sky as black rainclouds moved in, heralding predicted bad weather. She hoped it was the end of the moonlight for a while, or at least long enough to allow her to carry out her intended plan of attack.

With her rifle pushed ahead, she slithered along the ledge until she had a view of the roof of the old station and then braced herself, raising up on her elbows enough to see her target.

Her original assessment had not been quite correct. Two guards sat behind the defensive barrier at the base of the flagpole, and not the solitary one she had expected. One faced outward, peering into the night with his weapon propped in front. Echo thanked the gods for the intermittent cloud cover, without which the guard might easily have spotted her team when it first emerged from the forest.

The second guard sat behind the first, legs stretched out on the roof and fiddling with a rifle. This one faced towards Echo, head down and paying no attention to anything but the apparently malfunctioning weapon. She determined to take him out last; the possibility the rifle was faulty might give her a few minutes extra.

Staying alive 101, she thought. Make sure your gun is working before you need it to avoid being dead!

Visible beyond the edge of the roof was the ground-level barrier built around the ruined yard wall of the ancient outpost. Two more guards hid there, rifles at the ready, facing out and keeping low. They would be hard to hit from a frontal attack, their bodies well shielded by the makeshift fortifications.

Echo's team members were not attacking head on; by now they would be positioned as ordered, and as high as possible. With the curve of the fortification wall, each enemy soldier was exposed to attack more from the sides than from the front.

Carefully Echo took aim at the first of the rooftop guards, the one keeping lookout. Sighting on the intricate harness of his body armor, she pressed the contact on her rifle. A bright, pencil-thin beam lashed out, hitting him squarely in the back.

The webbing crackled with green electric current, neutralizing the enemy soldier as his suit stiffened. The second guard looked up and saw Echo, the malfunctioning weapon dropping from his hands as he lunged for the rifle of his downed companion and struggled to rise to a firing position. Another bolt from Echo's laser hit his chest harness and released a web of current through his body armor. His loud cry alerted those below as he toppled forward, temporarily unable to move.

At ground level the two remaining sentries turned towards the sound, raising their rifles as they searched for the source of the unexpected rear assault. They did not have time to retaliate; laser fire from the trees on either side of the encampment cut them down as they rose from cover. It took only seconds to dispatch all four guards; disabled by their own armored sortie-suits, they lay motionless where they fell.

Without hesitation, Echo climbed off the ledge and inched her way down the rock face to the roof. With barely a glance at the prone bodies, she scrambled to the flagpole, at the top of which flew the red pennant of the enemy, set in a metal socket.

Her rifle on her back, she wrapped herself around the pole and shimmied towards the top, reaching up until she could grasp the flag. With one heave, she lifted it free and dropped it.

In a split second, everything changed. Floodlights sprang to life, bathing the area for a hundred meters around in pseudo-daylight. At the foot of the pole and on the ground below, the enemy soldiers stumbled onto shaky feet, the electric current in their armor now off and their webbing glowing a dull red.

It was finished. Echo knew her rifle, as well as those of her opponents and companions, no longer worked. At her base, her other team members would know it was all over, their weapons also neutralized. Somewhere on the path between the camps, Jackson Cooney, the man who was always right, would be cursing under his breath as he saw his own harness and those of his force glow red.

Echo had claimed the opposition flag; the exercise was over.

# Chapter Two

FOR A BRIEF MOMENT, the cloud cleared again, but it no longer mattered. With the conclusion of the exercise, powerful lights flooded the clearing. Echo sat at the edge of the blockhouse roof, dangling her legs and waiting as her two sharpshooters picked their way through the grass towards her.

Below, the four defeated soldiers huddled together deep in conversation. They stood motionless with arms hanging loose, their heads shaking in denial as they stared at the ground, perplexed by the apparent ease of their defeat.

The failure rested not with them but with the tactics employed by their leader. These exercises always contained hidden flaws within the scenario, designed to allow the opposition to take you out if you failed to appreciate and cover your weakness. This approach was not general knowledge, and teams received no warnings beforehand, but Echo had worked it out early in her training. Her opponent for this exercise never had.

At her camp, the flaw was its location in a clearing surrounded by dense bush. A guard stationed inside could not possibly cover all approaches at once. A leader on top of his or her game would take advantage and attack from all sides, so Echo had positioned most of her team in trees outside the perimeter, hoping they would see what those further in could not. Anyone attempting to sneak in would pass beneath them and present a clean target without knowing they were in the line of fire.

Her opponent's home base sat at the foot of a sheer, barely scaleable, rock buttress. The deep split in the edifice, difficult to see from the old station itself, allowed an enemy sharpshooter to reach a position above and behind the defenders without detection. As expected, Cooney had failed to survey his surroundings. Echo found the crevice and took advantage.

Below where she now sat, her two companions reached the old wall. The first was Sergeant Akachi Khamisi, called 'Katch' by all. With his dark skin and deep brown eyes, the huge man resembled a walking shadow in the now floodlit clearing.

His tall, solid build gave him a bear-like aspect as he walked forward, waved an acknowledgement to Echo, and flashed his pearly white teeth. Despite ruthlessness in the field, he was a gentle man, his smile that of a close friend.

As he stepped into the clearing, he punched his fist skyward in a victory salute.

Private Sarra Corian strode in not far behind. In comparison to Khamisi, she was diminutive, but that did not limit her in any way. Her olive complexion, brown eyes, and dark brown hair made her appear more demure than was the reality. This woman was a born fighter. Lean and fit, she moved as fast as her bigger associate did, and her abilities as a sniper surpassed everyone else in the squad.

Echo sometimes wondered about this pair. There was no doubt Katch had strong feelings of attraction for Sarra, despite their complete physical dissimilarity, and that they were extremely close. They never betrayed their feelings in public, aware of the effect it might have on their work. To Echo, their friendship was obvious.

Both slung their now useless weapons across their backs as they stopped below.

"Easier than expected," Akachi concluded, looking at the huddled enemy group.

Echo nodded. Across the clearing, the members of the opposing team took glancing looks in her direction. They had followed the plan given to them, and she knew well where the blame for their defeat lay.

"Not their fault. Bad strategy on their leader's part."

A piercing whine shattered the night as a troop transport swooped in and landed beyond the ruined wall, sending the grassland debris in swirls as its massive feet settled to the ground. The ramp at the stern dropped, and a solitary officer stepped out, turned towards the blockhouse, and stood with feet apart, hands clasped behind his back.

Echo dropped from her vantage point and walked to the shuttle, then snapped to attention and saluted the motionless figure. Commander George Brenner returned the salute and smiled.

"Well done, Sub. You may have set a new record for this exercise." He reached out a hand to shake hers.

"Thank you, Sir. It would not have been possible without a first-class team."

"Or a less than equal opponent, I suspect," Brenner said, smiling again. "I think we should have found you a more fitting challenge; this kind of thing's a little below you now."

"Thank you, Sir. May I board my people?" Brenner stepped aside and waved her to the ramp.

A minute later, the ship departed, turning across the valley towards her camp to retrieve the remaining participants in the exercise. Less than half an hour later, all twenty were aboard, Echo and her squad seated to one side of the cabin, the opposing group on the other.

Across from her sat the leader of the enemy team, Lieutenant Jackson Cooney. He was of medium height, a muscular man in his mid-twenties. His black hair was so short as to be almost a crew cut, and his eyebrows met to form a bridge across ice-blue eyes that gave most people the willies. Those frowning eyebrows and glowering orbs made it quite clear their owner was livid.

"How can you take my flag before I even reach your camp?" he growled, tapping his feet with agitation on the deck. "You weren't on the path. How'd you get there so quickly?"

"We were there." Echo kept her voice as calm and businesslike as possible. "You walked right past us. You were so intent on where you were going, you forgot to open your eyes. You missed us."

"Don't tell me what I did or did not do, bitch. I'll…"

"You'll address your fellow officers with more respect, Lieutenant," Brenner said as he stepped down from the cockpit. "Your team failed because you used transparent tactics and did not allow for the obvious flaws in the defense of your flag. Sub Bourke, on the other hand, took a calculated risk, and it paid off. In the future, you will try to remember that the purpose of these exercises is not only to win, but also to show initiative."

Cooney sat back and went quiet, but his eyes never left Echo. She returned the stare, unwilling to be intimidated. The man puzzled her. Having trained together in the same squad for several months, they had developed an unusual relationship. Sometimes he behaved as nicely as could be and showed a distinct sexual interest, one never reciprocated. In his case, it was a lust-hate thing, but for Echo, one of simple dislike.

There was no doubt Cooney was a superb fighter, but he was no leader. Arrogant, rude, and authoritarian, the man's approach to leadership was one of total dominance and control. In Echo's eyes, that made him a bad officer.

It was common knowledge that he gained his position through influence, coming from one of the most powerful families on Brenton, the home world of Fleet's largest academy. His father, a senior administrator there, held enormous authority. Echo guessed Cooney did not share his father's talents for organization.

Luckily, this was only training. Assignment to a permanent squad and a task force would follow soon, and with luck, she would never see the arrogant fool again. Looking around, she noted Katch and Sarra seated forward of her. She hoped that when the fateful day came, they would be on her team.

She had chosen them to accompany her on the mission for good reason. They were intelligent and reliable, could be trusted to watch their fellows' backs, and never failed in their duty. They were also the best shots in the group, and her friends.

* * *

Hours later and back at the academy, Echo allowed the warm water from the shower to ease her frustrations. It felt good to wash away the dirt of the last few days and feel clean again. Soothed by the streaming water, she rubbed her soapy hands over her stomach and thighs, then closed her eyes and let the water run on her face.

At twenty-four, her body was trim and fit thanks to intense training. She kept her hair, now back to its natural light brown, cut short in the manner of all spacers. Her green eyes bore a look wiser than ever before. She was more self-assured, no longer the naive, young girl first discovered by Ben Teague in the forests of *Corros*. Upon leaving her home world, she had entered a new life both socially and physically demanding, and every day had grown more adept at dealing with the highs and lows of existence. The events of recent years had left marks only she could see.

To one side, the other participants in the exercise also showered. Beside her stood Katch, his glorious, dark skin flawlessly draped over muscles Echo found close to perfection. Beyond him was the smaller figure of Sarra Corian, oblivious to her surroundings as she washed soap from her black hair.

Echo often found herself secretly admiring Katch's physique—there was no denying he was a beautiful man—but she never acted further on her thoughts. For her, Ben Teague was the only man. Months had passed since she last saw him. Their last parting had not been on the best of terms, but it did not matter; he was still the most important person in her life.

It had taken Echo time to adjust to the showers. At the Academy, teams comprised both male and female, and as a general principle, all lived and worked together without favor or privilege, as they would in the field. The bathroom and locker room facilities were common to all, as were sleeping quarters for the ordinary soldiers. No concessions were given based on sex alone. It was something to which all adapted in time.

As a junior officer, Echo shared a twin bunk room, but at present she occupied the room alone so there at least, she found some privacy.

Until now, she had always enjoyed her solitude, allowing others in only when desirable. Here, that did not happen. Everyone coped and adjusted, kept their eyes in all the right places to ensure their companions' privacy, and expected the same in return. Not all behaved as thoughtfully as was required, sadly.

Turning to wash the soap off her back, she saw Cooney enter, a towel slung over a shoulder but otherwise naked. Nudity did not concern him in the least, and neither did respect for others. As he strode into the room, he made a point of running his eyes over Echo's body, raising his eyebrows in mock appreciation.

Echo turned away and ignored him as he walked to the far end of the room and the last shower. Katch threw a glance Cooney's way and then at the expression on Echo's face, then moved to place himself squarely between the two. Echo smiled her thanks and refocused on her ministrations, determined not to let Cooney get at her.

Ten minutes later, she sat in the locker room, dry, dressed, and occupied in lacing her boots, when Cooney walked out of the stalls, still naked but now with his towel around his waist in the fashion of a short skirt. Aware of Echo's presence, he stopped and stood in front of her. She did her best to ignore him.

"I suppose you feel pretty clever winning that exercise."

"Not particularly. It was easy." With her eyes down, Echo did not see the look of repugnance that swept across Cooney's face.

"I'd be careful of that smart mouth, little girl. Keep putting people down, and it's going to get you hurt one day."

"Oh, I'm sorry." Echo's voice took on an innocent and conciliatory tone. "I don't speak to everyone like that: only those who ask for it."

For a moment, Cooney said nothing and moved away, then stopped and turned back towards her, his nostrils flaring as he clenched and unclenched his fist.

"Don't think that's going to happen again," he said. "There's only so far you can ride on a couple of civilian bravery awards and a hero boyfriend. Oh, don't worry, everyone here knows you're screwing Teague, the captain who lost two ships and only got the second back again with the help of his little girlfriend."

Echo felt her patience grow thinner as her mood started to turn. True, Ben had lost his last two ships, but neither through any failing on his part. The first, on *Corros*, resulted from the incompetence of Ben's captain, a brand new commander who, like Cooney, received his commission because of his father, a senior politician on Cymbel 3. Promotion through social favor was one of the greatest failings of the Federation forces.

Pirates from Kerac 5, a dark world, took Ben's last ship, his first full command, through stealth. Fleet did not reprimand him; he handled the situation according to policy, and this time official procedure failed him. In time, he took the vessel back, and not just with Echo's help. If anything, those affairs had boosted Ben's standing, showing him to be an officer who could perform in difficult, spur-of-the-moment circumstances.

"Well, at least he's a real hero, not a wannabe. And yes, he and I have a relationship. That's the whole point here, isn't it?"

Cooney scowled, unsure of where she was leading. "What's that supposed to mean?"

"I mean he has me, and you don't!"

For a moment, Cooney's face blanched. His eyes narrowed, and Echo could have sworn smoke was rising from his ears. The hand not clutching the towel closed into a tight fist as his arm began to rise. Then he glanced up towards the shower-room doorway.

Katch stood calmly leaning against the door frame, watching the encounter with amusement. He raised an eyebrow in a questioning manner, his face passive. Cooney turned his attention back to Echo, dropped his hand to his groin, and clasped the towel suggestively.

"One day, Bourke, you're gonna get hurt so bad," he hissed. So saying, he turned and moved away between the lockers. Katch stepped forward and sat down on the bench beside Echo.

"Thanks, Katch," she said, continuing with her boots.

"You can report him for that, you know."

"Yes, but there's no point. We'll be rid of him soon, once we get our assignments."

"Don't be so sure." Katch shook his head. "Baby Girl, that arsehole has the hots for you, I'm guessin'."

Echo grinned up at her friend. "You think?"

"Oh yeah. He wants you bad, and he's pissed he can't have you. I figure he's also got the shits because this is the third straight time you've made him look like a fool."

"Yes, well, it's hard not to. He's hopeless at strategy and easy to beat. I'm not about to throw an exercise to bolster his ego, and I won't let my team down. I don't know what else to do about it. I'm a sub, and somehow or other he's a full lieutenant."

"I don't think I'd worry about that," Katch replied. "He got his commission through daddy's influence; you know that, and so does everyone else around here. Before much longer, you'll be promoted, while he isn't going anywhere. Another six to nine months and you'll outrank him, guaranteed."

\* \* \*

In her room, Echo sat on her bunk and sighed. It was not getting any easier. She had hoped the decision to join this squad would make a difference, but so far, all she had achieved was to show a superior strategic ability in training exercises and make an enemy of a fellow squad member who was technically her senior officer.

Months ago, she realized she was more suited to ground operations than flight duty, even though she now suffered less from the queasiness that plagued her on her first space journeys, from *Corros* to *Cymbel 3*, and from there to *Kerac 5* and back again. Having spent the return journey from *Kerac* awake on Ben's destroyer, she now had a better idea of what life in a small, tin can could be like. It required a particular mindset she was not yet convinced she possessed.

She was far more effective with both feet planted on the ground. The years spent in hiding on her home world, and the subsequent cat and mouse game played between her, Ben and the Tolleani, had revealed a peculiar trait in her personality: the high she got from being an adrenaline junkie made her a more effective fighter. The rush sped up her thinking and drove her on.

A year later, she experienced the same thing on several occasions during the *Kerac* affair, when she descended to the planet in an insubstantial emergency bubble and escaped from a terrified and lonely farmer armed with an ancient and unstable projectile weapon. It happened again when she joined the rebels on a critical raid into the mines of that planet to free Ben, the rebel leader, and hundreds of prisoners.

The sensation was intense, almost orgasmic, and undoubtedly addictive.

Echo stood and opened a locker to put away her gear. On the top shelf rested a small, transparent box, inside of which resided a golden medal. Across the blue and yellow ribbon stretched a gold bar, indicating she had won the award twice, firstly for *Corros* and again for *Kerac*.

The data block she and Ben stole from her old home world contained details of the experimental device that remotely disabled Ben's ship, and the gaining of that knowledge was proving a great boon to the human war effort. The data also contained incomplete schematics for a bomb that made a thermonuclear weapon look like a child's toy, and could destroy all life on a world without damaging the planet itself.

Her old mentor, General Molliner, had assured Echo that should they ever get it to work, humanity would never use it against a populated world, even an alien one. Over the last few years, she had learned that the best of intentions did not always follow through. Because of the device, her part in that business mortified her, and although the Civil Cross was an undoubted honor, especially when received twice, it was hard to reconcile.

Worst of all, she did not think she deserved either award. The stolen data was Ben's doing, not hers; she would have left it behind. Their subsequent escape was also a result of his efforts in repairing an old dispatch ship.

In the war against the pirates of *Kerac*, her only contribution had been to talk the few remaining rebels into fighting back one last time and show them how to use crossbows, effective if somewhat antiquated weapons, they could make with limited resources.

The real credit for overthrowing the Pace regime went to the rebels themselves and to Ben and his crew. Even David, a young navigation officer from the cruise liner she had arrived there on, did more than her by launching a backtrack beacon to lead the Federation to the forgotten world.

Neither affair concluded through her efforts alone. That was a prime reason for joining this team; she needed to prove herself, to do something where she could honestly accept that her contribution made a difference.

Beside the medal sat a small, velvet box. Inside was something else that caused her concern, a magnificent ring set with a large blue sapphire surrounded by clear diamonds. Ben gave it to her following the Kerac affair, telling her the design came from a famous ancient piece from *Old Earth*.

He had intended to propose to her at the end of the mission when the pirates took his ship. Afterwards, aware of her wish to enter Fleet training, he gave her the ring as a token of their relationship but did not stand in her way.

Now it was another cause for concern. After her decision to join the division, she and Ben had fought, and with him away on assignment, they had not spoken since. With no idea if their relationship was still on, she was unsure whether she had any right to keep it. When she knew beyond a doubt it was over, she would give it back, but for now...

Lower down, a crossbow sat at the back of the locker. It was a fine weapon, a work of art created for her by two of the artisans of Kerac. She no longer used it, but it would always remain a prized possession, more so than the medal.

She had another now, a smaller but more high-tech and powerful bow built from Carbon fiber and the finest of spring steel. Made to order by a private shop here on *Brenton*, the lightweight folding weapon fitted into a rack on the back of her battle harness.

The beauty of the Special Missions Division was that it was an ensemble of already-skilled individuals. Every member of the team brought his or her special abilities to the group, and while all were proficient in the standard weaponry, each carried their weapons of choice if they so chose.

Her two closest friends, Katch and Sarra, as well as being excellent snipers, were both knife experts. Katch carried a set of deadly throwing knives on his belt, and woe betides an enemy who came within range. Sarra, small, fast, and stealthy, kept a long, thin poniard on her right calf, a weapon able to stab through a skull as easily as a heart. Such weapons were not permitted during training exercises, but when the time came, Echo would carry her bow and her companions their blades.

A knock came on the door, and Sarra poked her head into the room.

"Have you heard?" she asked. "The news just came through; the push to take back the *Corros* system has started. Your Ben will be there, guaranteed, and your home planet will be ours again soon, I bet you." As quickly as she had come, Echo's friend disappeared.

Echo sat on the corner of the bed and stared at the wall opposite. She always wondered how long it would take to attempt a reoccupation of the system, considering how necessary the mineral mined there was to the war effort.

But her home? No, not anymore. It was a part of the past and would remain so, for now at least.

# Chapter Three

BEN GAVE A DEEP sigh as the ship thumped down on the hanger deck of the mother ship, the Fleet carrier *Pellargo*. His first mission in his new command was over.

This vessel was a stealth-fighter, similar to other destroyers but fitted with the latest dispersion-field generators. When activated, the field disrupted, absorbed or scattered any waveform that hit it, including light, sound, radar, microwave and any other kind of wave detection employed by the enemy. The ship was designed for clandestine operation, and that had been Ben's task in this battle.

Re-acquiring *Corros* had been a long, hard campaign. A fleet of small, fast and deadly robot drones, each a respectable attack-weapon in its own right, began the process by swarming through what Fleet hoped would be the least guarded of the wormholes to the system. *Corros* had three, two leading to human territories and a third opening to the *Cardoon* system, from which the initial enemy invasion of the planet came years earlier.

Tollean destroyers blocked the chosen entry point, as expected. No drone could match one of them, but the little robot fighters served to draw fire long enough for the larger Fleet contingent to enter and for the human crews to regain their mental acuity.

Any transition through a wormhole affected human responses adversely. For several minutes afterwards the mind mired in a state of foggy disassociation, unable to respond quickly or think clearly. Most non-crew would make the passage in a sleep chamber, but for operational personnel that was not an option.

Given time, an experienced officer adapted to the sensation, but only to a point, and so standard practice involved exiting a gateway with defensive shields up, just in case. With armed and alert enemy craft waiting at the other end, the drone fleet served as a valuable diversion and extra precaution.

Ben had entered with the second wave and with the dispersion field on maximum. As soon as his ship emerged it turned away from the conflict and, hidden from view, snuck away into the system at full bore, intent on closing the *Cardoon* gate to any warning drones the Tollean defenders might send.

Because of the planet's *Trilatenite* deposits a Tollean base now occupied *Corros*. The original alien research station was destroyed by the enemy's own experimental bomb, triggered by mines set inside its casing by Ben on the fateful day he and Echo escaped. At the time the Fleet invasion began, a full Tollean naval squadron guarded the planet, with three capital ships at each of the gates leading to human space. An orbiting Tollean carrier served as the enemy command center. The gargantuan alien vessel now lay at the bottom of one of *Corros's* oceans.

Thanks to good intelligence reporting, the *Pellargo* fleet knew what to expect, but the battle resulted in heavy losses for Fleet regardless. After weeks of intra-system cat-and-mouse maneuvers the battle was over and Ben was home, his ship parked in a bay on one of the vast hanger decks making up the forward section of the *Pellargo*.

The flagship, commanded by Admiral Lord Salazar Baquir, was one of the largest vessels in the Federation fleet. A colossus that could carry a thousand small fighting craft far beyond their normal ranges, it was also the beating heart of a swarm of larger ships ranging from gunships and destroyers to heavy cruisers.

Ben nodded to Jerry Bayer, his second in command, then rose from his seat and headed for the airlock, exhausted and looked forward to a long, uninterrupted sleep. No sooner had he alighted from the boarding ramp than a young ensign floated up, almost losing his balance as he attempted to snap to attention in zero-g.

*A newbie,* Ben thought.

"Pardon me please, Sir, but Lord Baquir requests your presence in his day room immediately." Without waiting for a response, the ensign saluted again, more carefully this time, and propelled himself towards the bay exit.

"Damn," Ben muttered. "No rest for the degenerate."

* * *

Fleet Admiral Baquir was not a man to whom Ben warmed easily. Without doubt a commander of the highest ilk, the man had a little too much of the bookkeeper about him for Ben's liking. More a manager than a fighter, he saw warfare as a business and did things by the numbers.

Baquir got things done despite his strict adherence to protocol, and most of the credit went to the large number of top-quality officers he managed to have transferred to his command. Ben liked to think he and his crew were a part of this squadron for that reason. All of the officers felt proud to be part of such a glamorous task force.

"Come in, Captain," the elderly officer greeted as Ben entered the day room and saluted. "Please, take a seat."

Ben did as commanded, still wondering why his presence was required. He was due for a stand down and a good, long rest. It was rare for the Admiral to deal direct with flight officers, that job normally being the domain of the Flight Commander, who now sat quietly in a corner of the spacious office.

"No doubt you're curious about what's going on," Baquir said. "Now that *Corros* is ours again—congratulations on your part, by the way—something else has come up. Have you ever heard of the Brixton Virus?"

"Yes, Sir." Ben nodded his head. "Only rumor though. Word travels, you know."

"Yes, of course. The damned thing first appeared on planet *Brixton 4*, hence the name. Rather a nasty beast—not actually a virus, but we're calling it one since it appears to work the same way. We've never seen anything like it before. It first came to our notice about three months ago and is now on eleven other planets; it managed to spread quite widely before we even knew about it.

"The problem is it has a long incubation period. Victims show no signs or symptoms, but are extremely infectious, and I do mean *extremely*. They carry it everywhere before they know they have it. During that time it invades every cell of the body and, at around ninety standard days when there are no more cells to invade, it hits hard; kills within a matter of hours, from complete and total failure of every system and tissue in the body. The fatality level is one hundred percent."

"No cure, Sir?"

"We're working on it, but haven't been able to come up with anything yet, mainly because the biology of the damned thing is unlike anything we've seen before. Our only defense against it is to test everyone trying to move between worlds. If we find the organism, the carrier stays quarantined right where they are and nobody else leaves or enters that world. We have whole planets locked down now, and we risk losing entire populations. You were aware of that I think, and now you know the details. We do have one lead to a cure, and that's where you come in."

"Sir?" Ben was at a complete loss as to what he could do to help.

"Ever wonder why we rushed this invasion, Son? Oh, yes, the *Trilatenite* is important, but it's not the only reason. We could have taken more time and prepared a little more. We didn't because of the virus.

"Several decades ago we discovered a rather special moon in the *Cardoon* System, right next to this one. You've never been there. It teems with living organisms very different to DNA based life. When we occupied it we kept it secret, and set up a scientific research establishment to study the life forms.

"The place is now under enemy control. They built a massive regional military complex on one of the other moons in the system, and they have our station.

"Our experts believe the virus may have originated there. It bears some similarities to samples sent in by our scientists years ago, before the Tollean takeover. The possibility exists the Tolleani are using the base to continue our research, and found something they were able to use as a biological weapon. Best guess is they released it into our worlds by infecting a prisoner and letting him escape back to our side of the lines."

"How can I help, Sir?"

"Another little mission, Captain, after you and your crew have rested, of course. As you know, the gateway you blockaded during this invasion connects directly with the system. The enemy used it to invade here in the first place, and they still control it."

"Yes, Sir. I am aware." Ben shuffled uneasily in his seat. It was obvious what was coming.

"Good. I need you to sneak into *Cardoon* and do a reconnaissance. Seven wormholes lead out from that star; hence its value. Three of those enter Tollean space, one to a neutral system, one to here and two to other human systems. Tollean procedure is to fortify any accesses to our territory with capital ships, and to post early-warning drones or gunships at any gate to an unoccupied system. Those between Tollean territories are not well guarded if at all, and again usually by automated craft. Like us, they don't have so many military vessels they can afford to waste them.

"When we counter-invaded, we sent several stealth fighters, including yours, direct to the *Cardoon* gateway to block it, so the opposing forces haven't yet had time to learn about this campaign. As far as they are concerned, *Corros* is still theirs. The other end of the wormhole will still be watched at this stage, but most likely by drones. They won't stay ignorant for long and the gate won't stay unguarded, so we have to act with haste.

I want you to ascertain the strength of the *Cardoon* base and find out how many enemy ships are guarding each passage to our space. If you sneak through without detection, you can poke around and see what the situation is in there."

"I can do that, Sir."

"Of course you can. Once the drone guard fails to report, the Tolleani will become suspicious, and will reinforce that gate, so getting home again will not be so easy. We can't avoid that."

"Yes, Sir. My crew and I are ready."

"Excellent. You need some sleep, but you'll have to leave as soon as possible. We estimate the Tolleani will bring reinforcements within a standard week. Unfortunately, we aren't ready to extend the invasion to there yet, so we'll continue to prepare the fleet while you carry out your reconnoiter. I have arranged for your ship to be refueled and re-armed while you and your crew rest."

*I prefer to do it myself,* Ben thought, aware the Admiral's orders always prevailed.

\* \* \*

Ben entered *Cardoon* with the dispersion field on full. As expected, a sentinel awaited, watching for something to come through what it still regarded as a safe gateway. Under normal circumstances it would send a demand for a valid recognition code, and failing to receive one, would send an alert to the base Ben intended to reconnoiter.

A guard drone could detect a gate opening, and would seek to identify anything coming through. Its detection signals would be broken and scattered by the dispersion field, with nothing returning to the source.

Without a response of any kind, Ben hoped it would assume nothing had come through and the gateway had absorbed the signal. So far, Tollean scientists had not been cautious enough to cover the obvious and program into their computers the simple fact a wormhole cannot open *unless* a ship makes a passage.

For normal operations the drones had lightning-fast response times and none of the failings of an organic being. Despite that, they could not deal with circumstances beyond their programming, and Fleet believed the Tolleani were still ignorant of humanity's newest invention.

The ship drifted from the gate at minimum power, the distance between it and the stationary sentry decreasing until only a few hundred meters separated the two. Seconds later the drone entered the dispersion field and registered the presence of the destroyer within. By then, it was too late.

Ben's defensive shields activated instantly, surrounding both vessels with a bubble of pure, electromagnetic force through which no emergency signal could escape. Another few seconds and the drone ceased to exist, disintegrated by a focused laser blast.

Ben turned his ship and drove into the star system at maximum acceleration. Part of his mission during the *Corros* campaign had been to prevent any warning of the attack escaping, but one could never be sure. If the guard drone had detected something amiss, a signal might already have been sent, and worse, a squadron of enemy ships could be on its way.

Conveniently, all the planets in the system were located close to the red dwarf star, and all the gates leading to human systems, including the one to *Corros*, were located on the star's ecliptic plane and currently in the same quadrant. After only a few days, a massive gas-giant dominated the screens on the control bridge.

It would have been easier to invade *Cardoon* immediately, but little was known of the alien presence there and the *Pellargo* fleet had paid dearly for the re-acquisition of *Corros*. Several standard months were needed to bring up reinforcements; such was the nature of space warfare. In that time, Ben could check all he needed to see, but by the time he was finished recent events would be known to the Tolleani, and the way home barred.

With the dispersion field on full the ship drifted in space, well away from the moon where the Tollean naval complex was located. Ben positioned his vessel so it did not occlude any other moons and as few stars as possible; only that way could his presence be detected. To any person or machine on the base the destroyer would be a patch of nothing, a black shadow against equally dark space.

"So, what have we got," he muttered under his breath, studying the figures streaming down his monitor.

Jerry Bayer shuffled in his seat and gave a low whistle. "Too much, I think," he replied. "It's a fortress." Jerry had been Ben's second since his first command following the escape from *Corros* with Echo. The man was with him on *Kerac*, and was someone Ben trusted without reservation. "There are fourteen capital ships down there, including seven cruisers and four destroyers. They might only be the start."

"For sure," Ben confirmed. It was certain at least three additional vessels, most likely two destroyers and a cruiser, guarded each entrance to human space. That meant at least six more to worry about, not counting smaller craft. The problems did not end there.

By now, the destroyed drone must surely have failed a routine check-in, and more ships were probably on route from this base to the *Corros* wormhole. The most likely scenario was they would assume the *Corros* system was lost, and post permanent guards on the gate. Those ships would send a report back to the base, and it would soon be on high alert.

On the rugged, airless moon, the base sprawled in a snowflake pattern across the dark, barren surface. At the end of each arm sat a ground weapons installation, each with massive plasma projectors capable of reducing to slag anything approaching uninvited.

"Nine primary cannons. We can deal with that, yeah?"

"I think so," Ben said. "We can send in *groundhogs*. Those guns all point up to space, since that's where an attack would come from. It would take several minutes to lower them, so a surprise, low-level attack might work." He checked the screen again, waiting for the ship's computers to complete their assessment. "It's not too bad really. I expected more ships here. We better scram before we push our luck too far."

\* \* \*

Fourteen days later, the ship once again drifted in space near the gateway through which they had arrived. The other two wormholes to human space had each provided a surprise. From the first the expected battle cruiser was missing, and from the second, a destroyer. Those ships and another destroyer now guarded the gate through which Ben had entered, and had hoped to depart from, the system.

"I guess by now they know we have *Corros*," Jerry concluded. "Those ships are on full alert. If we try to go through that cruiser will melt us."

"We won't get back that way," Ben decided. "The first gate we checked is less well guarded. There are only two destroyers there now, so we go out that way. We need to check out something else first."

Farther in towards the star, a second gas giant forged its way along a much closer orbit. It had numerous moons, but only one of those concerned Ben.

Considerably larger than *Old Earth's* solitary companion, the moon *Persephone* had a dense, cloud packed atmosphere, and according to reports, had vast water oceans and land masses so choked with alien life that even finding a safe place to land was difficult.

Throughout the history of space exploration humanity had found many, many planets and moons bearing life, and all had been something the human mind could comprehend. Life based on the DNA molecule or a similar variant was the norm in the galaxy, giving powerful impetus to the long held theory of panspermia: that all life spread across the stars from a common source.

*Persephone* was the sole exception so far discovered. Here, life evolved on a principal entirely different. Ben did not understand the details, but he'd read the briefings and knew living organisms on this moon were incompatible with and aggressive towards DNA based, and therefore human, life.

When first discovered many decades earlier, the scientific research base allowed scientists to study the moon's amazing life in safety. Of the gross plant life nothing proved of immediate use, but many alien chemical substances and compounds were now being studied in laboratories Federation-wide. Careers had evolved around the classification and researching of those forms, at least until the Tolleani invaded and took the system away from human control.

The microscopic life forms were something very different. Completely alien, they had no similarity to known, normal micro-fauna or flora. Most of them could not survive in a DNA based environment and stopped functioning; death was not the right word, as the organisms did not fulfil the requirements for living things as defined by science.

A handful had been discovered that did not cease to function, their potential effect on terrestrial life something scientists could not ignore. Life on *Persephone* was unique and deadly, and many of the old scientific principals needed re-writing as a result.

Some who studied these microscopic monstrosities believed the 'virus' now spreading across several of the worlds of humanity had many similarities to samples sent out from here before the Tollean invasion.

No human had been near the base since, and it seemed likely the researchers stationed there were long dead. The Tollean penchant for not destroying infrastructure unless necessary meant it was possible the dome still existed, retained for use by the enemy to seek out agents of biological warfare. The possibility was too great to ignore.

A dense cloud layer hid all but the tops of the highest mountain ranges. As Ben's ship passed above the supposed location of the research base, radio and thermal imaging gave some indication, albeit imperfect, of the surface below. Irregular breaks in the cover occasionally gave a short-lived view of dense jungle and rocky ridges.

This region featured a maze of gorge-like valleys divided by high, steep sided bluffs. The reports Ben had read advised thick vegetation choked those canyons and the bluff tops, but little of that was visible. Ben was unconcerned: Fleet had compiled extensive survey maps of the moon in the early days of occupation.

On-screen, a massive, multi-paneled structure emerged on the thermal imager. Perched on a flat ledge stepped into a sheer bluff, it registered as cooler than its surrounds, suggesting it was still intact and in use. The Tolleani preferred cool worlds, and for them *Persephone* was a hot, humid hell.

Not far from the base of the cliffs another structure, smaller than the primary dome, sat on the valley floor hemmed in by the native vegetation. It too was cooler, but to a lesser degree than the station. Within each were small pinpoints of higher heat, indicating living beings.

"Okay, it's undamaged and occupied," said Ben. "The enemy must be working there, so the boffins may be right about the virus. If there's one thing down there can kill us there could be others, and we need to control that. We have to get this moon back. Let's get away from here."

Several standard days later, the least guarded of the human-space wormholes in the system was only hours away when an alarm sounded on the bridge.

"It's a drone," Jerry reported, "a messenger headed for the gateway." Ahead, a small, autonomous device not unlike a backtrack beacon and used to carry messages between stars, cruised silently through space.

"Might be interesting," Ben said. "It's Tollean. Can we grab it?"

"I think so." Jerry adjusted course to bring the ship up beside the mindless machine, and minutes later, it lay in the hold awaiting attention when time allowed.

The gate was fast approaching. As before, only two destroyers still guarded the approach, each facing the point of potential where the wormhole would form when opened. Both hung motionless in space, shields up but on minimum power.

Ben dropped a hand to the console and flipped the cover on the controls for the disabling device. Most Federation warships now carried the weapon, stolen from Tolleani weapons researchers by him and Echo. It worked by sending a clandestine signal to link with the alien ship's computers, detecting and analyzing any and all systems on the ship, and then shutting down those it was ordered to target. In this case, Ben chose to disable the enemy's main generators, cutting off all power to the engines, weaponry and shields. He pressed the 'activate' switch.

Nothing happened.

"Damn!" he cursed. "Both are armored." The scenario was becoming more frequent these days. When first deployed the 'disabler' worked in every case, and gave promise of turning the tide of the war. Humanity had been losing, and the weapon at least allowed Fleet to even the odds. Now the Tolleani were wise to the device and most of their warships were shielded from its effects. The opposing forces were on a more level basis, but it appeared humanity's advantage was reaching an end.

The second the signal reached them, the ships' shields flared to full power. Ben hoped at the least, confusion would rein on the enemy bridge decks. His vessel was undetectable, but they knew they were under attack. Logic dictated the intrusion was coming from the wormhole, and they focused their attention in that direction, away from the human craft.

"Guess we just bust our way out," Ben said. "Tighten your sphincters, kiddies."

With both the defensive and dispersion fields on full, Ben drove the ship forward at a speed far higher than considered safe for normal transitions. The Tollean ships remained oblivious to the destroyer's presence as it flashed up and flew between them. The instant the gateway generator activated, they reacted, firing with everything at their disposal.

The rear shield glowed violet from the overload as Ben's ship cannoned into the wormhole and vanished.

# Chapter Four

THREE STANDARD FEDERATION WEEKS later Ben sat in the dayroom of Admiral Baquir, waiting and wondering once again why his presence was required. At the far side of the desk, the old man gazed through a hull port, watching the nearby flotilla as it spun a merry dance around the flagship, an illusion caused by the rotation of the section of the ship in which the office was located. After several more minutes Baquir turned towards Ben, a faint smile on his lips.

"Quite a show you put on, young man. You barely snuck out of there with your hide intact. You know that, don't you?"

The gate used by Ben to enter *Cardoon* was now without doubt the most defended passage into the alien held star system, and caution had dictated he leave by another path. The journey home had resulted in severe damage to his vessel.

"Yes, Sir. We were lucky." Ben shuffled in his seat, an itch of unease starting to worm its way into the back of his mind.

"You damaged your ship in the process!"

"Yes, Sir, but we got her home. I thought the information we gained worth the risk."

"Of course it was." The Admiral nodded his head in agreement. "However, I'm taking her away from you."

The statement hit Ben like a hammer. He had expected a censure of some kind, certainly, but never the loss of his command. He rose and snapped to attention.

"Sir, I…"

"Oh, sit down for the Gods' sake, Son. I'm giving you another ship; from here on out you will command one of the new *Infiltrators*."

"Sir?"

The admiral stepped across to his desk and sat at ease on the corner. Ben felt his concern fade; he knew Baquir well enough to know the man's manner. A reprimand was not why he was here.

"I have far too many commanders who got their positions through political influence or money rather than innate ability. We have a mission into *Cardoon* coming up which requires the use of an *Infiltrator*, and the commander who came with the ship I intend to send is a fool. You are a competent captain, prepared to take risks when necessary, and the only one in this task force who has been inside the system recently. You get his ship and the mission, and he goes somewhere he can't do any harm.

"Thank you, Sir. What sort of mission?"

"A rescue. Oh, the information you brought back will be invaluable for the invasion of *Cardoon*, but that's not why I need you. You also retrieved a Tollean message drone, correct?"

"Yes, Sir."

"Would you care to guess what we found in it?"

"No, Sir. I have no idea."

Baquir grinned. "Well, my boy, this is going to surprise you." Rising, he crossed to a bar and poured two glasses of a dark amber liquid, drawing a long sniff from one as he handed the other to Ben. *This is important,* Ben thought as he accepted the offering.

"Again, it concerns the Brixton Virus. We always suspected the damned thing was a gift from the Tolleani and came from *Cardoon,* from the moon *Persephone.* Your report that our old research station is still there and functional made it more certain. However, we now have absolute confirmation our suspicions are true."

"Sir?"

"The drone contained a message as expected, but not intended for the guard ships at the gateway as you thought. It was for us, the idea being that it would be able to use its identification codes to sneak through to a human system. It carried a self-destruct in case of failure. The contents were encrypted of course, but nothing our experts can't deal with. The individual who sent it did not want the gate sentries knowing what it contained."

"Why didn't it go off when we intercepted it? Wouldn't that be considered a failure?"

"The self destruct didn't activate. It was programmed to do so upon the detection of certain Tollean signals, not when being bundled into the hold of a Federation ship. We're not precisely sure whether it originated from the research base or the enemy naval station, or who sent it. We do believe that individual is a scientist or naval officer, not a drone engineer, and he got the programming a little wrong. Lucky for him, you found it before the Tolleani."

Ben kept his silence. *Cardoon* fell some years ago, and he had never considered humans could have sent it.

"Wherever it came from, it concerns the *Persephone* station. At least some of our scientists are still alive and prisoners; the enemy are using them to do their work. The message confirms the virus is one of a number of local genetic structures discovered and studied by them. It's fatal to humans but not Tolleani, so the enemy took it and let it loose on our worlds.

"Our surviving people on *Persephone* have the original organism, and a vaccine they developed unbeknown to their captors. The drone is a call for help. This creates a problem for us."

"Yes, Sir?"

"When we invade, the enemy will attempt to destroy the station and their prisoners—you don't need to know why. We need that vaccine and the original virus. In addition, there is someone in that base who is of vital importance to us. At this point of the war, he may be crucial to our success, so we have to sneak him out before they level the place. Now do you understand why you are here?"

"I think so, Sir. I'm going back in."

"Well guessed, Teague. You will take the *Infiltrator* and carry a rescue team in. This is critical and we don't have a team available at the moment; ours is on secondment to task force nineteen. I've arranged for a new team, and the quickest way to get them here is for you to go and get them while we're waiting for our replacement capital ships. We'll mount a small attack on one of the other gates to create a distraction while you slip back into the system. You'll drop the squad on the moon, where they'll have a set time to carry out a rescue mission and move the prisoners to a safe place.

"You will then take up position on the other side of the *Corros* gateway prior to the arrival of the invasion force. When we make the main push, it'll begin with a massive swarm of drones through the gate, followed by the destroyers. You will attack from behind, causing a distraction to keep them off us until our men can recover from the transition. With any luck, we can dispatch the opposing ships with minimal loss, and move on to the Tollean base in short order.

"My boy, this puts you in the hot seat. If you survive, you'll return to retrieve your people at the predetermined place and time. If you fail, someone else will pick them up, assuming we are successful."

Ben sat motionless, unsure of how to respond. He had not anticipated going back so soon, much less at the command of a new ship. The new *Infiltrator* was a remarkable vessel, a combination of light warship and troop carrier with full stealth capability, designed for front line covert activity. The job sounded straight forward assuming he could get through at the start and did not kill himself during the actual invasion, but there was a high danger potential. *Not so easy, maybe.*

* * *

The heat from the sun shimmered across the tarmac of the academy airfield on *Brenton* as Echo and the other eight members of her new squad quick-stepped across to the mission room. Rumor spoke of a new invasion push, and now she and the others would find out what their role would be, if they were to take part at all.

Training had finished a week earlier, and now the team was ready for assignment to a base ship, most likely a task-force carrier somewhere on the front that stretched across almost three hundred light-years of space.

In the last year Echo had gone from civilian to highly trained soldier of Fleet. She now knew the basics of flying a variety of aircraft and spacecraft, and could navigate with competency. Following her stint with the Special Forces, she would no doubt take the navigator position on a ship.

She possessed a wide range of weaponry, aircraft and spacecraft skills and a broad knowledge of the war, and in the last few days had undergone subliminal computer training in the Tollean language, as far as was understood from the handful of captives taken alive during military operations. This last minute training puzzled her, as there was no one with whom she could converse except others who took the course with her.

Being a member of a ground-missions squad would not save her from long periods in space, but at least the colossal carriers were better than the smaller battle-craft. Those enormous ships contained living quarters with centrifugal gravity, and far more facilities. Echo prayed it would be as comfortable as the old commercial liner she traveled on during her first attempt to reach the Academy.

The new team consisted mostly of individuals from the group she trained with, including Katch and Sarra, her closest friends and strongest supporters throughout the training period. Also present was Jackson Cooney, the man she detested above all others. He outranked her enough to make life uncomfortable should he so choose, and whilst that presented a slight problem she was determined not to let him get to her. Until now, an opportunity to cause difficulties had eluded him, but she had no doubt he would eventually try something.

The possibility had not escaped Katch either; he made a point of sticking close to her whenever possible. He was only a sergeant to Cooney's Lieutenant, and a conflict between the two of them would bode ill for him. Echo knew that fact would not hold her friend back. Katch knew that Echo could look after herself, but he was a good friend and constantly had her back.

The mission room contained little more than a small stage and dais, with rows of seats either side of a center aisle. Echo walked forward and chose a seat in the front row, her friends beside her. As the others took their positions Cooney moved to the opposite side of the room. The entire squad snapped to attention as a small huddle of men, led by the base commander, Commodore Martus Payne, stepped up and turned to face the room. Payne moved to the dais.

"Please sit," he said. "I welcome you all to the first official briefing of your new squad. This team consists of the highest achievers in our last training intake. You are the best we have, and you will have the chance to prove it."

*How in the hells did Cooney rank top ten*, Echo wondered. *Daddy again?*

The old commanding officer paused for effect, but he had already lost Echo's attention. Her focus was on the individuals behind him. Three men, one a civilian, the other two officers, stood at ease at the back of the stage.

One of them, Ben Teague, gazed at Echo with a curious expression, concern written bold across his face. Special service was a dangerous place to be, and she knew that his decision not to stand in her way was against every instinct he possessed. She could never hold that against him. Clearly, he had not expected her to be in this squad.

"I do not need to tell any of you that nothing said in this room will be repeated beyond it," Payne said. "You all know the rules. Your first assignment is a rescue mission of inestimable importance to the war effort. Your squad leader will be Commander Brenner, with whom you are all familiar." Payne indicated the second officer standing behind him. The Commodore stepped back, allowing Brenner to take over the briefing.

Echo's heart lifted. Brenner was a tall, rugged man, with grey eyes and dark hair, his impeccable appearance branding him as a career soldier. He had been her commanding officer throughout the training period, and she knew that he was a good and trustworthy man. That he was to continue as her leader exceeded her hopes.

"Thank you, Sir." Brenner turned his attention to the room. "I am extremely happy to see you all here. You all completed your training with top results, and this assignment will test everything in your respective skill sets." He paused a moment, pointedly glancing at Cooney before continuing.

"I have to say it is unusual to see a team such as yours. Normally we would spread our best graduates across the task forces, but in this case, we've made an exception. The upcoming mission is urgent and cannot wait until we have a team available, so we have formed a new one with me as the commander, especially for this assignment.

"The target is a scientific research establishment on a moon called *Persephone*, in the *Cardoon* System. This station used to be ours, but the enemy took it from us some time ago. They captured the scientists working there and established a powerful, regional naval facility on another moon in the system.

"In the near future we will launch a massed invasion to take that system back and destroy the base. The details are not important here. Before we do so we must retrieve certain personnel, materials and data from *Persephone,* and that is our task. I will lead the operation and the civilian gentleman on my left will accompany us." He motioned towards a nondescript, weedy individual standing next to Ben.

"Doctor Dewhurst is a mission expert. You do not need to know his purpose, but you *will* protect him with your lives. Am I clear?" The little man shuffled his feet and flushed with embarrassment as nods of acknowledgement came from across the room. He was a complete stranger, but if he was important, that was enough for Echo.

"Good," Brenner continued. "Our first-class travel plans will be courtesy of the officer on my right, Captain Ben Teague, with whom some of you are familiar." He threw a glance at Echo. "We will first join Task Force *Pellargo* in the *Corros* system. From there, Captain Teague will sneak us into *Cardoon* and place us at the top of the moon's atmosphere. We will descend to the surface and fly to our target using drop-sleds."

Echo swallowed the slight lump in her throat. She had trained on the sleds and handling one posed no problems for her, but they resembled the emergency bubble she used to land on *Kerac* 5 too much for comfort. Despite all her experiences since, that event remained as the most traumatic of her life, excepting only the day the Tolleani slaughtered her family and entire community on her home world.

"Once down we will make our way to the target destination, enter, retrieve certain information and materials and rescue certain personnel, after which we will make our way to safe ground. At a predetermined place and time a ship, most likely Captain Teague's, will pick us up and bring us home.

"If the invasion fails … well, you all knew there would be dangers when you volunteered for this duty. Fleet will do all it can to rescue us, but there are no guarantees." Once again, Brenner paused to let his words sink in.

"One last thing, *Persephone* is a unique and dangerous moon. It teams with life about as alien to us as it is possible to be. Its classification is zero percent Terran, and it's the only place ever found with this brand of life, hence our study of it. You can't eat anything, you can't touch anything unprotected, and virtually everything will try to kill you one way or another.

"Special full-body suits will protect you from the local life forms. Filter masks will allow you to breathe the air, which is high in carbon dioxide, methane and numerous air-borne nasties. You will carry everything you consume on top of your normal gear. You will follow a specific field-diet to eliminate any need to remove the suits, and you will not drink the water. Full details will be on your personal data readers once we leave for the *Corros* System, and you *will* study it!"

*Cardoon*! Echo realized why the name was familiar to her; it was one of the neighbor systems to where she had grown up. A system's neighbors were not necessarily those closest to it, but ones to which it was linked by a wormhole. Her old home system possessed three, one of them *Cardoon*, a red-star system currently in enemy hands.

Brenner nodded and stepped back, allowing the base commander to step forward again.

"That will be all," he said. "Departure will be at three-three-zero this afternoon from pad five. You have a few hours to prepare your kit. Dismissed."

Echo sprang to her feet with the others, saluted, and waited as the officers and civilian left the room. In turn, she filed out and walked across the tarmac towards the barracks. She looked forward to the mission—it was the sort of thing she joined the program for, and she was going to see Ben again. Perhaps they would have a chance to talk. Despite their falling out, she still loved him and could not get him out of her head, but how did he feel about her after their argument?

# Chapter Five

ECHO HAD NEVER SEEN a spaceship as large as the *Pellargo*. A torpedo shaped colossus, the ship hung in space like a gargantuan shark. As she looked through the shuttle port at the nose of the battle wagon, she saw the yawning maw that led to the bay where swarms of fighting craft docked. Several rotating portions of the vessel's midsection separated the forward airfield bays from the aft engineering modules

She counted her blessings. The crew quarters and training facilities would be in partial gravity, so at least her posting would be more bearable than on a smaller ship even though she would be weightless anywhere on the vessel other than the accommodation sections. It was doubtful space travel would ever be enjoyable, but after having been on several ships in the last year, she could now deal a little better than before with the effects of zero-g. This time it would not beat her.

"That's one of our biggest carriers," Sarra Corian commented from the next seat. "Its commander is Fleet Admiral Lord Salazar Baquir. He's an ace at his job, but a hard man to deal with."

"How do you know?"

"I keep my ears open; you should to." Sarra smiled at her companion.

Echo turned her gaze back to the docking manoeuvres.
"Yes, I should."

*   *   *

The barracks were in a gravity drum as hoped, and although
only one-third Federation standard, it suited Echo fine. Her
gear stowed, she focused on the routine of training to restore
peak fitness after several weeks in hibernation on the voyage
out.

During the next duty period she stood at a window in the
common room and gazed at the distant, bright, yellow orb, the
sun of her old home world. She had never expected to return,
but only a few years had passed since her escape and here she
was.

Fate?

The star was visible only briefly with each rotation of the
accommodation drum, as was the broad curve of *Corros* far
below. From numerous support ships that were part of the task
force now in orbit, shuttles carried machinery and personnel
down to the surface. The push to re-establish the colony and
restore the Federation's supply of the mineral *Trilatenite*, used to
build the wormhole generators in every ship, was a priority.
According to rumor Fleet intended to establish a full naval
contingent on one of the planet's moons this time around.

Echo doubted her old town of *Casta* would be re-
established immediately. Wiped from the face of the planet by
the prototype bomb detonated by Ben when they escaped from
the Tolleani, nothing remained of the site. Only an irregular

stain remained, stretching several hundred kilometers across the surrounding shattered mountains.

The other two mines and their respective towns were first on the agenda, starting with the air base where Echo and Ben had repaired the courier used in their escape. In time *Casta* would be replaced and the third mine recommissioned.

While she watched, the devastation of her old home appeared over the shoulder of the world. The blasted ground looked a little greener now as the stubborn, native plant life reclaimed its hold on the deeper gorges and those places further from the epicenter of the destruction. Given time, all signs of the bomb's legacy would be gone excepting the giant trees of the mountain rainforests. They would not return for an age. As Echo stood window gazing, Commander Brenner entered the barracks.

"At ease, team," he said as he seated himself on the end of a bench and motioned the group to gather round. "I thought I should bring you up to date. There's been a minor change to the mission plan—nothing that will affect your part in all of this. Our original intent was to go into *Cardoon* from here, but that way is now closed to us. The enemy knows we have this system back; they're moving in reinforcements and the *Corros* gateway is now heavily defended. They are expecting something.

"The new plan is to sneak in by a back door. We'll fly to a currently unoccupied system with a lightly guarded gate to Tollean space, and a small squadron will go through to make it look like we're opening up a new front. Captain Teague's ship, with us on board, will sneak in behind the attack and make its way through enemy territory to enter the *Cardoon* system by a safe Tollean gateway.

"It means traveling through a number of enemy systems, and we'll be several weeks in getting to our destination. Even the safe gates may have drone guards, so it'll be dangerous, but with luck we *will* get through.

"The bad news is the *Infiltrators* don't have gravity, so you'll be in zero-g the entire journey. To avoid problems you'll sleep most of the way, and you will use your wake time to exercise and prepare for the mission. Does anyone have any questions?"

Echo felt her stomach twist at the thought of all that time without weight, but shook her head in denial. That weakness would not defeat her, even if it meant a few weeks of discomfort. She was determined to persevere no matter what.

"Excellent," Brenner said, standing again. "Several destroyers will accompany us. Their objective is to throw the Tolleani a curve ball and get us in unseen. The flagship and the fleet will make its way to the *Tannis* system, from where the primary assault will commence after we've had sufficient time to carry out our task. With most of the enemy ships at the *Corros* Gate, the invasion should go more smoothly at *Tannis*."

Without another word, Brenner nodded to his team members and walked out of the room. Echo breathed a deep sigh.

\* \* \*

"Echo!"

Echo stopped dead in her tracks as a tall, familiar figure walked along the corridor towards her.

"Ben, I'm so glad to see you again." Unbidden, the frustration and insecurity built up inside since their argument came flooding back. She felt as she had the first time she saw him many years earlier. "You didn't speak to me at *Brenton*."

Ben reached out and wrapped his arms around her, holding tight for a few seconds before easing off. "I'm sorry. I didn't get the chance. It was all go while I was there, and on the way here you were asleep the whole voyage. It gets kind of hectic on the control deck. I should have talked to you sooner, I know, but here we are."

"I'm not normally allowed in this sector, and besides, we're both under orders."

"I didn't mean here, on this ship. Ever since our fight I've wanted to see you again. The argument... I was wrong."

"So was I. I didn't think about how you might feel when I chose to enter Special Forces. I followed my instinct." Echo raised her hand and placed her palm on his cheek, feeling the warmth of contact she so missed.

"Come with me. We need to talk." Ben clasped her hand and led her away through a series of side corridors to a part of the ship she had not seen before. He stopped at a cabin door, pressed his thumb to a reader and entered, drawing Echo in behind. Together they sat on the cabin's solitary berth, her hand still clutched in his.

"These are my private quarters when I'm on this ship, one of the advantages of being a captain. We won't be interrupted here. I want you to know…"

"No, I want to say something. I'm sorry; I should have talked to you before volunteering. I know you wanted me to be a navigator, but I don't do well in space. I'm a ground hugger, and the squad is where I'm much more comfortable. I…"

"Stop," Ben said. "You don't have to apologize to me, ever. It was my fault; I had no right to interfere. It's just that the Special Forces Unit is dangerous, and I worry about you."

For a moment, Echo sat and gazed at the man beside her. He had not changed much since the day he first stumbled into her shack on *Corros*, filthy and blood smeared. The sight of him mesmerized her. His body, two meters tall and perfectly proportioned, still looked fit and muscular, his pale blue eyes, light brown hair and bronzed skin—artificially tanned as in all spacers—were exactly as she remembered them.

She thought of the line of tattooed figures stretching down his right flank from armpit to hip. They were not visible now under his uniform, but she had always wondered what they meant. Ben always refused to tell her, and no amount of research gave any clue to their meaning.

"You know, if I *had* joined a space crew, it's unlikely we would've seen each other until the end of the war, assuming we both survived. I had no chance of being posted to your ship, and I might have been sent to a different sector."

"True," Ben agreed. "Mind you, the likelihood of your squad being assigned to this fleet was also pretty thin. There are thirty-one fleets spread along the front. And yet, here you are."

"Yes, here I am. So … where are *we*? You and I?"

Ben ignored the obvious question and peered at the floor for a few minutes, then lifted his gaze back to Echo. "Do you understand how dangerous this mission is? You'll drop from space to *Persephone* on a sled with almost no defensive ability. Once down, you'll be in enemy occupied territory on a world where the vegetation can kill you, not to mention the animal life. There's a fair chance you won't be retrieved afterwards."

"What will you do while I'm enjoying my holiday in tropical paradise?"

"I'm sorry Echo, I can't tell you."

"In other words you're going to be a part of the invasion, and you'll be in as much danger as me."

Ben nodded his head. "Yes, I guess so."

"Fine, so where are we now?"

Ben slid along the bunk until right beside her, and reached out to take her hands again.

"We're good, as ever and always. Yes?"

"Maybe we should be making the best of what time we have together on this ship." Echo leaned in to Ben and pressed herself against him, wrapped her arms around his waist and kissed him ardently. She accepted his anger arose from concern for her safety and not from lack of consultation. He was still hers, and she would not let him escape in the short time they still had together.

\* \* \*

An hour later, Lieutenant Jackson Cooney turned into the end of a corridor, paused as a door opened ahead, and pulled back around the corner. This sector, the space crew area, was off-limits for him. Nevertheless, curiosity led him to explore and he did not relish the chance of discovery. From the doorway, a young woman wearing fatigues identical to his stepped out.

*Bourke, you bitch.*

He could only see her from behind, but he could not mistake the woman he had come to hate, the one who had embarrassed him and made him look a fool far too often. Her unseen companion remained inside the doorway, but as he leaned forward to kiss her, the face of Ben Teague emerged.

Teague, your precious hero-captain.

Bourke was also out of her zone, but Cooney realized he could not report her without making it clear he was also breaking the rules. Being with a senior officer who *did* belong here, she would get away with it. He would not. Waiting for her to move on, he turned and headed back the way he had come.

He had entered the space-crew sector via the Special Forces officer's quarters, and intended to return the same way. It was another restricted place, but he had an excuse ready in the unlikely circumstance of discovery. He would report he was taking a message to Commander Brenner and wave a nondescript dispatch envelope in the face of his challenger. Nobody in the sector possessed the authority to dispute such a claim except Brenner himself.

Passing without a sound from one corridor to the next, he inched through the bowels of the colossal ship. The carriers were the largest spacecraft built by humanity, and were few in number. The interstellar equivalent of an old-fashioned, oceanic aircraft carrier, each served as the flagship of one of the Federation's thirty-one fleets, the personal vessel of that task force's commanding fleet admiral.

As Cooney approached the officer's wardroom, he noted the door was ajar, and detected voices coming from inside. Careful to remain silent, he snuck up to the door and positioned himself to overhear the conversation. One of the speakers was familiar: it was Brenner, his team leader. The other was one he had not heard before, but he could guess who it was.

This voice belonged to the 'specialist' Dewhurst, whom Brenner had introduced during the initial briefing on *Brenton*, a civilian who accompanied the commander everywhere. Since boarding the *Pellargo*, the two of them had remained always in each other's company. Cooney wondered how this stranger could be so essential as to warrant compromising the mission by the inclusion of an untrained civilian.

None of the team other than Brenner knew the exact objective of the mission, beyond the basic fact they were to infiltrate a research base, rescue someone and something, and then retreat to a predetermined place for retrieval. Cooney expected this individual must have essential knowledge of some sort, and was perhaps privy to who or what they were going after. He would be descending to the moon's surface on a duel sled with Brenner, and the team's orders were to protect him with their lives. Whoever he was, he was important. Cooney strained to hear the voices.

"…about two days through the jungle before we reach the target," Brenner spoke. "Based on the station construction plans, we should be able to enter the main complex through the greenhouse. The enemy will guard the entrance from the valley floor, but perhaps not so much that one."

"As long as we can get in without being discovered," Dewhurst said, "it doesn't matter how we enter. The prisoners, any still alive, will be in the dome. We find them, grab them and the base administrator, and get out as fast as possible."

"And the virus. You're positive you can identify it?"

"If the staff are dead? Yes, of course. I set up the lab myself, and I know exactly what to look for. If you can get me inside, I'll find it."

"Assuming they kept a sample."

"Please, Commander. There is no way they would not have done so. We stored and cataloged every specimen taken on that moon. It will be there somewhere. Besides, the message in the drone said it was."

"Yes, well let's hope that's still the case. It's your only priority, is that clear? The administrator is mine, and so are any survivors from the scientific team."

"I don't quite understand why the administrator is so important."

"You don't need to, Doctor, only that he might be critical to the war effort in the future. He may well be the most valuable individual in this whole blessed conflict."

"Fine, if you say so. Coffee?"

Cooney heard movement and edged away from the door, turning back in the direction he had come. With the wardroom door wide open, he would have to find another way back through the hangers.

Working his way back to his quarters, he smiled at his unexpected good fortune. Of everyone in the squad besides Brenner, he alone knew the mission objective. The person who they were to rescue at all costs was the base administrator; from the briefing data he had flicked through earlier, he knew that to be an elderly scientist named Arthur Mendoza.

The Squad was also to locate and retrieve a sample of some sort of virus, probably something to do with the plague now spreading across the Federation.

Cooney always operated on the principle that anything he knew and others did not was to his benefit and their detriment. It gave him power over them, which could only be good.

Especially over Bourke.

He outranked her, but only just. At least half of the team ignored the fact, and took little notice of him in deference to her. He could understand why; she was attractive and sexy. Those who were loyal to her were all men, except for the Corian woman. Most likely, they all had the hots for her. Perhaps even Corian. Maybe she preferred women; after all, she had never given him so much as a glance and he came from one of the finest families on *Brenton*.

As for Bourke, she was an ever-increasing pain in the side. The discovery she was to be a part of this team was infuriating and he hated the woman more than ever, if that was possible. Seeing her step out of Teague's cabin galled him. There was no doubt in his mind what they were doing in there.

Now he knew something she did not. One day the knowledge would prove useful.

# Chapter Six

AFTER A LONG AND dangerous voyage, and almost invisible against the blackness of interplanetary space, Ben's ship powered towards one of the lesser-used gateways to *Cardoon.*

His journey had begun with a small sub-group of the *Pellargo* fleet moving to a star regarded as neutral. With no rocky worlds and nothing else of particular interest, the system held no immediate value to either the Federation or the Tolleani. It was a neutral zone from which a single wormhole opened into human territory, and another to a Tolleani occupied system, each side maintaining a cursory military presence at their respective gates as a precaution.

Before any attempt to pass through the enemy gateway, Ben sent a captured messenger drone through, now reprogrammed for use by the task force and broadcasting Tollean recognition codes. It remained in enemy space long enough to discover two gunships guarding the passage, before carrying that vital information back to the sub-fleet.

Any Tollean warships, even the little gunships, represented a threat to be reckoned with, but they could not compete against destroyers. A swarm of several dozen unmanned robot fighters preceded the squadron, their intention to scatter and surround the enemy before attacking from all sides. The Fleet warships followed close behind, manned by crews who through long experience were hardened to the debilitating effects of wormhole passage.

Within minutes of the drones attacking, two things happened. First, the Federation ships arrived, operational and ready to fire. Without pause, they began a barrage of firepower against which the smaller Tollean vessels could not hope to contend. Second, an *Infiltrator* hidden within a dispersion field entered behind the main assault, unseen by the enemy forces as they busied themselves with the immediate task of survival against overwhelming odds.

The *Infiltrator* moved rapidly away from the one-sided battle, as the Tolleani battled for survival in the face of defeat. The diversion squadron would retreat, and within a week this end of the wormhole would be reinforced and impassable.

For Ben none of that mattered. The attack served only to let him sneak past the front line. From there he sought to reach *Persephone* by the least used Tollean gate. Via a series of jumps through empty or sparsely populated systems, he wove a tenuous pathway to *Cardoon*, flying through enemy occupied territory without detection.

In a matter of days, the invasion would begin with the *Pellargo* fleet bursting through the *Tannis* gate, the same Ben used to escape on his last mission. It would commence with a swarm of a thousand drones. Fleet Command knew the entrance to be heavily defended, and the unmanned craft would serve only as a distraction. The next wave would include almost a hundred capital ships and squadrons of smaller fighters.

Ben's task was to enter via the back door and drop the ground team in space above *Persephone*, and he always expected his biggest hurdle would be the final gateway to *Cardoon*. When the fleet arrived, he would play a cat and mouse game, hiding behind his dispersion field as he harassed the enemy from behind, unseen.

The battle for the *Tannis* gate would be Ben's moment of greatest danger. In firepower his ship equaled a light destroyer, and he had no concerns about its ability in a fight, but if he failed, Echo and her team would be in greater jeopardy, their retrieval doubtful.

The journey through enemy territory had been easier than anticipated. There had been few encounters as most warships stayed close to the front lines, but the chance always existed of meeting a ship traveling between stars or an automated buoy or beacon that might somehow detect and report the *Infiltrator's* presence.

To guard against the eventuality Ben made the entire passage with the dispersion field on full. In addition, the ship's computer stood ready to broadcast recognition codes from captured drones. The Tolleani did not yet know the Federation possessed them but that did not guarantee success, as codes often changed and in time Ben's would be rendered worthless. However, message signals could not travel unassisted through wormholes, and so word traveled slowly in space.

Now, after a long and stressful flight, the gate marking the way into *Cardoon* was only minutes away.

"Are we ready for this?" Ben glanced across to his second in command. Jerry Beyer nodded and focused on his job of guiding the *Infiltrator* into the gateway. Seconds later Ben felt the nauseating gut-twist characteristic of passing through a wormhole, never pleasant but for him only a transitory discomfort. Years of flight time allowed him to remain focused through the transition.

Wormholes were strange, inexplicable things. Rather than an actual hole, they were little more than microscopic, tube like energy fields stretching from one point in space to another. Where two harmonizing points existed in adjacent star systems, they created a link across deep space. Found usually in specific locations within a system, such as the Lagrange points of a planet's orbit or close to the star itself, they were a convenient way to traverse vast distances in a matter of minutes, since once inside, the normal laws of physics did not function.

The great breakthrough in space travel came with the invention of the Saitou-Radelick generator. The device formed a bubble, forcing the thread-like field to expand and flow around the vessel. As the ship traveled along the thread at a relative velocity many times faster than light, the sphere of force protected it from whatever strange physical reality existed within the wormhole. An insignificant number of ships met with disaster when their generators failed mid-passage. None had ever reappeared.

As the *Infiltrator* emerged in the *Cardoon* System, the sensors let out a loud buzz, warning of an alien presence. Not far away, an enemy supply ship approached, oblivious to the fact that something blocked the way. Because of the dispersion field, the alien vessel had no warning, detecting only a fuzzy occlusion in the momentary glare of the opening gate.

With the skill found only in an experienced pilot, Jerry Bayer shunted onto a new course to clear the way. The *Infiltrator* remained unseen as the Tollean ship approached, passed dangerously close by and vanished into the gateway, its captain no doubt puzzled as to why the gate had opened and closed seconds before his arrival.

"Get us away from here, now!" Ben directed, rising from his seat. Only two days away from *Persephone*, he still had much to do.

\* \* \*

In the small operations bay Echo concentrated on preparing her sled. All around, her teammates did the same, each responsible for his or her own vehicle. Echo did not like the drop-sleds; she had used them twice before during training, but this would be the first time where it mattered.

The sleds were five meters in length, and one and a half in width. Little more than an engine and fuel tank in a shell, they carried a single occupant laying prone in a shallow, groove-like cockpit along the top, covered by a transparent heat shield.

Once released from the hold, the little craft would descend at a steep angle into the atmosphere of *Persephone*, plunging like a meteor to a point where the air was dense enough to support normal flight. At that point, small airfoils would extend from the sides and the stern, transforming the sled into a miniature aircraft able to fly its precious cargo to the intended destination.

The designated rendezvous was almost halfway around the moon from the descent point. The sleds would drop well away from the research station and potential enemy activity in the hope they would avoid detection during the descent. Once down, they would fly at minimal altitude to a location two days march from the base, landing on a rare patch of open marshland. Unable to make the return journey to space they would remain forever hidden beneath camouflage, their mission accomplished.

At the front of the bay sat a larger sled, a two-man version for Commander Brenner and his strange, unexplained 'specialist'. Echo did not envy the experience awaiting the man. Her emergency bubble descent to *Kerac 5* had left her traumatized, and the memory remained with her to this day.

The sled was not quite so bad; she could control it herself, and knew how to fly it well. For a man like the specialist, who in all likelihood had never been on anything like it before, this would be a descent into the depth of the hells. She expected he would spend the first part of the journey with eyes closed, praying to his personal gods.

Glancing up, she saw Ben approach the Commander. The two conversed for a moment then Brenner nodded, and Ben turned towards Echo. He took her gently by the arm and led her to one side.

"Are you ready for this? Those things aren't all that safe."

"I've flown them before. I'll survive."

"See you do. I'll never forgive myself for bringing you here if anything happens. You're still the amazing girl I met on *Corros* years ago. I have something for you." Reaching into his flight suit, he retrieved a tiny device about the size of a computer memory wafer, with a small pressure pad in the center.

"This is a rescue beacon. Carry it on your person, under your suit. If you're stuck, press the center; it'll send a distress signal pinpointing you to within a few meters. It's only detectable a few hundred clicks into space, but if I'm near enough, I'll hear it."

"Thanks. I won't forget." Echo smiled as she took the object and slipped it inside her body suit. She loved that he worried so much about her, but hoped the device would never be necessary.

"One last thing. I just reported this to Brenner, and I'm telling you as well. We just detected some kind of signal hitting the hull, just briefly. Something may have gotten through the field; it isn't perfect, after all. It could be anything, but there's a small chance we've been detected, so as soon as I drop you I will be away from here. Make sure you and your team get down into the clouds as quickly as you can."

"That's our plan," Echo replied.

Ben looked around, gave her a quick peck on the cheek and headed for the bridge. She had no idea what he would be doing during the invasion—despite her digging he gave nothing away. She knew it would be equally as dangerous as her job, and she prayed to the gods he would get through unscathed and be ready to pick her up again when the time came. In less than an hour, they would be in position over the surface of *Persephone* and her mission would begin.

\* \* \*

Barbus Koll was in the foulest of moods, his usual state of mind these days. A walking stick clutched in one hand, he hobbled along the corridor towards his private surveillance room. Once again life had taken an unwanted turn and dumped him in a place so close to oblivion it made the other assignments of his career like holidays in comparison.

The previous low point had been his posting to the planet humans called *Corros*, to nursemaid a trio of insufferable scientists while they conducted dangerous weapons research. It was an easy if frustrating assignment until the day the animal turned up, ruined his life and brought him to this juncture. He kept an image of it burned into his mind, of the long, pale hair and the odd weapon it always carried.

It hadn't taken long to work out it was a human female, and to his detriment he never bothered to do anything about it. In the end it teamed up with an escaped human pilot to destroy the base, and his life with it.

While he chased them in a hover-scout, the experimental bomb the scientists had been working on somehow exploded, destroying everything over a radius of almost one hundred kilometers. He alone survived, his craft smashed, his bones broken and life hanging by the smallest of threads. A rescue ship arrived only hours later to find him laying unconscious on the tarmac of the old human air base. Koll had never forgotten the animal and never stopped hating it, or humans in general.

Limping into the surveillance room, he slumped into the solitary seat and switched on a monitor. From here he could watch everything happening in this stinking dome. He spent most of his days alone in his private spy hole, waiting to catch someone committing a dereliction of duty.

As he stared at the screen the constant ache from his shattered leg plagued him. After his rescue from *Corros* it took an eternity to recover and he still carried many reminders, his limp not the least of them. Of course he submitted a full accounting of how a squadron of terran craft attacked his base, erasing it from the surface of the planet. He survived only because he was out surveying the other mines. The enemy knocked him out of the sky and left him for dead.

His superiors did not believe the report in its entirety, he suspected. After his release back to active duty he received punishment for dereliction, his wife and family abandoned him and he was reassigned to this, the deepest cesspit in the galaxy. Even humans did not like it here, and in his experience they were not particular.

Overall, he considered himself fortunate. He could have been drummed out of the service, and was lucky not to have been sent to the slave markets. Not that this isolated moon was much better.

His new command consisted of a huge, rectangular, glass structure on a wide ledge on a steep mountain slope rising up from a vegetation-choked valley. The humans called the place *Persephone*. After the initial conquest of the system and the construction of the naval base, he was assigned here as security coordinator.

Tolleani could not easily breathe the native air, but the dome allowed a reasonable level of comfort. One of Koll's first commands had been to adjust the internal atmosphere, originally modified for humans, to suit himself. The prisoners did not cope well with the change, but they could breathe it, and had no choice but to put up with it. Not many of them still survived; it was incredible how weak these creatures were.

That he should have fallen to this, the nursemaid of a bunch of pathetic animals, irritated him. He was not technically in charge of the station, but in reality he filled that role. The original commander left several months ago, and his replacement took little interest in matters of administration. Koll knew why.

Ronus Kemmin, a Tolleani of a very different breed, first arrived here with a squad of personal guards; Koll soon learned they were not here to protect the new commander, but to guard him and prevent him leaving. He was a scientist and academic, a nobleman with great power on several of the home worlds, and a political prisoner of the Crown.

The Emperor feared Kemmin, and loath to assassinate him outright because of public backlash had sent him here where he could do no harm. Koll suspected the order to remove him would come one day, and the sooner the better. The accursed nobleman interfered little in the running of the place, but when he did, it infuriated Koll.

Kemmin's minders departed soon after their arrival, after transferring their charge to Koll and his guards. They left behind a standing order not to interfere with the prisoner except in an attempted rescue or an invasion, in which case he was to be executed immediately.

In the meantime, Koll tried not to attract the new administrator's attention. Kemmin required regular reports of events and got them, but they never contain anything of importance. This was Koll's command, and no piddling member of the nobility whose only claim to power came from an accident of birth was going to take it away from him. Kemmin lived on borrowed time, and if Koll ever got his way that time would soon pass.

Attention on the monitor, Koll spotted a brief blip on the screen and a line of nondescript symbols. A signal had been sent from one of the surveillance satellites he had ordered be placed around the moon. The flash lasted for the briefest of seconds, indicating the fleeting detection of a body approaching the far side of the little world. It did not re-occur.

Koll scratched his head, positive there was nothing due today. Despite the nearby presence of the naval base, visitors rarely came here. It was a forgotten corner in a quiet system. One warship remained here on rotation, as well as the shuttle he kept parked at the back of the landing platform behind a stack of containers. Nothing else ever came near other than supply ships.

The signal, if a ship at all, did not indicate anything coming from the base. It gave no clearance transmission, and appeared to have come from open space somewhere on the other side of the moon. There was a minor gateway out there, a short distance from *Persephone*, but it led to a safe Tollean system. Koll tapped the intercom.

"Pac?" For a few seconds he heard only silence, and then a voice replied.

"Flight Leader Pac here." The voice was that of the captain of the three-man fighter currently assigned here. "What do you want, Koll?"

"One of the buoys detected something on the night side of the moon, coming in from LG2. It disappeared in a second so it's probably either a meteoroid or a ghost signal. I want you to take your ship around and check."

"You don't think I have better things to do than investigate meteoroids?"

"You've done nothing but play *quads* since you got here. Do as I say or I'll file a report to your superior."

"Fine!" The line went silent.

Ignorant bloody pilots.

Koll leaned back in his chair and stared at the monitor, willing the indicator to flash again. It did not.

*Never mind,* he thought. *The exercise will do the fool good, instead of him sitting down there in his ready-room gambling with his crew.*

Maybe, with luck, they would intercept a ship, perhaps one coming to steal Kemmin away. If so, Pac would either bring it down or capture it. *That would be a real feather in my cap—possibly even regain a little of the favor I lost after the* Corros *business.*

# Chapter Seven

ECHO LAY ON HER belly in the shallow cockpit of her sled, waiting for the signal to launch. Through the transparent heat shield, she watched the other sleds around her. To her left the bay doors opened wide, the moon *Persephone* looming beyond.

The side to which they would descend was in semi-darkness, shrouded by the moon's strange night but still visible in the gaseous glow from the tiny world's gargantuan host. A pearly, mottled and broken cloud layer, difficult to discern in the dim light, blanketed the entire surface. That was good; the cover would shield the drop-sleds against visual detection from above as they flew to the rendezvous point further around towards the day side.

On readouts just centimeters from her face Echo noted ten numbered indicators, each confirming the status of one of the squad. Number one was the sole double sled, carrying Commander Brenner and the civilian specialist, Dominic Dewhurst. Nothing else had been explained about him to the team members. They understood only that they were to get him to the laboratories at the research base at all costs. That, and the main objective, to rescue the administrator and any researchers still living.

Indicator number two was Cooney, and three, Echo. The little flashing symbols would serve to keep each member of the squad informed of the others' status. The sleds' computers would keep all within close proximity during the descent and the flight to the target landing area. If anything happened to anyone, she would know.

Brenner's sled lifted from the deck and slid through the open door into space, followed by the others in quick succession. Clustered together, they began a steep descent. Ben had dropped them right at the top of the atmosphere, only a few kilometers above the surface, and then sped away to the next part of the *Infiltrator's* assignment.

Echo flew the craft with ease. Outside the shield, the temperature began to rise as the tiny ship plunged through the first wisps of thin upper atmosphere. A casual observer, were they able to see through the clouds, would see a meteor shower, small fragments plunging to their extinction, a not uncommon event on most worlds.

Closer to ground level they were both difficult to detect and hard to attack, but during the descent they were vulnerable. Echo prayed they would land without detection.

She was wrong.

"Alert," Brenner's voice came over the intercom. "Spacecraft approaching. Looks like a fighter, closing fast. I'm pretty sure we've been sprung. Everyone take whatever evasive measures necessary and reacquire at the target point. Out!"

Echo's heart sank. Her vehicle had nothing in the way of offensive weapons, its defense ability limited to a capacity to maneuver quickly. A return to space was not an option—not that there would be anyone waiting there—and her only choice was to vanish into the clouds.

Without hesitation, she took manual control and increased the angle of descent to vertically plunge the remaining thousands of meters into the cloud banks. Seconds later, the electronic sensors withdrew into the hull and the heat shield turned black as the little craft plummeted through the denser atmosphere. Echo was alone, for now.

The sled dropped lower, a shining fireball amongst several as the squad sought refuge from the attacking ship. The cloud cover drew nearer and small foils pivoted out from the hull, transforming the sled into a small aircraft.

Seconds after the wings dispersed, something hit the fuselage with a solid jolt. A powerful stream of turbulence sent the tiny craft into a roll as something large and fast tore past. The shield clear again, Echo strained her neck to look for any damage, spotting a blackened patch on the shell. Something, most likely one of the needle beams the Tolleani so loved to use, had glanced off the skin. At this height, the little boat was easily able to survive insignificant damage like that.

Echo saw her attacker disappear into the distance. The enemy pilot had flown his ship down to cloud level in pursuit. Unfortunately, it was a fighter capable of flight in both space and atmosphere. Echo and her team could turn and flip their rides on a dime, and by the time he turned and came back, she hoped she and her companions would be safe in the clouds.

Faced with imminent danger, she once again felt that familiar, electric thrill of adrenaline coursing through her veins, the crucial hormone that heightened her awareness and drove her on.

Far ahead, an exhaust trail slashed across the sky. The attacker, larger and faster than the sleds, had come from behind and shot straight through the group, its shock wave scattering them like leaves in a breeze. The contrail showed it to be in a steep bank as it prepared for a second, head on attack. This time there would be no mistakes.

Echo could not afford to hesitate. Her heart beating wildly, she dipped the sled's nose and plunged once again towards the ground. Around her, several of her fellow squad members did likewise.

The sled slammed into the top of the dense cloud bank as Echo battled to regain level flight. Her companions might be anywhere around or in front of her, but the sleds' linked computers would ensure no collisions occurred.

Seconds later, her little ship dropped below the cloud and skimmed meters above the jungle that carpeted the moon's land surface. Echo banked and turned in the direction of the rendezvous point, the computer guiding her. Their arrival had been detected, but if the squad could survive long enough to disappear into the forests unseen, the mission might not be a complete loss. The enemy ship could fly in atmosphere but not low to the ground, and she needed to lose it before landing.

On the control panel, two indicators were dark; two sleds were down. With the team scattered in all directions their attacker had chosen to chase others. Echo breathed a long sigh and praised her luck.

Outside, streaming rain blocked out what little light existed and left lines of moisture streaking the heat shield cowling. This was a wet world, the precipitation almost constant. Echo watched the sensors closely, aware of the possibility of flying into something solid and unforgiving in the limited visibility. Once again, she glanced at the panel; only seven lights remained active: three of the squad members were gone. She swallowed the lump in her throat, and pressed on.

The clouds hung a hundred meters above a carpet of endless vegetation, the dark shapes of trees rushing below in an unbroken array of mottled blue-purple sentinels. Echo dropped to barely above treetop level and began the flight towards the research dome. In time, the little craft crossed a coastline, and the forest blanket gave way to a dark ocean.

Hours later, another coast appeared and Echo entered a long, broad valley, almost flat bottomed with mountain ranges along both sides. The station, according to the briefings, sat at the far end, on a ledge of the bordering hills.

A mass of tangled plant life choked the valley floor, across which snaked a sluggish brown river. Day was just emerging, although beneath the dense cloud the dim light was not much better than an average moonlit night. Showers marched in grey, sweeping curtains, a strong wind squalling in from the shallow sea.

Somewhere in that unpleasant morass of alien life was the place chosen from the survey maps of the early scientific surveying teams, where the remainder of the squad would land and regroup.

Echo's craft slowed until it flew at a speed just above stall. She had long since switched back to automatic control, the computer far more capable of making a safe landing than her. Without warning, the trees gave way to dense, grass-like vegetation on a flat, open field. Not far from the tree line the sled stalled, and dropped in a less than gentle manner on the grassy hummocks.

As the engine powered down, Echo released the shield and jumped down beside the hull, her laser pistol in hand. She realized she had been holding her breath and exhaled, willing herself to calm down as she took in her surroundings.

The steady drizzle restricted visibility to little more than a hundred meters. A stream, its waters dark and sluggish, flowed nearby to join the river Echo had seen on the way into the valley. She felt the breeze against her body; it was warm, despite the driving rain. This moon was a humid hothouse.

The water here was acidic and unpleasant for humans, the air unbreathable. Like all members of the squad, Echo wore a skin-tight body suit molded from a synthetic material that allowed her unrestricted movement, kept her warm and dry, and with the form-fitting helmet covering her head, protected her from the environment.

The headgear contained a filter mask to help her breathe, communications equipment for interaction with her team, and computer navigation to keep her on track. The field harness, still stowed in its locker, contained extra oxygen as well as pockets for nutrient tablets, water and any other anticipated needs.

Other than the rain and wind, the grassland, now revealed to be a marshy bog, seemed benign. Beside Echo, the weight of the sled was already forcing it to settle into the spongy surface. All around, the night looked deserted and free of any threat. Satisfied there was no immediate danger, Echo scrambled back into the cockpit and checked the readout. Of the ten drop-sleds that set out, only six remained. All remaining indicators flashed green, placing them, like her, on the ground. *Small mercy,* she thought.

The attacking craft had moved too fast for clear identification, but Echo had seen enough to recognize a Tollean spacecraft with atmospheric capability, and not an aircraft. It could fly in air, but because of its speed could not maneuver safely at low altitude. Once the squad reached the shelter of the jungle, the enemy would find them impossible to locate, but they had lost the advantage of surprise and the Tolleani would be waiting.

On the dashboard, indicator one was dark. Captain Brenner had gone down over the ocean and the team was now without its leader. Echo had not anticipated that. To make the situation worse, Brenner's sled carried the so-called 'specialist'. As far as she was aware, only he and the Commander possessed the full knowledge of the operation. To Echo, that was an unforgivable oversight; the entire mission was in danger of failure before it had begun.

Her attention back on the moment, Echo checked the direction finder strapped to her forearm. A beacon indicator, set at an ultra-low level and undetectable beyond a radius of five hundred meters, flashed in the dim light. With Brenner out of the picture, sled two called all survivors of the descent to its location.

*Cooney!* A full lieutenant, he had assumed command. "Damn," Echo cursed under her breath. If the mission was to be salvaged, having an incompetent in charge was not the ideal beginning.

She fought to overcome the adrenaline that coursed through her veins as she set about preparing her gear, pulled the field harness from its stowage, slung it over her shoulders and tightened the restraining straps. From another locker she removed something she never went anywhere without: her crossbow.

Cooney often laughed about her insistence on carrying the weapon, but in a stealth situation it had its uses and had proven its worth on her previous adventures. This was not her original, lost on arrival at the planet *Kerac 5*, nor the magnificent work of art created for her on that world. It was her new one, commissioned on *Brenton*. Its sleek, black, deadly frame weighed very little, but packed a punch unmatched by either of the previous timber and steel weapons.

Slipping it up and over her shoulder, she dropped it into its snug cradle in the harness. Last, she took a quiver of arrows and strapped it to her thigh. With the bow, her standard issue laser rifle, pistol and knife, she felt ready to take on anything that might come her way.

Last of all, she pulled a camouflage sheet from a pocket in the cockpit, draped it over the sled and secured the corners as best she could on the spongy ground. Nothing about the machine held any interest for the enemy—it was a basic device —but there was no point in making it easy for them to find her. On this surface, her tracks would vanish quickly, and in time, the sled would sink below the surface of the bog.

Satisfied the craft was invisible from above she glanced at the direction finder and headed towards Cooney. Progress was slow over ground covered with high clumps of long, tough blades and patches of saturated moss that swallowed the unwary foot without warning. Between them, the treacherous surface held hidden, mud-filled holes that were difficult to avoid. After stumbling into one and sinking up to her knee in sludge, Echo found it easier to move from one clump to the next, using them as stepping stones.

Thirty minutes later she located Cooney crouching beside his covered sled, talking in a hushed voice to another squad member. As she drew closer, she recognized Tandie Applegate, one of Cooney's camp followers. A few meters away two more figures crouched near the stern of the vehicle, their insignia identifying them as Serge Petrovsky and Echo's friend Sarra Corian.

"About time you got here," Cooney snarled as she stopped beside him.

"Worry about yourself." Echo turned to scan the surrounding grasslands. One surviving team member remained out there. Within seconds she noticed a movement not far away, as the shadowy form of Akachi Khamisi scrambled towards them, jumping from grass tussock to tussock as she had done.

"Watch your mouth, Bourke," Cooney reciprocated. "I'm in charge here now, and you'll show some respect."

"Fine, Sir!" He was correct, although she had always held strong concerns about his ability to command. Until they worked out a plan of action, it was not worth the fight. Khamisi joined the group and squatted beside Echo.

"You okay, Baby Girl?" His ubiquitous grin flashed through the faceplate of his helmet.

"All good. You're the last in, so we need to move out of here. We can find cover over in those trees."

"I'll decide that," Cooney interrupted.

"Of course, Lieutenant. And your orders are?"

For a moment, Cooney stared at her. He had doubtless expected a fight over this, and Echo's compliance took him by surprise. "Follow me, everyone." With those words, he moved away in the direction she had indicated.

"You know," Katch said. "If he's going to pull rank, the best way to get him to do anything is to recommend the opposite. His dislike of you will probably make him do the exact thing we want."

Echo grinned at her friend. "Let's wait. He might surprise us." With a deep breath, she moved to follow the one in the group she least trusted to lead.

The dense vegetation surrounding the grassland looked like a terrestrial rain forest. Tall, tree-like structures with dense canopies reached towards the clouds, their lofty trunks shrouded in twisted vines and leafy tangles struggling to seek out what little light was on offer.

As the squad moved under cover, the treacherous ground gave way to harder but no less wet terrain, the forest understory choked with a host of giant, broad-leafed plants. Where it seemed impossible for such to exist, flower-like structures blossomed in a multitude of shapes and iridescent colors, reaching out to catch the drops of rain falling from the canopy. Echo gazed around as she walked; all around her was beauty, but deep inside she knew it was not real, and nothing on this moon was harmless.

The tendrils waving from some plants could give a vicious sting according to her briefing data, and a corrosive dampness dripped from others including some of the flowers. Thank the gods, Echo thought, for Fleet's technology experts. The suits she and her companions wore would protect them from harm as they worked their way through this tangle to reach the research base.

Several hundred meters from the clearing, the team halted in a drier place, and turned to their new, self-appointed leader.

"So," Echo said, "we've lost four of our number including Commander Brenner, and Dewhurst. What are your orders, Lieutenant? Where to from here?"

Cooney remained silent, staring at the ground.

"Considering that Dewhurst is gone," Katch said, "the mission is looking a little shaky, wouldn't you say? Only he and the commander knew our purpose here and without that knowledge it seems a bit pointless to continue. Wouldn't you agree, Lieutenant? Perhaps our best course of action is to head for the extraction point and wait for rescue."

*Smart*, Echo thought, realizing Katch was employing his own theory on how to control Cooney.

"You presume too much," Cooney replied. "They were not the only ones briefed on the true purpose of this mission. I also know."

"Why would they tell you and not us?"

"I would have thought you could figure that out for yourself, Bourke. In case of an emergency someone else needed to know, and as second in rank I am the obvious choice."

Echo choked back a retort. "Then perhaps you might like to fill the rest of us in. Otherwise Katch is correct."

For several seconds more Cooney said nothing, continuing to stare at his feet as if deep in thought. "You all know this is a rescue mission. The primary objective is to rescue the base commander and any other survivors. The commander is the chief scientist, a genetics expert named Arthur Mendoza. He ran the whole shebang before the Tolleani took over. It appears he managed to sneak word out telling us he and some of the others are still alive. For some reason he is critical to the war effort and we have to get him out at any cost. Most of that you know."

"Didn't know his name," Katch muttered. Echo knew this to be a lie—Katch, like her, had read all of the data provided.

"Well, I do. The message said they have a virus of some sort there, apparently the one that is spreading across our worlds. To make a vaccine we need the original strain, and that came from this hell of a moon. That was Dewhurst's job, in case Mendoza is dead by the time we reach the station. He was Mendoza's colleague at one stage, and his task was to find the virus in the labs and retrieve it. That's just as important as rescuing Mendoza."

"So we have to enter the dome one way or another," Echo said, "locate a scientist who could be anywhere, identify and steal a single item from a laboratory storage, and then escape again without being seen. All this with the enemy already knowing we are here. They'll be waiting for us."

"Too much for you, Bourke?"

"You're the boss. I think we have zero chance of pulling it off." *Let's try a little of Katch's theory.*

"Too bad. Get your asses together. We leave in five."

As Cooney turned away and began fidgeting in his pack, Echo turned to Katch. He smiled and turned his thumb up in recognition of a job well done. She winked back; Katch considered the lieutenant a coward who, if Echo had insisted on pushing ahead, would have abandoned the mission.

Applegate was his close friend and would back him regardless. Petrovsky would blindly follow anyone, and the lieutenant pushed him without mercy. At least Echo's friends had her back.

# Chapter Eight

PAC SETTLED HIS SHIP outside the dome. While he waited for the engines to wind down he glanced through the cockpit window at the landing platform. He was technically the commander of any ships assigned to this station but with only his three-man fighter present, that meant little. His ship was the only craft stationed here, along with the personal shuttle Koll kept out of sight behind a wall of storage containers at the rear of the pad.

Pac spent most of his time battling boredom, playing games of chance with his crew in the ready room, from morning until night. A few more weeks remained before another pilot from the main base relieved him, then another short stint at the naval base and he could rotate out to somewhere more civilized.

The biggest annoyance here was that insufferable security coordinator. Pac's prime directive was to guard the scientist Kemmin and he did not answer to Koll, but the fool behaved as if that were so and continually tried to order him around. When he did comply, it was usually to avoid argument and because there was nothing else to do on this forsaken moon anyway.

Even going outside the dome for long periods was irritating. The high methane content of the air made Pac feel sick after a while. Those poor humans Koll kept prisoner in the dome could not go outside at all without breathing filters, having evolved on a planet with a much lower carbon dioxide level in its atmosphere.

Pac took a deep breath. Finally, the first real excitement he had experienced in the weeks since he arrived here. He had no idea what Koll saw whilst ensconced in his little spy hole, but on the far side of the moon Pac had discovered a swarm of small ships dropping down from space. They could only have been one of two things, either a human attack, or an attempt to rescue Kemmin from his pseudo-prison.

The first was unlikely; this system had a substantial Tollean military presence, and a small attack force could not come through any of the war-front gateways without detection. The intruders, most likely a rescue attempt by the damned scientist's supporters, must have arrived through a Tollean gateway. Despite his confinement here by the Emperor, Kemmin was an immensely powerful Tolleani and many political factions wanted him free.

To preserve the Emperor's integrity, the official navy line was that *Persephone* was a scientific research base and not a prison. As a scientist, Kemmin was posted here as the administrator, and was not a prisoner. That should have ended the matter.

It did not work quite that way. Somehow, Kemmin got messages out and received them as well. Pac assumed that the Tollean Lord had some supporters at the main base, and they were facilitating his communications despite orders from higher up.

Pac scrambled down to the tarmac. As he turned towards the airlock, it did not surprise him to see Koll just outside the outer door. The fool had no patience and took his job much too seriously.

Again, from extreme boredom, Pac had done some background checking. He knew that Koll's demotion into this job was the result of a past incident involving the loss of his entire command. According to rumor, he was assigned here on a 'not to be promoted - not to be transferred' basis, but Pac doubted Koll knew that. Everyone at the base did, and Koll was a standing joke there.

"Well?" Koll demanded as the commander walked up. "What did you find?"

"I encountered a landing force. I suspect whatever you detected was the ship that dropped them. Some sort of small landing craft I've never seen before, each carrying a single pilot judging from their size. I'm not sure how many there were, but I managed to knock out four of them before the rest dropped into the cloud cover."

"Why didn't you pursue them?" Koll eyes glared and his face twitched as he shuffled on the spot, supported by his walking cane.

"Wake up, Koll. You know as well as I that trying to pursue them below the cloud cover would have risked my ship. It's a space fighter, not an aircraft. If you want to chase the rest, call the main base and have them send over a ground force."

Pac gazed impassively at the coordinator. He knew Koll did not like being answered back to by anyone he considered his inferior, which was more or less everyone. "I suspect it is an attempt to rescue our special guest. If any of them landed safely, I doubt they will be able to get here in one piece all the way from the far side of the moon, considering what is out there. You might like to send some of your guards after them if you are concerned. I am not!"

"You will show a little more respect when you address me." Koll's voice was low and distinctly threatening, a threat Pac knew the fool could not fulfill. Koll pivoted on his walking stick and marched back into the airlock.

Pac feigned a snap to attention. "Yes, of course, sir!" As Koll vanished inside, Pac wondered what it was about Kemmin that enraged the coordinator so. He knew the scientist was important and powerful, but not exactly why or how. The name was from nobility and it was the crown that exiled him here, so perhaps he was a distant member of the royal family. It was something worth looking into; with luck, he might discover why he had orders to kill Kemmin if certain events ever occurred.

Not that that would ever happen. The Tollean lord's little sidekick had already paid him an enormous sum to protect his master, more than Pac could ever hope to earn in the forces. That fortune would be waiting for him at home when the war was over, so he would happily consider turning a blind eye if the time ever came. Of course, orders were orders, and it all depended...

\* \* \*

Echo slashed her way through a tangle of broad, fleshy-leafed plants as she forced a path along the banks of the valley's main watercourse. On Cooney's orders she was at point, the hardest position in the column, but had managed to find a relatively easy route through the jungle. She had reached the river after only half an hour, and located animal paths that made the journey somewhat easier.

Old surveys of this region revealed that a tributary stream flowed close by the greenhouse, the smaller structure set on the valley floor below the main station for the study of local vegetation. By following the watercourses, the distance traveled was greater due to the twists and turns, but time taken was shorter compared with forcing a way through the unbroken jungle.

"Everyone take a break," came Cooney's voice over the suit radio. "Bourke, stop where you are and everyone else close up."

Echo sighed and sat down on the ground. Katch slumped down opposite her, his head shaking as he buried himself deep in his own thoughts. The dome was close, and despite the short range of the radio, both knew it was not smart to be broadcasting at this stage. Cooney's indiscretions would serve them ill, but there was little either of them could do.

Feeling a touch on her leg, Echo glanced down. Only centimeters away, one of the beautiful, flower-like denizens of *Persephone* turned slowly to face her, slim tendrils reaching out until they licked against the impervious fabric of her suit. With deliberate slowness, it wrapped itself over the synthetic surface. It was not the first plant, assuming that was its nature, that had tried to investigate her since the beginning of their march, but the squad now knew how to deal with its kind.

Watching on, Katch took his pistol from its holster and turned it to the lowest setting, sufficient only to produce an uncomfortable heat. With the weapon aimed at the center of the flower, he pressed the contact. After a few seconds, the plant flinched, released its grip on Echo and drew back into the leafy mass from which it had emerged, leaving a faint, greasy smear on the fabric of her suit. From the briefing material, Echo knew it was probably corrosive, but the suit would handle it.

Ten minutes later the group was preparing to move on when Echo noticed a disturbance further along the riverbank. Holding up a restraining hand, she pointed her pistol in the direction of the intrusion and waited.

It was unlike anything she had seen before, a large bug-like animal with an ovoid carapace about a meter and a half long, and supported by crab-like legs, three on either side. The creature's multicolored, cream and blue-green shell was hard and jointed, like the exoskeletons of Terran crustaceans. Each foot ended in three toes, and from the front of the carapace two smaller limbs extended to what looked remarkably like multi-jointed, three fingered hands. In one of those, the creature held a torn piece of vegetation.

There was no discernible head, but a long, flexible snout extended from the front of the shell, tapering to what might have been a small mouth. No eyes were apparent, but from the top of the snout extended a long, flexible proboscis, the end of which swelled to a flat pad of a darker color, possibly a sensory organ of some kind. At what Echo assumed to be the tail end, twin rod like extensions extended vertically, creating a 'v' shape reminiscent of an old-fashioned, rabbit-ear aerial.

The creature scuttled onto the animal track just meters away from the group and then stopped as it sensed it was not alone. Turning, it pointed its snout towards Echo and shuffled a little closer, its proboscis waving in the air and stretching towards her.

Petrovsky raise his rifle. Echo held her hand out to stop him from firing. The creature had done nothing to indicate an intention to attack. That was a nice change, she thought, considering the number of smaller 'things' that had assaulted them since their arrival.

The animal moved forward, first in Echo's direction and then towards the other nearby squad members, showing a clear curiosity as it 'examined' each in turn. Then, without warning, it withdrew and ambled back into the jungle, presumably having decided they were neither food nor threat.

"What a monster," Petrovsky mumbled. "Haven't seen one of those before. Nothing about that in the briefing material."

"Yes, well," Echo replied, "just be thankful it isn't dangerous."

"We don't know that," Cooney said, stepping up behind them. "Move on, Bourke."

As Echo turned back along the path, she stopped to peer into the dense vegetation where their strange visitor vanished. Pushing the brush aside, she faced a hole over a meter in diameter, neatly bored into the steep slope backing the riverbank.

"I think we stumbled on that thing's home," she said. "We're using its pathway."

# Chapter Nine

THE RECTANGULAR GREENHOUSE SQUATTED on the flat valley floor, hemmed in by dense vegetation that in places grew right to the carbon-glass walls. From one end, an enclosed, glass-covered walkway extended in the general direction of the cliff face.

The primary dome perched fifty meters higher up on a broad, natural ledge. The original intent of the builders had been to position the structure above the native vegetation and the dangers it contained, while the greenhouse used to study the jungle plant life sat on the valley floor.

Echo knew from the briefing data that the walkway extended into the station via an airlock, and then through two sub-basement levels cut deep within the rock below the dome. A narrow path skirted the base of the greenhouse and disappeared towards the cliff face, to a second entrance that allowed direct access from the basements to the outside world.

Following the perimeter wall, Echo strained to see inside. The glass was filthy, coated with the grime and slime of the local environment. Vague shapes loomed through the greenish smear, betraying the presence of structures within, some appearing to be monstrous plants and others, crops growing over high trellises. A full height glass partition divided the enclosed space in two, and in the section farthest from the airlock floodlights blazed down from the roof. Echo reached an exterior door and searched for an opening mechanism as the squad moved up behind.

"No handle or electronic panel. It looks like it opens only from the inside."

"We force it," Cooney said. "The mission depends on getting into the station from this greenhouse. We'll never get in from the valley-floor or the landing pad without being detected."

"I doubt we can break in here without setting off some kind of alarm," Echo said. "Don't forget the Tolleani are expecting us. They'll be waiting. Besides, that glass is several centimeters thick, so we can't get through it without using the lasers."

"I don't give a flying f…"

A ghostly face appeared beside the door, face mask pressed flat against the pane. It was human, an elderly woman with tangled, gray hair and dirt-streaked skin visible through the grime of the glass. The eyes were wide with alarm, the nose and mouth covered with an air filter. After a few seconds she seemed to steady with recognition, and focused on the nearest member of the squad.

Echo stepped forward and raised her hand in acknowledgement, trying to make the person inside understand they were friends and pointing to the Fleet badge on her body suit. The woman nodded, and then peered about to make sure the way was clear. She pointed towards the entrance and then vanished.

A minute later a soft clunk came from the door as it swung open. The owner of the face appeared, waving Echo to enter.

"Quick," she said. "Keep your filters on; the air in here is the same as outside."

The team, now reduced to six weary souls, passed through to a gravel walkway in a place that could have been a terran herbarium or greenhouse but for the strangeness of the plants. The looming vegetation grew high and dense, almost wild in its nature and encroaching onto the pathways in many places.

"This way," their host whispered, moving away toward the center divider. "Hurry!"

The dividing wall separated the dome into two distinct chambers, with a single, closed, glass door providing access between the two.

"We can talk inside," the woman mumbled, fumbling with the handle on the door. Once through, she removed her face mask and beckoned the squad to follow to a small, clear area. "This air is Earth normal. You can open your helmets now."

Echo took a moment to take in her surroundings. From the clearing the first chamber was no longer visible, hidden by high, vine-covered trellises that formed a barrier wall; nobody entering from the walkway would be able to see the cleared area.

The space held a handful of simple items: a seat and table, bedding folded on a camp stretcher to one side and a makeshift kitchen on another, with boxes of assorted cooking utensils. A structure at the back of the clearing resembled a common, alloy garden shed, and rows of vegetables and fruit trees filled the remaining space beyond. Without warning, the old woman rounded on the squad.

"Who in all the perditions are *you*? Where did you come from? What are you doing here? Took you long enough! Who *are* you?"

"Whoa, slow down, lady" Cooney replied, pushing his way to the front of the group. "We've been sent by Fleet. We're here to rescue you and anyone else who is still alive. What's your name?"

"Oh, yes, of course you are." The old woman shook her head absently as she backed away. Her eyes still darted about with the same, vague wildness seen through the glass. Echo wondered if she was completely sane. "I'm Margritte Alban ... Albandier, researcher first-grade, genetics ... yes, that's it. I'm a genetics expert. I look after the vegetables."

"What?"

"I grow the food to keep the others alive." She waved a hand in the general direction of the cliff-side station. "That's why I'm here. You must excuse me; I've not had visitors in a while. You're quite safe here with me. Really, you are."

Albandier's gray hair fell in sparse, dirty strands to her shoulders and beyond. She seemed only half-aware at times, but her piercing, gray eyes glistened with a burning spark of intelligence. She was old, perhaps in her seventies, but her wiry body moved with the ease of a younger person. Grimy skin hung loose about a frame surprisingly upright for someone of her apparent age. The clothes she wore were filthy, unwashed for a considerable time. Without paying any further attention to the squad, she turned away and began to shuffle items absentmindedly around the table.

"You have no guards? You work here unsupervised?" Echo asked.

"Yes, my … oh, you're a girl, aren't you? There's a guard just inside the walkway airlock. He doesn't come in here unless necessary, because I keep the first chamber at *Persephone* normal. Those arseholes can breathe it for a while, but they don't like it any more than we do. They hate the smell of our air as well, and that's what's in this section. I stay here, and they let me do my work. They think I can't go outside, but we always kept a few filter masks and environment suits stored in here. Why did you say you were here?" The old woman took a deep breath.

"Our mission is to rescue the base commander and any surviving scientific staff," Cooney said, stepping between Echo and the old woman.

"Oh, well, you're looking for Artie Mendoza. He's up in the station. Those monsters force him to work in the labs."

"Any others?"

"Oh yes. At least eight or nine of us are still alive, I think … not sure. I've been alone down here for weeks, so I don't know any more. Used to be thirty-six, but most are dead now. Yes … all dead." She turned, went to the makeshift galley and began to pour water from a jug into a saucepan, having apparently decided she was finished answering questions.

Cooney turned back to the group. "Loopy, I'd say."

"Not as loopy as you think, boy," a firm voice came from the direction of the stove.

"Yeah, well." He frowned at the old woman before turning his attention to the team. "We'll rest here and then try the walkway. We…"

"You can't enter that way, boy," the old scientist interjected again. "Those monsters changed the airlocks so they can only be opened from the inside, and there's an armed guard, like I said. You won't be able to use the valley-floor entrance either; more guards are in there. If you want in without raising the roof, you'll have to sneak through the air-conditioning plant and ventilation ducts."

Putting her pot aside, she moved to the side of the clearing and sat cross-legged on the dirt floor, fussing about her clothing as she made herself comfortable. Satisfied that everything was in order, she looked up and made a gesture to the ground around her, indicating that Echo should sit. "You want my help, or don't you?"

Echo stepped forward and squatted, followed by Cooney when he realized she had taken the initiative.

"You can show us the way in?" he asked.

"Not *show* you, boy, *tell* you. I'm an old woman." She turned her head towards Echo. "To reach the ducts you climb up the cliffs. No way am I hauling these old bones up there. I can tell you how to get in and where to go once you are inside, presuming you can do that much without wetting your diaper."

Cooney glowered as Echo nodded her understanding. Albandier seemed to address her more than Cooney. Whenever he opened his mouth to speak, she threw him a withering glance and an insult, then returned her attention to the person she had decided was in charge.

"This place has four entrances…"

"Three," Cooney corrected her.

"Four! The principal airlock leads in from the landing platform up on the western end of the ledge. Just inside is a room where the aircrews spend their days. You won't pass without being seeing, and the captain of that ship on the pad is the most competent arsehole up there." Albandier sniffed, and shot another look of disapproval at Cooney.

"Then there's the walkway airlock, just through there at the other end of the greenhouse. The third way in is about three hundred yards through the jungle, that way." She raised a hand and pointed in the general direction of the cliff. "It's a direct access to the valley floor. We used it to go out on excursions, collect specimens and so on. Both airlocks lead to the lower basement, and an elevator and stairs connect up to the plaza. The bottom level is full of storage tanks, you know. Everything we need to run the place is in there, from hydrogen, oxygen and water, to fuel for the machinery we use—used. You can't breathe, eat or drink anything on this moon, you see."

"What if we can open the airlocks?" Echo asked, earning another sharp stare from Cooney. "Would it be possible to overcome the guards?"

Margritte shook her head. "The jungle airlock? Not a chance, my dear. You might have been able to a week back, but according to my minder, the guard was strengthened a day or two ago. Something's going on, I expect." She arched her eyebrows.

*I wonder what that might be*, Echo thought. "Okay, what else?"

"About thirty meters in, the corridors from the airlocks join to form a single tunnel that runs to the basement. The outside entrance has two guards, I think, but there's only one at the walkway entrance, in a room just inside. He's my minder."

"He doesn't come in here?"

"Only on rare occasions. I live here now, and he leaves me alone as long as I behave. I grow the food for the prisoners—my colleagues—who are still alive, and he comes to collect it.

107

He hates coming in here. He prefers to stay in his guardroom and he's made it into a comfortable little cubbyhole. They don't think anyone can enter this way because the exterior door is alarmed."

Cooney looked up. "What, the one we came in by?"

"Don't wet yourself, boy. I bypassed the alarm ages ago. I'm smarter than those fools think I am. I do just fine for a *loopy* senior-citizen."

The Lieutenant ignored the obvious slight. "Any chance we could overpower your guard?"

"Oh, certainly. He spends half the time asleep, I expect. You couldn't do it without setting off the alarms though. The lock will only open from his side, so you would have to smash through. The other guards would be waiting for you at the junction in the corridors."

"Doesn't the guard think you will escape?"

Margritte regarded him as she would an irritation removed from her shoe. "You *have* been out there, haven't you, boy? You didn't just get dropped off by the stork?"

"Of course not, but…"

"Then you know what this moon's like: beautiful but deadly. They don't think I keep environment suits in here, but I do—lots of them. Even so, I wouldn't spend longer than necessary outside; my suits aren't half as effective as those things you're wearing seem to be. Anyway, where would I go, for the gods' sake?"

"What about the fourth way?" Echo asked, trying to guide the rambling old scientist back on course.

"Oh, yes, the door at the back of the station. It leads through to the power plant and ventilation-systems buildings, to allow maintenance. It's locked from the inside, and as hard as my old daddy's heart."

"So how do we get in?"

"Through the ducts, my dear. The conditioners suck in air from the outside, run it through solvent and membrane filters to remove the nasties, modify it and then pump it through ventilation shafts to everywhere inside. You can sneak into the plant room quite easily and open a maintenance hatch into the ducts. Follow them to where you want to go."

Echo tapped the readout on the forearm of her suit. "Are you sure Arthur Mendoza and the others are still alive? Can you tell us where they are, exactly?"

"Oh, certainly. Pity I don't have a map."

"I do, of sorts." Echo shuffled across beside the old woman, raising her arm to show a basic schematic of the plaza level on the small screen of her forearm readout. "Can you tell us which building they are in?"

The woman stared at the image for a moment, sniffed, and then raised a shaky finger. "Artie and at least one more will be in the labs, here." She pointed at a block towards the outer side of the station floor. "Ever since those monsters got here they've been forcing us to work for them, on pain of being tossed out into the jungle without suits if we refuse. They keep two of us in the lab almost all the time. The others, if any are left, will be here." She indicated a smaller block nearer the back of the structure. "That used to be general quarters, but they use it as a sort of jail now."

"So we need to reach the laboratories," Cooney interrupted, calling up the base schematics on his own readout. "The ventilation system vents onto the circular walkway. We can crawl through the ducts, and make our way from there."

"Yes. The main feed pipe leads to a ring duct that circles the station below the walkway—big enough to crawl through and it'll take you anywhere."

"So we go to the junction and on from there to the labs?"

Albandier glanced across to Cooney's screen. "Yes ... right," she muttered.

"And the accommodation block," Echo said. "We bring the prisoners out as well. How many environment suits do you have here, Margritte?"

"Oh, lots. When my fool of a minder cleared out the storeroom to make his personal den, he threw everything into the walkway, intending to throw it out later. I snuck the suits in here before he got around to it and put everything else outside so he wouldn't check. They're in the storage shed."

"Enough for your surviving colleagues?"

"Of course."

"Only one guard is posted at the walkway entrance, so when we come back out that's the obvious route. We can collect you and the suits on the way through." Echo glared at Cooney, defying him to contradict her.

"Really, Dear," Margritte said. "I'm much too old to be running around outside. I will stay here. Some of the others as well, I expect."

"We're not leaving anyone behind. We'll look after you."

The old woman nodded patiently and smiled, climbed to her feet and returned to her cooking pot. Echo wondered how much chance the elderly scientist had, even with help. Cooney shuffled across and squatted beside her.

"I would remind you, Bourke," he whispered, "that I am in command here. I will decide where we go, whom we rescue and how we escape. You would do well not to cross me. Do so, and I guarantee you will regret it."

A broad, heavy hand landed on Cooney's shoulder. The grim face of Sergeant Khamisi hovered only centimeters from his.

"You may be in charge," Katch said, his words calm and studied, "but that doesn't make you the most competent. You should listen to the opinions of your team. By the way, I know I'm only a sergeant, but if you make any more personal threats to Sub-Lieutenant Bourke or any of the rest of us, *I* will make sure *you* never leave this place. Now, anything about that you don't understand?"

Cooney's face turned a deep scarlet. He scrambled to his feet, walked to the edge of the clearing and began sorting through his gear. "Everyone rest," he muttered. "We're all exhausted. We move in six hours. Bourke, you have the watch on the door to the first section. Khamisi relieves you in three hours." With that, he turned his back on the group.

"That wasn't too smart," Echo said, taking Katch's hand. "When we get back he'll have you drummed out, or disciplined."

"That is a risk I'm prepared to take, Baby Girl." A warm, friendly smile spread across the big man's dark face.

# Chapter Ten

SEVERAL HOURS LATER ECHO sat cross-legged on the ground a few meters from the door through to the inner section of the greenhouse. It was locked on her side to make sure nobody entered unannounced, but there was little point in arguing with Cooney's orders for a guard.

It was a pointless exercise. The door was the only way between the chambers, and the Tolleani could not enter without making a great deal of noise. If the enemy discovered the squad it would be trapped, the only option being to cut through the glass walls and escape back to the jungle. Margritte Albandier assured them that would never be necessary. She had an emergency exit, but declined to reveal its location, saying she would do so if, and when, it was necessary.

Soon after Echo first began her watch, the elderly scientist appeared, sat for a while and chatted. The woman had taken a liking to her and a strong dislike to Cooney, so Echo took the opportunity to ask about the station. Thanks to the open plan layout she did not expect problems moving around inside, but any knowledge was useful.

To fit the available space on the cliff-side ledge the dome was rectangular with vertical sides curving over in a series of flat bevels before merging into a flat roof. The residential, administration, services and laboratory buildings sat around the perimeter with a clear plaza at the center.

A fountain and park-like gardens once filled the space, with plots for vegetables and fruit trees brought from other worlds. It was a wasteland now, allowed to wither by the alien security chief who considered maintaining it a waste of time, effort and precious water.

The air inside had been modified for the Tolleani, and whilst breathable by humans it was not ideal. Something in the Tollean mix also upset the plants, which when combined with the lack of water and care, struggled to thrive. The gardens had failed long ago and the health of the surviving scientists had deteriorated.

Their loss prompted the first alien administrator to allow Albandier to establish vegetable gardens in the greenhouse, since humans could not eat Tollean food and he needed to keep them alive for his research. The cunning old woman took the advantage and created a jungle nightmare to hide her from prying eyes and keep her minders at bay.

Inside the station, a raised, concrete walkway ran inside the glass walls, providing a serendipitous viewing platform to the outside. A ring of ductwork beneath the structure carried conditioned air to all buildings and open spaces, and vents projected up through the plascrete to send air into the dome proper. These provided the means to enter undetected.

"You need to be careful of Koll, the chief of security," Margritte said. "The Coordinator, they call him. He's a nasty piece of work but easy to spot. He walks with a limp and carries a cane. My minder bitches about him incessantly. The rumour is he lost his previous command to the last man, and that's where he got his injury. I'm guessing he was dumped here as punishment, and now he takes it out on everyone, human and Tollean alike."

"You understand their language?"

"Enough, Sweetie. Despite being shut away down here for months, I still pick things up pretty quickly. There are a few brain cells still working in this old head." She tapped a finger against her skull, her white teeth glinting in the dim light.

"So this security chief—he's in command here?"

"Debatable. He thinks he is, but another Tolleani up there called Kemmin has a lot of sway. He's a civilian, and technically the real boss. This is a scientific base and he's a scientist. He replaced the first administrator they sent, but I sense something different about him. I don't know much about him and I'm not sure whether he's in charge, or a prisoner, or both, but all the guards hold him in awe. I think they pay him more respect than Koll. He keeps to himself and rarely comes down here."

Suddenly the old woman looked behind, stood and walked away, ending the conversation without warning as was her habit. As Echo contemplated the locked door, a rustling noise came from among the plants. Standing, she moved closer to the disturbance.

In a small open space behind a dense clump of shrubs, Margritte Albandier sat cross-legged on the ground, her eyes closed. She was not alone; before her squatted an animal like the one Echo had seen by the riverside on the way in. It squatted motionless on its crab-like legs, less than a meter from the old woman. She extended her arms, and grasped the creature's hand-like forward limbs.

The strange creature's tentacle-like proboscis stretched out to the old woman, its pad resting on her forehead. Albandier's eyes were closed, her face as serene as if deep in a dream. She smiled.

The creature drew back and Margritte opened her eyes, saw Echo, and motioned her forward.

"It won't hurt you," she whispered, motioning Echo to sit beside her. "Sit still and do nothing."

Unsure how to react, Echo sat facing the strange, crustacean-like alien as it rocked sideways, wary of this new intrusion. After a moment of uncertainty, it turned towards her.

"I encountered one like this on the way here. It ran into a hole in the riverbank."

"It came here to me. I knew you were approaching the greenhouse; I was expecting you. These creatures are the prime species on this moon, and they are my friends."

Slowly, cautiously, the creature stretched its probe forward, hesitated, and then moved a little closer. Echo flexed her head back at the approach, unsure of whether to let it touch her.

"It's alright. It wants to communicate with you."

Communicate?

The pad on the end of the proboscis touched Echo's forehead, and her head exploded in a swirl of color. The instant contact occurred, the world of the surrounding greenhouse vanished and she found herself floating in a sea of mist. A loud hum, like the buzzing of insects, filled her mind as images formed in the mental haze.

For a seeming eternity Echo allowed herself to drift with the sensations, until the images began to take shape. An impression appeared of her with her teammates, standing on the path by the river; this creature was the same she had seen earlier. Emotions not her own flooded in, mixed with a sense of curiosity and a degree of cautious acceptance—friendliness. The vision shifted, and she saw the Tolleani, then sensed fear, apprehension and concern.

Echo realized what was happening. The creature was indeed trying to communicate with her, but its methods were so alien she could only comprehend vague impressions and sensations. She perceived many things, but one was clear beyond all else; the animal was terrified of the Tolleani!

The proboscis withdrew, and Echo turned to see Margritte smiling at her.

"It's intelligent," Echo gasped. "I sensed emotions—fear."

"Of the monsters, yes. Not of us. The Tolleani get bored and hunt them. Other than playing card and dice games those mongrels have little else to do."

"This is the same one I discovered earlier. It showed me an image of myself."

"It's how they communicate. They pass images, sensations and emotions, even thoughts through the proboscis. Our minds aren't well adapted to interpret, but I've become quite good at it in the last few years. They are *excellent* at understanding us."

"Where do they come from? Do they live out there, in the jungle?"

"In a way, yes. Their homes are underground. They come to the surface through burrows, but most of the time they stay below ground—more so since the monsters started killing them."

"How did it get in here?"

"There's a hidden entrance to their tunnels inside this part of the greenhouse. They made it when I began living down here. The Tolleani won't find it easily—not without a thorough search."

"They have a city under the station?"

"Yes, but more like a giant warren. It's quite an amazing place," she said. "They are not just intelligent—they use tools and build structures, even buildings of sorts."

Echo watched as the creature scuttled across the clearing and through a gap in the tangled garden vines. As it left, Margritte turned towards her.

"Their entrance is inside the storage shed over at the back. I leave it open sometimes, so they can come in and say hello. You might think it strange, but they are the only company this old girl has most of the time."

Margritte's brow creased, her eyes focused intently on Echo. "Listen to me, Sweetie. This is our great secret. Life on this world is different to anything we've seen before right down to the cellular level, and our boss Alfie Mendoza never allowed anyone here besides scientists. I've studied these creatures since we found them. We call them Kylax; they are intelligent, and technology users at a primitive level."

"You've been hiding this?"

"Yes. We thought if word of their existence got out to the general public the over-attention would destroy them. They are only the second technological species we've discovered, but unlike the Tolleani, the Kylax can't defend themselves against the likes of us. Imagine what would happen to them if the media got wind of this, and everybody decided they *had* to get a look.

"Now the entire race is under threat from the monsters, who see them as prey for sport and nothing more. I let *you* see this because I believe I can trust you. I *need* to share this with someone else, in case none of my colleagues get out of this place alive. Someone has to tell the right people. You *will* do this for me, won't you?"

"Yes," Echo said, a little taken aback. "I'll make sure the authorities know about them. You have my word."

# Chapter Eleven

MARGRITTE LOOKED UP TOWARDS the ledge, fifty meters above where the team crouched in the undergrowth. The old woman had donned an environment suit and led them outside the greenhouse to a point at the base of the cliff below the rear end of the research dome. She pointed further along the cliff face.

"There's a steel staircase leading up about a hundred meters further along—usable, but the bastards keep it under observation. They have a camera up there."

"Then why did you bring us here," Cooney snapped.

"Patience, boy. You can climb up here. This spot is beneath the view of the camera, so you won't be visible."

Cooney bristled at the old woman calling him a boy. He looked up at the rugged rock face and shook his head with doubt.

"Come on, boy, I'm sure a big, strong lad like you can scramble up there." Margritte made no attempt to disguise her contempt.

"Yes, but you can't, I'm guessing."

"Don't be an idiot. I'm too old to go scrambling up cliffs, as I told you before. This is as far as I go—from here you're on your own." Turning on her heels, the elderly scientist shuffled back towards the greenhouse. As she passed Echo, she stopped.

"You be careful, Sweetie. That fool is heading for trouble."

Echo nodded, but said nothing.

"If you come by on your way out, I'll see you then, but I'm too old to be running around this jungle. Remember; through the duct, turn left at the T junction and you will come out near the labs."

"Left."

"Yes."

"One last question. Do you know how many of the aliens are up there?"

"Oh my word, yes. There are eighteen. That fool security chief has twelve guards, none of whom are especially loyal to him. There's another Tolleani, the one I mentioned before. The chief actually runs things, but technically, that one is the base administrator. He has a little sidekick who acts as his personal servant: Tolleani, but tiny, maybe a dwarf or something. Those two won't bother you at all; they're friendly. The three from the warship rarely come out of their ready-room, so they won't be a problem unless you try to go out through the administration block."

"You know a lot about them."

"I keep my wits about me, Dear. I'm not so old I don't know what's what." Margritte tapped a finger on the faceplate of her environment suit, smiled, and ambled back into the bushes.

The cliff climb was not as difficult as expected, the cracked and weather worn rock laced with a multitude of hand and footholds. Less than half an hour later, the quad reached the ledge and gathered against the dome footings.

The electronic map on Echo's forearm readout did not include the air conditioning unit, but thanks to Margritte Albandier, Echo had a good idea of where the squad needed to go. The way in was through the main exterior air intakes, and the elderly scientist had given her a detailed description of the layout.

The squad needed only to enter the air conditioner plant, climb into the network, and crawl through to the interior ventilator grills. Either branch of the ring duct would serve to access the walkway, but according to the old woman, the left alternative led closer to the lab, their ultimate target.

Margritte's knowledge was amazing, Echo thought. Here since the beginning, she had been instrumental in the dome's commissioning, and knew every corner of the complex. Letting her stay alone in the greenhouse to feed the human captives was a poor decision by the enemy, one they would no doubt live to regret.

The broad, cliff-side outcropping had been blasted flat to provide a firm surface for the construction of the dome, and beyond the far end of the structure, a plascrete barrier rose fifteen meters, stretching from the edge of the shelf to the vertical cutaway of the mountainside behind. Only a single, solid security door broke the wall.

A small reactor and the generator that provided electricity for the station sat on the far side. Echo noted the cooling pipes for the plant running down the cliff-face from a water source somewhere on the plateau above. More pipes ran over the outer rim, carrying the waste coolant down to the valley floor and the stream she had followed on the way in.

The team squatted in the lee of the skirting wall beside the conditioning plant, a block-like unit that sat against the rear of the giant, armor-glass habitat. The point where the squad intended to enter was one of several wide intake grills just meters away. Secured by bolts from the outside, it would take time to open, but was the only option.

Echo craned her neck towards the camera mentioned by Albandier, high above her head. It began to turn, arcing away from the direction of the ladder-like stair to scan across the jungle.

Cooney groaned. "The old woman didn't say anything about it moving. We'll be seen."

Katch glanced up at the device. "Maybe not. It's not looking down here. It's pointed towards the valley floor." After a brief pause, it reversed motion and returned to the original position.

"Whoever is on the other end," Katch continued, "is more concerned with the approaches to the bottom of the service stair. They haven't considered anyone might climb the cliffs, and they aren't looking down here at all."

"They don't climb," Echo said. "Their feet aren't adapted to it."

Reaching into his field kit, Katch retrieved a multi-spanner. "What worries me most is that they are watching this area at all. Those bastards are expecting us, and that does not fill me with confidence." Without another word, he crept around the skirt of the dome until he was beneath the nearest grill and began removing the retaining bolts.

Inside the opening, a wide duct led into darkness. A stiff, continuous draft of raw, native air flowed in to the conditioning units, where it was filtered, sterilized and the individual gas balances modified. Katch crawled in until level with a service hatch on one side and, with another tool from his field harness, proceeded to cut through the hinges. In less than a minute a hard thump popped the panel, allowing it to fall away and clatter to the floor outside.

"Everyone in here, quick," he barked, jumping through to the interior of the structure. "This will cause a change in pressure to the conditioners. If it stays down too long it might trigger an alarm." As soon as the last squad member was through, he lifted the hatch cover and used his laser pistol to spot-weld it back in place.

The interior of the blockhouse was dark, hot and humid, and hummed with the monotonous drone of machinery. Several block-like conditioning units and the pipe and ductwork that attended them filled almost all the space. A single, heavy duct ran to the inner wall, carrying conditioned air for distribution through the station.

A solitary metal door led through to the dome proper. Echo grabbed the latch wheel and gave it a wrench; it was frozen, or locked.

"Secured from the other side," she said, "as Margritte expected. We'll have to use the air system."

Close to the point where the main duct passed through the wall was another inspection hatch, secured with lug nuts. It opened without resistance.

"You have the honor of going first, Bourke." A grim smile spread across Cooney's face. Echo did not argue. Bucking the lieutenant was a pointless exercise—he was in command, and took no notice besides. Significantly, he always placed her at point in the most dangerous situations, with himself well back in the line. Without a word, she hoisted herself through the hatch and into the confined conduit.

The interior was small, only a meter square but clear of obstruction. Crouching, Echo shuffled forward as the others clambered in behind. A strong draft blew from the plant, useful if they lost their way or the light from their torches failed, she thought. If one followed the direction of flow, he or she would sooner or later reach an inside vent.

That should never happen. According to Albandier, the main duct that circled the dome below the raised perimeter walkway was the only one they could actually get through. Echo did not expect to find a maze in there.

Sarra Corian lifted the faceplate of her helmet to take a sniff. "Stinks in here," she said.

"That's the Tollean air," Echo said. "They've changed the mix to suit themselves. We can breathe it, but keep your masks on. It's not pleasant."

"How do you know what it smells like?" Cooney asked.

"I've smelt it before." For a brief second her memory flashed back to the time she spent trapped in the storeroom of the alien commander's quarters, her father's old office, on *Corros*. "I'll tell you about it sometime ... not now."

Beyond the wall, the vent joined the main circuit at a 'T' junction, just as described by Albandier.

"Left" Echo directed. "Margritte Albandier said that would bring us out closest to the laboratory block."

"Right," Cooney's voice sounded from somewhere behind. "Go right."

"No, Margritte was quite clear. Left!"

"Don't argue with me, Bourke. I heard her when we were discussing this back in the greenhouse. She said right."

"She said…" Echo sighed. "Fine, you're the boss." She crawled away in the specified direction. *And you're wrong!*

Behind her, Katch crawled on all fours, his height a definite disadvantage in the confined space. "Everyone be careful," he said. "This duct is carbon-steel. If we make any noise, they'll hear it outside. I would prefer to *not* find us facing a wall of pointing guns."

Echo looked behind. "Where's Cooney?"

"Bringing up the rear," Katch whispered. "Where did you expect him to be?"

Echo nodded and crawled forward, stopping at a point one hundred meters further on where a narrower channel branched upwards. Easing into the confined space, she stood.

"I can get up here easily enough. You should be able to make it okay, Katch, but you'll find it a bit tight for working so I'll open the grill. It's about two meters up, facing in to the plaza, by the look of it."

Braced against the sides and using the joins on the ductwork as toeholds, Echo shimmied upwards. The tube passed through the plascrete walkway, the outlet grill sitting about sixty centimeters above the pedestrian surface. Through the narrow gaps between the slats, she could look out across the body of the station but only a few meters to either side. Bright light flooded the dome interior; getting out would mean exposure, and would be dangerous if any alien guards were in the vicinity.

Bracing herself, she examined the inside of the grill. On one side were hinges, indicating the vent was a door that opened out like the hatch they had used to exit the air conditioner intake. On the other side two nuts secured a single latch to the metalwork.

"Pass me up a set of pliers," she whispered to Katch.

As Echo waited, a shadow moved to block her view. A tall figure stood only meters away. Dressed in the drab, matte-green uniform of a Tollean guard, he faced away towards the central courtyard of the complex. Echo signaled for everyone below to keep as quiet as possible.

For several minutes the new arrival stood motionless, his weapon slung casually over his shoulder. Echo wondered how many of his fellows were also on the beat. If alone, he was certain to move away in time, to a point where his view of the ventilator would be hidden by a solid, waist high barrier that ran along the inner edge of the walkway. If he had companions, they would be at the other side, and he would not be leaving soon.

The situation remained unchanged after ten minutes. Not wanting to alert any other guards with the brilliant flash of a laser blast, Echo struggled to reach over her shoulder to wrestle the crossbow from her back in the confined space.

A faint alarm sounded, and without hesitation the guard turned and walked toward a nearby stairwell. Perhaps it was a change of shift, but there was always the possibility the squad's entry had been discovered.

Another five minutes and he had not returned, so Echo set about the task of removing the nuts from the inside of the latch. Once clear, she used the pliers to jiggle the bolts through the thin metal frame to release the plate from the outside, then knocked the grill loose and eased it open.

The vent exited to a narrow platform with the glass of the dome wall on the outer side and the barrier at the inner. A short distance to either side, the walkway ended against the upper floor of one of the building structures, each with a single door. Echo wondered if one of them might provide an alternate route down, a safer, more hidden descent to the plaza level than the nearby open stairs.

Scrambling up, she eased herself through the vent opening, dropped to the walkway surface and assumed a crouching position, rifle in hand and ready to cover the others as they followed behind.

Echo adjusted her face mask to exclude faint leaks from the air; it was not so much a worry, but every time she smelt a whiff, memories she preferred not to re-live came unbidden into her mind. Careful not to expose herself, she rose up to look around.

Almost the entire complex was visible beyond the barrier. Echo recalled from her briefing material that the station staff used the main courtyard below as a retreat when stressed, somewhere to remind them of home while spending months at a time confined on a hostile, alien world. The fresh crops once grown there supplemented the dried and packaged kitchen fare brought by the supply ships.

Now it was a brown, depressing place, the gardens were dead, and the fountain no longer flowed.

"Surprise, surprise," she muttered. "We got it wrong." He *got it wrong*. "The lab building is across the courtyard."

"How can you know that?" Cooney looked at the base schematic on his forearm readout, his brow wrinkled with concern. The individual blocks on the plan, whilst shown, were not marked as to purpose. "Shit!"

"Margritte told me what to look for: a three story, white block without windows, with ducts leading from the roof, through the glass to the exterior. I see only one building of that description, on the outer side. We should have turned left, like she said."

For a few minutes, Cooney remained silent, sending an angry glare in Echo's direction. "Perhaps it might have been better if she had mentioned it to me instead of you. And you should have advised me."

"And maybe you…" Echo stopped herself before she said something she might later regret. He was right; for a brief moment she wondered if she was letting her dislike of the man cloud her judgment. "Yes, sir. What are your orders, Lieutenant?"

"We work our way around at this level. We can use the barrier as a shield to avoid being seen." With a scowl, he pushed past her.

Buildings interrupted the walkway at four cardinal points. The team moved back towards the one at the aft-most end of the dome, assuming it the easier course, as the presence of the aircrew at the other end meant three more aliens to deal with at that end. Echo expected if that crew became aware the dome was compromised, they would most likely board their vessel and prepare for takeoff. The ship always came first.

Almost certainly, the enemy knew the squad was on the planet and would be waiting. From her experiences on *Corros*, Echo thought it unlikely the security chief would have sent his men out looking for them in the jungle. These creatures hated heat and extreme moisture, as evidenced by the cool air and dryness of the station. They also disliked hunting in darkness or discomfort, so all twelve were likely still inside.

With no exit at the rear excepting the one to the atmosphere plant, and that secured from within, the guards would concentrate on the airlocks. Some would be at the main entry and others down in the sub-basement at the lower exits. Their orders would be to stop ingress, and it might be some time before they realized their perimeter had already been compromised.

With twelve guards between three weak points that meant two or three, perhaps more, at each airlock, a number easy to handle on the way out. The lower locks were within meters of each other, compounding the problem. At least one guard was inside the dome, and there was a possibility someone was watching the scientific team prisoners if any were still alive. Margritte had assured Echo they were.

The segment of walkway ended at the rearmost building of the dome. Echo crept along in the lee of the barrier, crossed to the entrance and slipped the latch. Inside, a featureless, empty corridor led past several closed doors to another exit at the far end, one she hoped led out to the next segment of walkway. Keeping as silent as possible, she crept through.

The laboratory block was the next structure around the perimeter. Once inside, the team found an identical hallway leading through. Echo gingerly tested the handles on each door in turn. Behind the last, a stairwell led down towards the ground floor of the building.

"Everyone, keep as quiet as possible," she whispered, moving to the top step.

# Chapter Twelve

THE LABORATORY BLOCK CONSISTED of white corridors, white rooms and glass lined cubicles. Outside the ground-floor stairwell exit a camera perched high on the wall, a small red indicator blinking hypnotically on its side. With her pistol set to maximum intensity, Echo fired at the camera, punching a blackened hole through the plastic case. The light snapped off, a faint curl of smoke drifting up to the ceiling. Satisfied, Echo pressed on as the other members of the team moved up behind her.

Through the window-walls the squad found laboratories, specimen rooms filled with strange, alien plants growing in glass environment flasks, and the odd meeting room or office. Each was deserted. Where a significant group of scientists and support personnel once worked there was nothing but emptiness and silence, bar the constant background drone of the ventilation system. Snatching a quick look around a blind corner Echo stopped, then motioned the squad to stay back. Seconds later Cooney stood behind her.

"What's holding it up, Bourke," he whispered.

"There's a glass wall down at the end looking into another lab, and a guard sitting outside. Looks like he's half-asleep. I can see two men in the room behind him."

"That'll be our target. The old woman said the Tolleani keep Mendoza in one of the labs most of the time."

"We can't be sure yet. And are we positive he's the base commander?"

"He was at the time of the enemy takeover, according to the records. Take out the guard." Immediately he stepped back.

"Yes, sir!" Echo raised her pistol, fired, and the alien slumped from his chair with a neat hole drilled through his skull. Echo sighed; she had killed before, but never as a calculated act of war. What bothered her most was her complete lack of hesitation, such was the degree of hatred she bore for the monsters responsible for the death of her family and the loss of her youth.

The door to the lab was unlocked. The occupants turned their heads as Echo entered and raised a hand to her lips, motioning silence.

"Who are you?" one of the men whispered, standing to face her, his face white with shock. Before Echo could reply, Cooney burst into the room beside her.

"Lieutenant Jackson Cooney, Fleet Special Operations. We're here to rescue you. Is one of you the chief science officer?"

The man who rose to greet them, young and perhaps in his mid-thirties, was dressed in a once-white but now grimy lab coat long overdue for a good clean. His mop of ginger hair screamed for lack of care, a matching beard of several weeks' growth and wild, green eyes completing the archetype image of a man on edge. Uncertain how to respond, he said nothing. After a few seconds, his eyes lit with understanding.

"That would be Arthur." He raised a shaking hand and pointed towards his companion. "Arthur Mendoza, Chief Scientist." The second man remained hunched in his seat at the back of the room, unmoved by the events unfolding around him. "He was the boss before the aliens took over."

Mendoza was a beaten man. Older and smaller than his associate, and stick-thin, his gaunt, drawn face was worn and lined with worry, his dark eyes dull and devoid of light. Grey, thinning hair hung in limp strands down to his chest. His shoulders slumped beneath a shabby lab coat, giving him the aspect of a man overwhelmed by circumstance, who no longer sought to fight back. He peered from one member of the squad to the next, saying nothing, only vaguely aware of their presence.

"Then he's the man we came here to rescue," Cooney said.

Nobody noticed the minuscule surveillance camera set high in a corner at the far end of the lab.

\* \* \*

Barbus Koll, marginally short of apoplexy, slammed his fists onto his desk and glared at the monitor. The enemy was inside, actually inside despite his precautions. How could this happen? The chance of these humans trekking unharmed across country to the station were minimal considering the nature of everything on this moon, but somehow they had done so regardless of the relentless rain, the choking vegetation, the heat and the poisonous atmosphere.

Koll's defenses had been well prepared, or so he thought. The days when he underestimated these creatures were long gone, swept away by the events on *Corros* and the death of his prospects for advancement in the military. Nevertheless, the animals were here right under his nose, and without any of his guards having discovered their presence. *Humans, for the ancestors' sakes.*

Expecting an intrusion, he had posted men at all three airlocks and sealed every other known access into the dome, but the infiltrators had found a way in regardless.

It was clear where he had failed. *The ventilation!* To reach the atmosphere plant meant climbing an almost sheer cliff face, and the only practical way up was the service stairway. Koll had a camera watching it and knew they had not come that way. They must have scaled the rock itself.

Tollean hands and feet were not well suited to climbing and such an approach had never occurred to him. The infiltrators must have climbed up beneath his camera, and entered through the ductwork. There could be no other answer.

Other cameras positioned through the station had picked up the humans' presence. The first warning came when one of the units in the laboratory block failed. Others detected the intruders and allowed Koll to follow their movements. They were not who he had expected and it appeared their objective was the scientists; this was not an attempt to snatch the exile, and Pac was wrong.

*Six of them,* he thought. *I can deal with this.*

Seconds earlier he had ordered the guards to re-disperse from the sub basements. They were on their way to the elevators, leaving three of their fellows guarding the lower level airlocks. In another few minutes, his trap would be ready to unleash. Seven armed soldiers would be waiting for the enemy invaders the second they set foot outside the building.

Koll would use Pac and his useless crew to support the one remaining guard at the main entry, just in case there were more of these creatures outside. He had already made it quite clear that if Kemmin escaped, the responsibility would be Pac's due to his complete underestimation of the threat implied by the small descent craft intercepted earlier. Pac did not yet know it was human intruders. It irked Koll that the commander took little if any notice of his admonishments, but now the situation had changed.

It escaped him why the scientists would be worth a rescue attempt like this, one bound to fail and hardly justifying the risk. They were not working on anything significant; their sole purpose here was to study the strange life of this moon.

Only their research into a number of virus-like micro-forms had been of any value. At the time of the invasion the scientists were studying one particularly dangerous organism, and due to a lab accident Koll had discovered that the strain was deadly to human kind with one-hundred-percent fatality. He seized it as a valuable weapon of war.

He had been, annoyingly, unable to take credit for the discovery, as the previous administrator had taken the praise and removed it to the naval base where human prisoners were held. They were infected and allowed to escape. With transmission by touch, through water or air, and with a long incubation period, the infection was unstoppable. According to latest reports, it had spread like a wild fire through Federation space before the enemy even suspected a threat.

Koll spent long nights pouring over every report from up the line. Several had mentioned Terran fleets were deploying a new kind of disabling device, and its use had enabled the humans to even the odds in a war previously weighted in the Emperor's favor.

Those stories troubled Koll; the descriptions matched an item developed on *Corros,* something he had thought destroyed by the explosion when the scientists' own bomb vaporized the base, but now... Perhaps those damned animals stole the data when they escaped; he could not know for sure, but if a connection were ever made it would mean serious trouble for him for not reporting the invention before its destruction.

Koll flicked on the intercom. It was time to give that damned commander a swift kick.

"Pac? There are six enemy infiltrators in this station. They are human, the remains of the invasion force you failed to destroy. Their objective is the scientists, not his lord almighty Kemmin as you so wrongly presumed. I will hold you responsible if they escape via the landing platform. You and your men will stop loafing around over there and join the guard at the exit, and you will do it now!"

\* \* \*

Arthur Mendoza peered up at each member of the squad in a vague, half-aware fashion, and then returned his attention to whatever he was writing as if no one else was present. His companion stumbled around the bench and rushed over to the new arrivals. Stopping in front of Echo, he held out a hand in greeting.

"Bernie Greer. I'm Doctor Mendoza's personal assistant. He's a little poorly today, I'm sorry."

Cooney stepped forward and pushed Echo aside. "We're here to take Mendoza and his work out of here."

"Thank the gods. You'll have to take it easy though. The Doc's been under a lot of stress, and his mind ... well, just be careful with him. He's been forced to do things for the enemy, things detrimental to humanity, under threat of the others being executed if he didn't comply."

"Others?" Echo asked.

"There are five more of us locked in the accommodation block, and one down in the greenhouse. There used to be more, but the Tollean security chief who runs this place has killed everyone else. He's a real bad case, that one."

"You work for the Tolleani?" Cooney asked, his face set in a grim frown. "That's treason; even under duress you should have refused."

Greer, a man of significant stature, rounded on the lieutenant, placing his face just centimeters away. "The Doctor is a civilian scientist and an elderly man, not a trained mercenary or soldier. He's spent his entire life trying to find ways to benefit humankind, and the other scientists here are and were close friends and dedicated people like him. If he had not done as those alien bastards asked, the rest of us would be dead by now."

"Nevertheless..."

"He's gone out of his way to make up for it. We developed a vaccine. A message was snuck out by..."

"Yeah, fine, we got it." Cooney brushed the man aside. "The virus?"

"Yes. It's here." From a nearby cabinet Greer retrieved a small box and opened it to reveal four glass phials. "The red one is the original strain released on humanity. The green is the antivirus, and the blue a vaccine to prevent infection. That's what Mendoza and I have been spending our time on here. The security chief doesn't have the vaguest idea. As long as he thinks we are working on something for him, he ignores us and we keep plugging away. The orange phial…"

"We don't have time for a lecture." Cooney grabbed the box from Greer's hand and shoved it into a pocket on his harness. "Get ready to leave here, now."

"What about the other scientists?" Echo asked.

"We don't have time…"

A face appeared at the corridor window of the laboratory. A diminutive alien peered through the glass at the people inside. He was short, thick set and without a doubt Tollean, his head barely extending above the frame of the window. His fur covered face showed the same emotionless gaze Echo had seen before. For a brief second he stared at the group, and then disappeared along the corridor."

"Damn," Cooney cursed. "Whatever that was, it'll raise the alarm."

"No," Greer said. "That was Torrick, the assistant of Ronus Kemmin, the alien who officially commands this place."

"I thought you said the security chief runs the place."

"He does. It's a funny situation. Kemmin is technically in charge, but he's under exile by royal decree and not permitted to leave here. Koll is his jailer, but he's terrified of him. Kemmin's a friend. He's the one who sent…"

Cooney shook his head negatively. "No Tollean is a friend. We don't have time to discuss this. We have what we came for, so we need to go." So saying, he grabbed Mendoza by the arm and hoisted him to his feet. A soft whimper escaped from the old man's lips as he tried vainly to resist the rough treatment.

"Go easy with him," Greer barked. "He's weak."

"If you want to come with us, do as you're ordered."

As Cooney hauled the old scientist away from the bench and towards the door, Greer stepped back to the refrigerator, removed a second phial box and secreted it inside his lab coat.

Echo fell in behind as the group departed the room. "Lieutenant, we need to find the other scientists"

"No time. The little alien will raise the alarm, and we'll never get away."

"No, he won't," Greer countered. "He's a…"

Cooney ignored him. "My chart puts the elevator to the basements in the blockhouse opposite this one. We'll have to cross on the ground level." Echo checked her own read-out.

"No, you have to rescue my colleagues," Greer shouted, his face flushed pink. "And Margritte Albandier, down in the greenhouse."

Cooney stopped in his tracks and turned on the civilian, his face flushed red with anger. "I am in command here. We came for the base commander—that's Mendoza—and the virus samples. Nothing else! Think yourself lucky you get to tag along as well." Without waiting for a response, he turned and rushed from the lab. Greer looked at Echo, a silent appeal in his eyes.

"I'm sorry," she said. "He's the boss. We'll work something out, trust me." Her deepest instincts told her to go after the other prisoners, and she knew Katch and Sarra would back her if she chose to do so. Without a doubt it would lead to courts-marshal for all of them; Cooney would argue they disobeyed the orders of a senior officer and placed the mission in jeopardy, and with the help of his powerful father, he would prevail. Unable to see an immediate solution to the problem, she motioned Greer to precede her and followed into the corridor.

Cooney predictably ordered Echo to take point as the team headed towards the building exit, so she clenched her jaw, forced back a retort and moved to the front. She did not fear danger, and even got a rush from it, but it was obvious the lieutenant was still placing himself in the least dangerous position. No doubt, he would love nothing better than to see her cut down by enemy fire.

The way out of the dome was more difficult and more dangerous than the path in. With the scientists in hand an escape through the ducting was not possible. Greer would be fine but Doctor Mendoza, an elderly and infirm individual, would never make it through the ductwork and down the cliffs without exposing them all to certain capture.

The aliens would soon be alert to their presence, if not already. The little creature who had seen them in the lab, although a dwarf in stature compared to the others, may have reported them to his superiors by now if Cooney was correct.

Conversely, Greer was adamant the little alien was a friend. If so, they might be all right.

At the front entry to the building, Echo eased the door open a crack and looked outside. The only options to re-gain the jungle were the three airlock exits, and to reach any of them meant crossing the open plaza.

The landing pad was the easiest choice, but was not without problems: guards would be at the exit, and although Echo doubted it, the crew of the ship on the platform might back up the guards. They would be armed; that was certain.

If the squad managed to escape, the alien ship might be useful if accessible. Like all graduates from the Fleet academy Echo could fly a variety of spacecraft at a pinch, as could all other members of the team, but this was an alien vessel and it was doubtful any of them would be able to handle it in an emergency. The main difficulty would be in understanding the various controls, but thanks to her training in the Tollean language, even that was possible.

The other two routes out, to the greenhouse and direct to the valley floor, involved passing through the sub-basement area deep beneath the station, accessible by elevator or by a winding stairway. Either way posed dangers, passing through points where a trap could be waiting.

Access to the basement was in the accommodations block at the inner side of the dome, both elevator and stairwell opening from the front of the structure out to the plaza. Greer insisted the other station personnel were in that building, so it was the way Echo intended to lead regardless. Despite Cooney's intransigence, she refused to give up on them.

At first the courtyard, viewed around the corner of a doorframe, appeared empty with no sign of movement apparent. Something flickered at the edge of Echo's line of sight. A Tolleani guard hunkered behind a block-work wall about thirty meters to the left, stealing a quick glance every few seconds at the entrance door where Echo crouched. Further observation showed more Tolleani hidden nearby.

"I think your little mate turned us in," Echo said to Greer.

"No, he wouldn't do that. He's a friend. He hates those guards, and the security chief especially."

"Well, there are several of them hiding outside, waiting for us to step through this door. We'll be caught in an inescapable crossfire. We can't go this way."

"They must have spotted us with the cameras. The damned things are everywhere."

"Doesn't matter how they know we are here. They do, and we have to find another way out. Can the lift be accessed from the mezzanine walkway?"

"Yes. If we can get to the accommodations building, we can go down from there. The internal stairs connect and go all the way to the basement levels. We can go after the other staff members and continue on down, or take the elevator from the ground floor."

Echo led the squad back the way they had entered and turned up the stairs. From the mezzanine door, she looked to see if there were any guards, and spotted a figure squatting on a set of open stairs from the ramp to the ground level, only the top of his head visible.

"Katch, I need you." Akachi stepped forward, with Cooney right behind him.

"There's a guard in the stair well about fifteen meters out. He's keeping down and watching this door, and he *will* be armed. We need to distract him enough to take him out."

"We go out with weapons hot—get him first." Cooney said.

"He's covered pretty well. He won't be easy to hit before he gets one of us. Katch, can you dive out and do a dash to the ventilator? He will have to lift up for a good shot at you, and I can take him down."

From over her shoulder, she drew the carbon-fiber crossbow from her back, retrieved a bolt and fitted it to the weapon. "I'll try to get him before he fires, and take him down without alerting the others below. With luck, it'll buy us time to reach the next building."

Cooney nodded and said nothing, no doubt overjoyed at the possibility of one of the thorns in his side being removed. Echo did not like placing Katch in jeopardy like this, but the man was fast and would willingly take the risk.

Without a word and with Echo poised, he took a dive through the doorway, hit the surface at a roll, and continued until he came to rest behind a ductwork pillar identical to the one they had used when entering the dome. The entire movement took only seconds, too quick for the enemy to react.

The guard watched the ventilator, his head and the tip of a rifle still barely visible. He did not rise further or attempt to fire. Echo cursed beneath her breath; the alien was cautious, waiting for a clear target before exposing himself.

Katch peeked around the edge of the ductwork pillar and saw his action had failed to achieve the desired result. Turning to look at Echo, he made a small hand movement she understood to mean 'get ready'. Seconds later, he rolled from his cover to the open walkway and lay on his stomach with his rifle aimed at the door of the next building entrance.

It happened in the space of a breath. Believing his opponent was unaware of his presence, the alien guard rose to line up on his target. Echo, ready and waiting, fired the crossbow and a silent killer thirty centimeters in length lanced through the air and buried itself in the side of the alien's neck. The body dropped silently. Without hesitation, Echo rushed from the doorway and across to Katch, the others close behind.

"That was unbelievably stupid," she said, a smile on her face. A set of gleaming white teeth flashed back at her; the man's bravery was beyond question.

# Chapter Thirteen

WITHOUT PAUSE, ECHO LED the way to the door of the adjacent building. The encounter with the Tollean guard had not been as silent as she would have liked, and she prayed his fellow guards had not suspected anything.

When they realized not all was well they would rush to the stairs occupied by the now dead alien, but by the time they discovered the body Echo intended the squad to be well on its way to the basements. With heads down, they ran for the door of the next block and passed unhindered through to the next part of the walkway.

The mezzanine stood two stories above the plaza level. Most of the buildings had three stories, the exception being the administration block at the landing field end. Once inside the top floor of the innermost structure, the team entered the stairwell and began the descent.

At the second floor, Greer called for Echo to stop, and pointed at the exit. "The others are being held in the accommodation quarters, through there."

Cooney pushed his way forward. "Maybe you didn't hear me well enough. The enemy know we're here and any minute they're going to come through that door above. We don't have time to go after your friends. We have what we came for, so we head for the basement." He turned his glare on Echo. "Any problems, Bourke?"

Echo glared at her supposed commander. He was livid at the idea anyone should contemplate going against his orders, and he held his rifle with the tip pointing in her direction. He undoubtedly wanted grounds for having her court marshaled if they survived this business, but she was resolved never to give him what he needed.

"No problems at all, Lieutenant." Echo kept her voice calm. "Greer, we can't risk a delay to look for the others now, not since we've been discovered. There's a Federation war fleet out there, and with luck they'll be able to come for your friends when we take back this system." She winked at the scientist, head angled to avoid Cooney seeing her do so. Greer's face, white with fury, calmed a little. He nodded acknowledgement and turned on the lieutenant.

"Once we make it out of here I *will* see you are indicted for cowardice, and for deliberately abandoning citizens of the Federation to save your own skin." He turned, stepped past Echo and proceeded down the stairs.

Three levels below, they entered the lower basement. From the stairwell exit, Sarra Corian put a well-placed shot into the elevator control panel. By now, the enemy would be well aware their prey had slipped through their fingers, and once they worked out where the squad were heading would not be far behind. The fused controls would force them to take the stairs, delaying them long enough for the team to reach the airlocks.

"How many of those bastards did you see upstairs?" Cooney demanded of Echo as the group gathered.

"At least four," she said. "Maybe more. With only twelve guards the security chief must have pulled them off the entrances. There may be less of them to deal with down here than we thought."

"Good. I'll take point from here. You bring up the rear." Cooney spun on his heels and headed in the direction of the tunnel. Echo shook her head. With the likelihood of more guards behind than in front, he once again chose to place himself in the safer position.

Rank upon rank of huge plasteel tanks cluttered the sub-basement, filled with everything from fuel for machinery and ships, to separated gases for making water for use in the labs, or pumping up to the air conditioners for modifying the air in the dome. Somewhere in a dark, distant corner pumps burbled away at drawing in the outside atmosphere and separating anything useful, including oxygen, helium, hydrogen and trace elements. At the outer side of the chamber, the exit tunnel bored through the bedrock towards the base of the cliff. One hundred meters in, another passage branched to one side.

"That branch leads to the outside airlock," Greer said. "Straight ahead and we come to the exit leading to the greenhouse walkway."

"We go by the outside exit," Cooney announced without hesitation. "It gets us to the jungle quicker, and to more cover. Bourke, you watch our asses while we take out the guards at the lock. Khamisi and Corian, take point."

*And the enemy fire*, Echo thought. Her friends were the best in the squad, and they would cope. She turned to face the rear as the others moved on towards the branch tunnel junction. Her heart pounded with the familiar awareness of adrenaline coursing through her body; she treasured these moments, the almost ecstatic thrill she got in the presence of danger.

As she backed away a loud thump came along the tunnel from the direction of the basement, indicating the guards were not far behind. Without knowing how many were following, Echo could only continue to retreat, her rifle raised. Against more than one assailant her crossbow was of little use.

Two Tolleani crouched at the airlock, facing the tunnel with weapons raised. With nowhere to hide they were exposed, but ready and waiting. The second the squad appeared, they reacted. Katch and Sarra dropped to the ground and returned fire, bringing both guards down.

Katch pushed himself to his knees, and turned. Tandie Applegate lay motionless on the floor of the tunnel. She had been behind him when he dropped, and took the full enemy blast in her chest. She now lay face down with no sign of movement. Katch rolled her over, and shook his head. No one could survive the massive trauma caused by the enemy barrage; she would not be going home.

Whilst he examined the body, Sarra rushed to the lock and grabbed two environment suits from a rack. Thirty seconds later both Greer and Mendoza were clad in insulated, grey coveralls, boots and gloves, their heads and faces covered with soft helmets and faceplates with air filters. The delay was unacceptable, but nobody survived unprotected in the alien environment outside.

With both inner and outer airlock doors open, the team rushed out to the path leading into the jungle. Katch turned and waited. "Echo," he yelled. "We're clear. Get out of there."

Only meters away along the tunnel, Echo crouched facing the junction. "On my way. You get out now. I'm right behind you."

Somewhere deep in the back of Katch's mind a premonition told him he should not leave, but he had a job to do and it included not leaving the civilians to the erratic care of Lieutenant Jackson Cooney. He turned and followed the others, heading for the cover of the surrounding vegetation.

Echo dived for the exit. A meter from the inner door something slammed with numbing force between her shoulder blades. Her muscles paralyzed by a bolt of high intensity energy, she lost all control and collapsed, her vision fading to darkness.

\* \* \*

Barbus Koll hobbled along the corridor and glared down at the prone body lodged halfway through the airlock. In his hand he held a stun pistol, something he kept for hunting. The weapon paralyzed a target's nervous system with electrical energy, disabling without killing, and allowing him the pleasure of disposing of his prey later, at his pleasure and at his own pace. From the open airlock he saw the last of the enemy vanish into the vegetation.

"Get this one up to the pen," he shouted as his men gathered behind him. "It could prove useful. And get rid of the other bodies."

One of the guards stepped forward. "Yes, Coordinator. What about the others?"

"There are only four of them left, and they are hampered by two of their scientists. Take three men and go after them. Their trail will be easy to follow so don't come back until they are dead—every last one of them! Command will be interested to learn human infiltrators have entered this system without their knowing about it."

Koll strode away, leaving the guard to ponder his fate. He peered out at the gray overcast and the constant drizzle of rain, and swallowed hard.

On the way back to the stairwell, Koll cursed his guards for letting the enemy get past. It certainly did not pay to underestimate these human creatures. One thing he was sure of was their unyielding sense of loyalty to their own kind; in most cases, they would risk their own lives to protect or save those of others. He did not understand this attitude, but it was something he believed he could use to advantage.

He had expected the intruders to attempt a rescue, and had been waiting where the other human scientists were imprisoned. The rescue did not eventuate. In what he understood to be an atypical manner for humans, the intruders bypassed the floor and headed for safety. It galled him; why could these worthless animals not act as expected?

\* \* \*

Consciousness crept back, and the memory of events in the tunnel flooded Echo's mind.

It was deathly quiet.

Against her first instinct to open her eyes and jump to her feet, she stayed still and listened. The surface beneath her was hard and unforgiving, and bright light filtered through her eyelids. The same foul odor of Tolleani modified air once smelled in her father's office on *Corros* filled her nostrils, and she realized her face mask was gone. She lay with her back flat against the tiles, so her field harness and crossbow were also missing.

After a few minutes of silence, she eased her eyes open a little, waited for them to adjust to the glare of the overhead lights and then opened them a little more. She was on a floor, looking straight up at a ceiling. All around, metal bars reached up through her peripheral vision; she was in a cage, roughly four meters square.

Propped on her elbows, she looked about. Her prison filled the center of a room devoid of windows, and she faced what she assumed to be the back wall. She tried to twist around for a better view, but stopped as a shock of pain shot through her body, a legacy of the battering her nervous system had taken from whatever brought her down.

Braced for the expected torment, she rolled on all fours and pushed herself to a standing position. In front of her, seated in a chair by the solitary door into the room, was a Tollean guard. He stared blankly towards her, his body motionless. For a moment he resembled a statue, with no sign of movement to betray life. Something rested in his hands and a short, ornamentally embellished cane lay on the floor beside him.

Echo had never been this close to a living Tolleani before. On *Corros* she once saw one from a distance, in her home village. He was the commander of the alien contingent based there. She had also seen several bodies close up. This one looked similar, but to her they all looked much alike.

Dressed in a green and red uniform, he sat with legs spread wide apart. Like the others of his kind, this creature had most peculiar feet. There were two small digits, each ending in a claw, with a bigger one, also clawed, on the inside. On the outer side of each foot, a second larger digit extended almost at right angles to the others. The feet were clad in open, sandal-like shoes. A dark, leathery hide covered his feet and hands.

The creature's hands also possessed four digits, with two fingers and two thumbs, one to either side, that closed together like a pincer. The overall body shape was humanoid, but it was in the face where the true alien quality showed the most.

Short, fine hair covered the facial features. Devoid of emotion, the thin lips remained silent, the cat-like eyes cold and dull, and the ears poking high above the head. Those characteristics were burned indelibly into Echo's mind. She would never forget the creatures that destroyed her home. Without moving, she flicked her eyes over the rest of the room. Besides the cage and the guard, the chamber contained only the door, and in one corner, a table on which lay her helmet, harness and weapons. She realized what the alien was holding; in his strange hands, he held her crossbow.

Trying to remain calm as her heart fought to pound its way from her chest, she faced the Tolleani and eased herself down, fighting against the pain to sit cross-legged on the floor. Her captor's eyes remained fixed on her, his body as still as a statue. For a second Echo almost spoke, but thought better of it. She would wait for him to make a move.

Barbus Koll stared at the creature as alarm bells jangled somewhere in the back of his mind. He knew this animal—he was sure of it—but he could not work out quite how. It was female, judged from the body shape. He was not surprised; unlike the Tolleani, who never allowed their women to fight, these beings had no concerns about placing theirs in danger, and from what he understood, many were included in their fighting forces, some in positions of command. *Imagine that!*

Koll had long ago learned that humans had two sexes just like the Tolleani, and he was quickly forming the conclusion that the more dangerous of the two was the female. Beyond the scientists imprisoned here, his experience of human females was limited to two examples, both on *Corros*. One was a prisoner taken from the enemy ship his pet scientists bought down with their disabling device, later allowed to escape carrying the viral weapon back to Federation territory. The other was the damned creature who destroyed his base on that world. He never saw that one close up.

From his office window, he often used binoculars to watch it as it observed him in turn from a ledge beyond the airfield. It usually lay on the rock with an ocular device obscuring its face.

The only other time he saw it was the day he lost his command. The two animals responsible had run across the tarmac to steal a scout craft, seconds before a destroyer stationed there launched itself skyward in a colossal explosion, along with the nearby administration buildings.

Soon after, he saw them from behind as they ran away from where he lay injured and barely conscious on the space field at the deserted human military base.

*Surely this could not be the same creature?* That animal had long hair, while this one's was cropped short. The color was identical, and he knew these creatures cut their hair, so that was not definitive. This one wore a skin-tight suit made from some kind of rubberized material, presumably what allowed it and its fellow infiltrators to move through the jungle on this moon without harm. The captive's helmet included a set of filters for carbon dioxide, methane and pathogens, allowing them to breathe the unpleasant native air.

What fazed him most was the object in his lap. It was a weapon the like of which he had seen only once before, and from a distance. The animal on *Corros* carried something similar to this one. Despite its high-tech construction, it was a primitive device, designed to shoot a sharpened rod at a target. It was simplistic for the advanced human technology, but no doubt effective; a bloodied shaft removed from the corpse of one of his men bore the evidence.

Koll detested history—it was not worth the waste of time —but recalled once reading that his own race used similar projectile weapons long ago, when still a single-planet species. It puzzled him why a sophisticated military force would use such a thing today.

In the back of his mind, a nagging voice insisted this creature was the animal he had encountered before, the one that destroyed his career, and his life.

Motionless and careful to give nothing away, he watched as the prisoner assumed a sitting position and stared back at him. Could it be the same one? It seemed unlikely; the odds were far too high. Nevertheless, that niggling doubt refused to dislodge itself.

Koll frowned as the small figure of Torrick, the creepy little manservant of the bane of his life, lord-high-bloody-almighty Ronus Kemmin, opened the door and entered carrying a tray.

"What do you want, ass-wipe."

The diminutive alien stared at him, unfazed. "I brought food for the captive," he replied, his head held high. "Perhaps you would prefer that it starve to death before you have a chance to torture it?"

"Careful how you speak to me, you little shit. Your precious boss can't protect you as much as you think he can."

"You don't say?" Torrick ambled across and leaned down to place the tray at the bars of the cage. He looked up and one eye closed in what might have been a Tollean variation on a wink.

Echo tried not to react. The little alien stood and walked from the room, slamming the door as he left. Echo remained motionless. The presence of real food reinforced the feeling of hunger growing in her belly. It was many hours, depending on how long she had been unconscious, since she had eaten anything but field tablets, and the smell from the food the midget left her was enticing. Nevertheless, she resisted making a move.

What occupied her mind the most was she understood the brief conversation that had just taken place; the subliminal language lessons received during training had not been in vain. She would never let her captors know, but the fact she could understand them gave her an advantage.

Braced against the residual pain in her body, she determined to out-wait her silent captor. From the way he tried to order the little alien, this was no common guard: he was probably the security chief spoken of in such glowing terms by Margritte Albandier.

# Chapter Fourteen

THE REGION OF SPACE ahead was far from empty. Five Tollean vessels, three more than Ben expected, sat a thousand kilometers ahead. Somewhere beyond lay the gateway through which the Federation forces would attack.

A fraction of a millimeter in diameter, the wormhole was not visible. The gate potential was a generalized region, several kilometers in radius, within which a gateway generator could create a link between the microscopic wormhole and a spacecraft.

This gateway was unusual. Located near the Lagrange L5, a Trojan point on the orbit of the star's largest gas-giant, its position moved around the yellow star with the planet. As a way into the system, it was unreliable and rarely used. It led to a neutral star, and was normally guarded by only two enemy vessels. Fleet chose it for the invasion for that reason.

Ben sat back and tried to summarize the situation. Three destroyers and two cruisers were inadequate to deny entry to the massed forces soon to arrive, but they could cause considerable damage. Losses at this early stage were unacceptable, but perhaps unavoidable. The real battle would take place once the main body of the fleet arrived and approached the Tollean base.

A heavy weight rested on Ben's shoulders. The Tolleani were expecting something to happen, and had bought in reinforcements. He could only speculate on what raised the alarm, but two possible causes came to mind.

First, the Special Forces team dropped at the moon *Persephone* had been detected. Once they were identified as human an alert would have been sent to the naval base. It took only seconds to discount the theory. If discovery had occurred and a warning dispatched, it would take time for ships to relocate. Ben flew straight here, and would have arrived first.

In all likelihood, he gave the game away when escaping the system at the end of his reconnaissance mission, months earlier. The enemy no doubt assumed something was in the wind, and had called in extra forces in case.

The Tollean military did not know Fleet would come through this particular gateway, so there would be reinforcements at the others as well. They would remain on station until word came of an attack elsewhere, by which time it would be too late to stop the incursion. Instead, they would head back to the main base to assist with its defense.

The guard vessels ahead would do their best to cause mayhem, undoubtedly ordered to pick off anything that came through the gateway without question. Once overwhelmed, they would try to lead the fleet away until their fellow ships could rejoin the main defenses at the base, and that is where Ben came in. He sat between the aliens and that base, his mission to block any warning signals if possible.

His ship floated motionless in space, undetected. With the dispersion field on full, and with the vessel positioned to avoid detection by light occlusion, his presence was unsuspected. The

*Infiltrator* was not an attack craft, but that did not make it either defenseless or powerless. Larger than Ben's previous command —a front line destroyer—it possessed almost as much firepower, especially as fitted out for this mission.

Ben turned to his first officer, Jerry Bayer, "So, this is going to make things difficult."

"Yes, sir. We need to send a signal through, to warn the Fleet."

Ben nodded. His orders were to conduct a stealth attack on the two ships expected to be here, thus creating a distraction while the first wave arrived, an event slated to begin in just one hour. The Fleet needed a warning to expect more than double the anticipated resistance.

The prearranged plan was still the only option, but carrying it out without committing suicide in the process could prove difficult. Ben planned to return to *Persephone* after the attack and recover the rescue team, and damage to or loss of his command would jeopardize the lives of everyone on that moon.

"The second we attack they'll know we're here and start a search for us. Our dispersion shield is good but not perfect, so a concerted attempt will still detect us in minutes. There's no way we can compete against two cruisers and three destroyers."

"How about we turn off the shield and run," Jerry said jokingly. "We might lure some of them away."

"Unlikely. They'll know something is going to happen here, and they won't leave. I think we have no choice but to carry out our original plan. We can attack four of those ships at once, so that's what we do. That should draw their attention long enough to get a signal through. Then it becomes a game of cat and mouse."

Five objects launched from the nose of the Infiltrator, four fusion torpedoes preceded by a messenger drone aimed at the gateway. Little more than a missile containing an engine, fuel, a wormhole generator and a guidance computer, the device would alert the fleet, signaling that the first part of Ben's mission was successful, and to expect more opposition than planned for.

Before firing, Ben had moved his ship in as close as he dare, relying on the hope the enemy ship's crew were focused on the gate and not their own backsides. Computerized detectors would guard the rear, but the buoy broadcast a captured Tollean identification sign.

The code was almost certainly out of date, but would confuse and delay. An old code received from within safe territory would be referred to operators, rather than initiate an instant, automatic response. With luck, the missiles would reach their targets before the Tolleani boosted their protective fields to cover their sterns, the most vulnerable point of any spacecraft.

Ben swung his ship away to a new course the second the weapons launched. The minute they passed beyond the dispersion field the missiles became detectable, and he did not intend to be in the same spot when a retaliatory attack occurred. He would jump from one point to another, causing confusion if making detection more likely.

The Tolleani were not sleeping on the job. They spotted the messenger quickly. As expected, their automatic defense systems picked up the broadcast security code and identified it as valid but obsolete.

The enemy computers referred the matter for the attention of the duty operator. The torpedo buoy passed between the cruisers, whose commanders only now become aware of its presence, and that of its escorts. Alerted, one of the destroyers turned away from the gateway, re-positioning to defend the sterns of its companions.

The torpedoes swept up to the turning destroyer, ignored it and continued on course for the other four ships. They targeted the drives of the enemy vessels; with those damaged, the warships would be severely limited in their ability to fight.

As they passed, the defending destroyer's computers locked on their point of origin and a barrage of plasma bombs poured into the space Ben's ship had occupied only minutes earlier. The Infiltrator was invisible to the enemy, but they knew it was there. The stern shields of the other vessels, not normally used due to their hindering the drive systems, had not yet fully activated.

Two missiles hit shields and exploded, their nuclear hellfire spreading in a distorted field of violent incandescence, but doing nothing to disable their targets. The other two found their way unerringly to their objectives. The stern of a destroyer disintegrated in a blinding blaze of light, while the second missile glanced off the hull of one of the cruisers, exploding and causing peripheral damage to the ship's exterior, but not affecting its battle capability.

Far ahead, the signal buoy plunged into the gateway, and blinked out of sight.

"It's through," Jerry announced, waving his hands above his head. "It actually got through."

Ben nodded, continuing to throw the ship through multiple course changes, shifting every few seconds to make it difficult to pinpoint. By now, his presence was known but not his location. He kept dodging, knowing they would not fire again unless they could find a target, but there was a limit to how long he could keep it up. He prayed for the arrival of Fleet.

Minutes after the buoy vanished, drones poured from the wormhole, streaming in a nose-to-tail line that dispersed to set up an overlapping shield-wall across the center of the gate. Hundreds more followed, moving out to attack the four remaining sentries.

Computer controlled drones could do little damage to the larger, front-line warships, but could not be discounted either. Their purpose was to distract, not destroy. Only seconds later, the leading capital ships began to come through, the first of almost two hundred.

As the drones swarmed, the Tolleani stopped their search for Ben, more concerned with the immediate threat of the tiny attackers and their annoying stings. Ben's ship was now back on the direct line to the Tollean base, the dispersion field turned to maximum strength. He hoped if the enemy got a distress signal away it would hit and dissipate on the shield, providing extra hours for the forces of humanity to gather before they faced the full force of resistance.

The battle took less than half an hour. Surrounded by the Federation's best, the five enemy ships were overwhelmed. None surrendered, but constant pounding reduced them to harmless, scrap-metal hulks. As the last fired a final volley, Ben powered down his shields and moved forward towards the battlefield.

Ahead, the colossal, cigar-shaped, Fleet carrier *Pellargo* nosed from the bubble of the gateway, then moved away to clear the gate for the follow up contingent.

Ben breathed a sigh. The 'beachhead' invasion had gone better than planned, considering. Six destroyers, a cruiser and several hundred drones were lost before the alien ships succumbed, but the bulk of vessels survived safe and intact. More importantly, he and his crew still lived.

*   *   *

Katch forced his way through the undergrowth as the fronds of unpleasant local vegetation slapped persistently at his faceplate. Ahead, Bernie Greer stumbled on, little more than a grey, shapeless form in his environment suit. Further on, Sarra Corian and Serge Petrovsky carried Mendoza at high speed through the jungle, one on either side of the failing scientist. In the lead. Cooney ploughed ahead along an animal path like the one used to reach the dome.

Two days had passed since the escape. The Lieutenant had bypassed the greenhouse, and continued across the valley floor until they reached the river. From there he followed the watercourse towards the ridge designated as the rendezvous point.

*Persephone* possessed a strange day to night arrangement, orbiting as it did a gas giant. So close was it to the massive world that it was tidally locked, making a full day-night sequence equal to the moon's orbit around its master, a fast transit of a little over forty-six hours. One side, the one always away from the planet, had twenty-three hours of day, and a night of the same length as it traversed the far side of its parent world.

The station was on the side facing the moon's host, and the sequence differed slightly. The night still equaled twenty-three hours but the reflected glow from the gigantic planet always lessened the darkness. The orbital plane of the moon almost equaled that of the gas giant's passage around the star, so the day period broke midway, with a brief pseudo-darkness as the moon passed through the planet's shadow.

The daily eclipse had fallen. The radiated light from the overhead orb might have still been sufficient to allow easy movement if not for the cloud cover and incessant rain, and progress was difficult.

Katch cursed under his breath, angry with himself and with Cooney. After leaving the airlock and reaching the shelter of the dense foliage, he had stopped, turned and crouched with his rifle aimed at the exit, intending to provide cover for Echo as she followed him out. He watched as she collapsed face forward in the inner doorway, hit from behind by enemy fire.

He had begun to rise, his first instinct to run back, but as he did so an angry voice stopped him.

"Stand down, Khamisi," Cooney had ordered, moving in beside him. "If you go after the body we lose you as well. She's dead, and you will focus on the job at hand."

"We don't know that," Katch spat back. "We can't abandon her in there. And there's Applegate, as well."

"They both knew the score when they went in," Cooney bought his face centimeters from Katch's. "You will do as you are ordered. Bring up the rear, soldier." He twisted away and waved the others to press on.

Katch did not move immediately. Two guards edged forward. One grabbed Echo by the heels and dragged her away from the entrance, while the other stood nervously in the hatch, peering out as he searched the undergrowth.

Unable to act without going against Cooney's orders, Katch turned and followed the remainder of the squad and its charges, swearing to himself that if they got out alive, he would personally make sure Cooney answered for his litany of miscalculations and poor judgment.

The Lieutenant had not attempted to rescue the remaining human prisoners who, according to Greer, had been only meters away at one point. He also refused to retrieve Margritte Albandier from the greenhouse, something he should have done regardless of her insistence she was too old to go running through the jungle.

Worst of all was his refusal to go back after Echo and Applegate. A military court-martial would exonerate him based on his statement it was impossible due to heavy fire. If Cooney walked free, Katch determined he would find a way to extract justice for his friend's death. There was always a way!

Ahead, he saw something clinging to Greer's back. A small, multi-limbed creature crept up towards the man's neck. Picked up from some piece of vegetation, it was doubtful anything so small could get at him through the environment suit, but those were not as resistant to intrusion as the purpose-made outfits worn by Katch and his fellow squad members.

He turned the intensity of his pistol to minimum, hot enough to cause the creature discomfort without hurting Greer. When the man paused for a moment, Katch fired at the alien beast; it dropped from the fabric and scuttled away through the undergrowth. Sensing the heat, the scientist moved a hand to his back, turned and grinned, realizing what had happened.

"Thanks. Lots of nasties out here."

"Little thing, green and purple, with six legs and a long tail."

"Oh, shit. Deadly bite, that one. Thank you again."

Greer turned and pressed on in pursuit of the others, Katch following behind. Katch liked Greer. The man had a sensible head on him, and an instinctive feeling said he might be a useful ally in the future.

There was also the second phial box. Greer had produced a small transport case in the lab, saying it contained the virus, antidote and vaccine. When the lieutenant snatched it and turned away, Greer retrieved another and secreted it in his own clothing. Only Katch and Echo saw him do it. Katch wondered what was in the second box; he had a reasonable idea, and guessed it was worth protecting.

\* \* \*

The guard was brooding, Echo was certain, but with a face frozen and emotionless it was difficult to tell. It sat without movement other than a slow fingering of the crossbow it was holding on its lap.

*Who are you? Why are you so interested in me?*

In a manner she hoped appeared calm and controlled, Echo examined the cage. Another tray of food remained un-eaten beyond the bars. Again, she felt the first traces of hunger, but did not intend to eat anything from the plate. It was probably safe, something from the garden maintained by Margritte Albandier, but she could not be certain. Better to leave it alone for now.

Whilst on missions, special-squad soldiers survived on formulated supplement pills; the skin-tight protective suits they wore made ablutions of any sort difficult at best. In a corner sat a bucket for use if necessary, but she had no intention of doing so except as a last resort—not in front of a monster who watched every move she made.

The alien stood and shuffled across to the table, his movement hindered by a noticeable limp. The cane leaning against the wall by the chair was not ornamental; at some time in the past, he had suffered a significant injury.

Perhaps, Echo thought, if he had been injured in a close conflict with humans he carried an intense hatred, and she was sure she would become the target of his bitterness in time. For a few minutes he shuffled through the items on the bench, picking up and examining her laser rifle. He reached for her pistol but stopped and turned as the door swung open.

Another Tolleani strode in and stared at Echo. This one stood taller than the first and had the same emotionless features. He was somewhat older, the fine body hair grayer and the face less angular, more rounded with the softening of age, as was often the case with elderly humans.

The newcomer's clothing did not look like a uniform. He was dressed in colorful pants and an elaborate, embroidered smock-top Echo at first thought to be silk. She corrected herself; silkworms came from *Old Earth* but clearly, the Tolleani possessed something similar.

He wore the most unusual boots she had ever seen. Worked into a mass of intricate designs and patterns, the leather tops extended up the creature's calf almost to the knee, with zips down the outside to allow fitting. At the base, the boot became a semblance of the typical alien sandals, purpose designed for their strange, angular feet.

After studying Echo for a few seconds, he pivoted and peered at the guard.

"Why did you not advise me you captured a human," he asked. Echo froze, now alert. She understood every word the newcomer spoke.

"It is not your business, Kemmin; this creature is my prisoner, not yours."

"I am in command here as much as it galls you. You should have advised me."

"I am the coordinator here, and I have no obligation to tell you anything. I run this station, not you." The security chief bridled at the intrusion; he clearly hated the new arrival.

"You are in charge of security, nothing more. I am the senior person in this facility, and I am your superior despite my unusual circumstances. You will keep that in mind in future." Kemmin turned his attention back to Echo, having dismissed the chief from his thoughts.

"This is my prisoner, and you have no authority over me," Koll blustered, his anger mounting. "Get out, now!"

Kemmin remained silent for a second, before rounding on his opponent. "Do not forget I know about your past. I am aware you lost your entire last command and destroyed your own career prospects by insulting a superior officer. This posting is a last resort for you, is it not?"

Echo remained motionless, following the conversation as well as possible. The lack of emotion made it difficult, but the body language indicated Koll was both furious and afraid. He stepped away from the table, one hand moving towards the pistol on his belt.

"That would be unwise, I think," Kemmin said. "I appreciate one day you will be ordered to eliminate me or at least try, but at the moment I am alive and well. You have no termination orders unless this system is invaded, and I have many friends on the major worlds. Do *anything* to upset me and you will be recalled and drummed out. You have already lost your career, your wife and your children. Cross me, and you will end up in the slave markets. Kill me and your family will join you. I have given my supporters orders to that effect, so be careful what you do next."

Koll's hand dropped limp at his side. He knew Kemmin got messages to and from the outside Empire, but had never been able to pin down how he did it.

"Much better," Kemmin said. "I thought you wiser than to anger me, Koll. Even confined here I am still an extremely influential Tolleani, and you would do well to bare it in mind in future. Now get out; I wish to speak to the captive—alone."

"N … no! The human is mine. It doesn't know our speech."

"Really?" The tall Tolleani turned his gaze towards Echo. "Do you understand us? Perhaps you would prefer we talked in your own language?" He spoke the last sentence in perfect, almost accent free Tantallic, the prime language of the Federation.

"How dare you talk to my prisoner in that foul language!"

"Of course, you don't speak it yourself, do you? Get out!"

Kemmin lifted his head and studied Koll over his flat, snub nose. He said nothing, letting his eyes convey the force of his threat instead. After a few more seconds, the chief barged past him and stormed through the door, slamming it behind. Kemmin turned and addressed Echo again.

"That fool can be infuriating. Someone like him should never be in charge of good Tolleani. It is a travesty."

Echo did not reply, feigning ignorance.

"There is no need to keep up pretenses. I was watching you during my conversation with Koll, and I am aware you understood every word spoken. You *can* understand me, can you not?"

Echo held her silence.

"Very well. I will speak your language if you insist. No? In that case, I will leave you alone for a while to think on it. You need not worry about Koll. The fool is terrified of me, and I will make sure he does not interfere with you. He refuses to acknowledge the fact, but some of his guards will obey my orders before his. Some are loyal to me, and the rest fear me more than him."

# Chapter Fifteen

KATCH HUNCHED OVER THE figure that lay motionless on the wet ground. Twenty minutes earlier Mendoza had collapsed, battered and exhausted, his tired, old body unable to cope with Cooney's brutal race through the jungle. Determined to reach the rendezvous in time, the Lieutenant had set a blistering pace, ignoring the drenching rain, the humidity and the needs of the civilians now in his care.

Sarra knelt at the other side of Mendoza's inert form and looked up at Katch, despair in her eyes. "I can't be sure—we don't have the facilities here—but I'm guessing his heart can't take the exertion. If he dies, then so much for our mission objectives."

To one side Greer squatted on the ground, his distress obvious despite his face mask. Earlier, he had privately admitted to Katch that he viewed the older man as a father figure who had mentored and guided him through many years of his career. A younger and stronger man, Greer had helped to carry his friend for hours on end, but lacked the stamina of the trained military personnel; he too was close to exhaustion.

At that moment, Cooney pushed through the surrounding vegetation. "How long before he can be up and moving again?"

"Not!" Sarra snapped back. "He'll die if we try to move him anytime soon. How's that for your mission directives, Lieutenant?"

"Shut it, Corian. Start giving me lip and I'll bring you up on charges along with your black buddy."

Sarra rose to her feet, her eyes glaring at Cooney's racist slur, but stopped as Katch reached across to place a cautionary hand on her forearm.

"Don't give him the pleasure, Girl."

She scowled at her superior officer, bent down to fumble in her field kit, and then began administering a stimulant to Mendoza.

Katch frowned at Cooney. "We need to stay put for at least a half hour. He needs time to recover his strength."

"We don't have time. Those Tollean soldiers are close behind, as well you know. We'll give away our lead."

"Listen to me, you ass. You decided this man was the one we came here to rescue. If so, then he's important and we've already lost most of our squad getting him this far." Katch stood, and positioned himself less than a meter from the lieutenant, his eyes cold and hard, and his voice low and menacing.

"When we get out of this I intend to lodge a report that you deliberately abandoned the other civilian prisoners in the station, including the Albandier woman, to preserve your own skin. I'll also state you unreasonably placed Sub-Lieutenant Bourke in constant positions of extreme danger, and refused to allow anyone to try to help when the enemy shot her. You may think your daddy's power and money will save you, and that reporting Corian and me will absolve you, but think again.

Even from a prison cell I can make your life a misery; Fleet doesn't like cowards. We stay here until Mendoza can go on. If that means taking on our pursuers again, then we will. We're not afraid of them, even if you are."


Cooney froze at the insubordination. It was clear grounds for court martial when they returned to base. True, Khamisi was popular among the ranks and could make life difficult for him, but only if the man survived. The same applied to his little girlfriend.

In a pocket of his field harness Cooney still carried the case taken from Greer. That was the crucial thing; if Mendoza died, he, Lieutenant Jack Cooney, would still receive credit if he returned with the phials unharmed.

Without question, he was the most efficient of the four surviving members of the squad, and the most capable of seeing the mission through. Petrovsky would do whatever he was told. Khamisi and Corian would choose to rescue a dying old man, and risk failure of the mission in doing so. If the old scientist survived and his work did not, it was unlikely the research was repeatable elsewhere, so the phial box was critically important and was firmly in his possession.

He turned back towards Khamisi, noting the sergeant had his hand on his laser pistol. That constituted treason, enough to get the man incarcerated for life. Furious, the Lieutenant moved back along the track and found a sheltered spot. He would allow fifteen minutes, no more.

On time to the minute, he returned. He would not allow the squad to stay here longer, positive they had given away their lead. The Tollean guards had pursued doggedly since their escape, twice caught up, fired on them and lost them again; they were likely only minutes behind. The rendezvous was a day away, with the pickup scheduled for tomorrow. Cooney intended to be there no matter what.

"Alright, pick him up. We're moving … now!"

Katch stood, his rifle on the ground beside him, his pistol holstered. "No point. He's dead. You pushed him too hard. Another black mark for my report."

"We still have the viral material. That's more important. I intend to deliver it to Fleet with or without you."

"Without, I think."

"What?"

"We're not going with you. Sarra and I will go back and rescue the remaining prisoners, and find out what happened to Echo and Tandie. We'll take the risk the invasion will succeed, and hope for a pickup later."

"You will do as you are ordered!" Cooney's face flushed a bright pink as he realized his control of what remained of the squad had evaporated. "This is a direct court-martial offense: desertion under enemy fire."

"Fine. Too bad."

"I could shoot you where you stand for this." His hand dropped to the butt of his pistol, then froze as Sarra Corian's rifle muzzle pressed against the side of his head.

"Alright, stay here and die! Those guards can't be more than minutes behind us." He spun around and waved at Greer and Petrovsky to precede him.

"No," the young scientist said. "I'm going back with them." He raised a hand towards Katch and Sarra.

"You'll do as I say! This is a military situation and I am in command here."

"Debatable. I'm a civilian, and not obliged to follow your orders. I think I stand a better chance of staying alive with them than with a psychopath like you, thank you." Greer crossed his arms in defiance and stood his ground.

Cooney's face flushed red, visible even through the visor on his helmet. "Psychopath?" he screamed.

"That's what I said. That's what we call people like you. Psychopathic personalities—people who care only for themselves, don't consider others and don't learn from their mistakes. As a scientist, I don't consider *you* mentally stable enough to lead, so I have no obligation to follow you. I go with the sergeant."

Again, Cooney lacked a response to the man's stance. In truth he could not force an ordinary citizen, and if he tried to shoot either Khamisi or Corian, the other would take him down seconds later. One avenue remained open to him.

"Are you with me, Petrovsky, or are you a traitor as well?"

"No, Lieutenant. I will continue with you." So saying, he gave Katch and Sarra a final glance, shook his head with regret and turned away along the animal path with Cooney close behind.

Khamisi, Corrian and Greer squatted by the body of Mendoza.

"What did you have in mind?" Greer asked.

Katch examined the vegetation around them. "We think like Echo, and we hide. Cooney is right: those guards will be along any moment. They'll be following the trail that idiot created smashing his way through this mess, so we work with that. I'm sorry, but we'll have to leave your friend's body here. Follow me."

They carried Mendoza's body to one side and left it near the track, then hid in the nearby undergrowth, kept silent and waited for their pursuers to arrive.

Katch peered through the tangled undergrowth. These Tolleani were instillation guards, not jungle-trained ground troops, and like Cooney, they would choose the easiest course. Rushing to catch their prey again, they would follow the smashed vegetation and the boot marks in the mud. At first, Katch had considered ambushing them, but there was no guarantee he and Sarra could take all three out. At this point, he could not afford any injuries. He would let the enemy pass unhindered to pursue the Lieutenant.

The strategy mimicked the one Echo used in their last test exercise on *Brenton*. It worked once, and Katch prayed it would do so again. As far as he was concerned, not all was yet lost. After escaping from the station, he had talked privately with Greer during their sparse rest breaks and now knew several things Cooney did not.

Greer had the second carry case, with an identical set of phials to the one taken from him in the lab. He had taken an instant dislike to the lieutenant when they first met, and when the first set was snatched from his hands, he took a precaution and retrieved another, keeping it concealed.

In his opinion, Cooney was far from being the most reliable person to carry such a treasure. Katch knew where Greer kept the second box, and could retrieve it quickly if anything happened to the scientist.

The plan was sketchy at best. Albandier stated there were only twelve guards in the station, and four of these died during the first incursion. Four more, one of whom was now dead, had tracked the squad across the face of this god-forsaken moon, leaving the last four in the dome along with the aircrew from the ship on the landing pad, and the security chief.

Upon receiving word of the invasion, which by now would be under way, the aircrew had most likely left to join the battle. If so, the guards and the chief were all that remained.

Greer and Albandier had spoken of two more Tolleani, an aristocratic individual who theoretically administered the station but was in reality a political prisoner, and his personal assistant, a dwarf Tolleani, the same who discovered them in the lab. Greer assured him they were no threat, and in fact, were friends, having done considerable to make the life of the prisoners easier in the past. Try as he might, Katch found that hard to accept.

The situation was a puzzle, he thought. Cooney insisted the target of their mission was Mendoza, who commanded the base prior to the alien takeover, but Katch remained unconvinced. The old man had been a brilliant mind, but nothing about him indicated he would be critical to the war effort in the future. He wondered which represented the more valuable prize, an elderly scientist in poor health, or a Tollean aristocrat with a wealth of knowledge about the enemy empire. Such a prisoner would be a catch indeed.

A few minutes later, sounds of pursuit came through the vegetation. From their position off the track, Katch, Sarra and Greer waited as several sets of feet thumped past. For a moment there was silence, followed by muffled voices as the aliens examined the body of Mendoza. Then, convinced they were close to their pray, they moved on.

One ... two ... three. Three sets of flat feet moved fast as they tracked the human flight. With the one killed somewhere back along the track, it confirmed there were only four guards back at the dome.

Ten minutes after the transition, three dark figures emerged from cover and moved in the direction of the research station.

\* \* \*

The aristocratic Tollean had wandered back into the room several minutes earlier, placed a small electronic contrivance on the table and activated it. He then stood outside the bars and studied Echo for a moment.

"Our security coordinator seems to be most enthralled by you." Kemmin spoke in almost perfect Federation Tantallic. "Something about your hair color and your odd weapon."

He pointed up to the security cameras in the corners of the ceiling. "The fool installed those when you were first brought here, while you were unconscious. He has microphones in here as well but this device will block both of them. I prefer he does not listen in to my conversations." He took the seat by the door, propped an elbow on a knee and supported his chin on his hand. After a few moments, he straightened and looked around the room.

"Your people built this cage, you know. They used it to study some of the larger life forms on this planet. There was a magnificent six-legged creature in there when I first arrived here. Dead now, of course. Koll did not give any thought to it, and it starved to death."

*A Kylax*, Echo thought. Intelligent beings, one of which she had communicated with in the greenhouse at Margritte Albandier's insistence.

"Interesting creatures, those," Kemmin said. "I'm positive they are sentient, but I've not been able to prove it. Every time I try to bring another one of them here to examine, Koll finds a way to foul it up."

*Koll! The security chief's name!*

"He and his guards use them for sport. They hunt them out in the jungle when it gets slow around here, which is most of the time. They stun the animals and bring them back as playthings. Thankfully, the creatures have become wary now. They live underground and usually stay there during daylight hours. Koll and his cronies won't go into their tunnels."

Kemmin shifted position, leaning back in his seat.

"So, why is he absorbed by you? It is not because he's never seen a human female before; there are a number of them here as prisoners. What is so fascinating about you? Have you met him before?"

Echo did not respond, sitting motionless on the floor of the cage, staring straight back at the alien.

"Still not talking, I see. You should understand, human, I am not your enemy. I appreciate the Tolleani humans usually see are not the best and finest of our species, and based on someone like Koll you would think we are all callous, heartless warmongers, but that is not at all the case. Most of us are peace loving and would much rather the conflict with humanity end here and now. It is our Emperor who wants war, not us. He seeks absolute power and sadly, controls our military and police forces."

Again, Echo forced herself not to respond. She did not trust this individual, but something about him struck her as different. Apart from the more elaborate, decorative clothing he wore, he appeared more sophisticated, with a gentle, more subtle manner, and a definite arrogance.

Margritte and Greer both mentioned he was a prisoner, a scientist with enormous political influence in the Tollean Empire, sent here to keep him on ice. As the administrator of the base, he technically commanded over Koll. That much she understood, and also the fear the security chief had of him; that was apparent from the conflict when Kemmin first entered Echo's cell.

"Perhaps he encountered you somewhere before?" the alien asked. "I can't imagine where. Most of his career has been in the expeditionary space force, and the closest he would have come to one of you before arriving here would have been during a short stint as a base coordinator on one of your worlds we conquered a few years ago in the star system next to this one."

Echo raised her head. "*Corros?*"

"Ah, she speaks. Yes, I believe that is what your people call it. The latest word is you took it back again recently. So, we are talking now, yes?"

"What did the other … Koll … have to do with *Corros.*"

"Oh, he hates the place. I suspect he blames it for his fall through the ranks to his current ignominious position. Of course it was his own arrogance and incompetence got him here, not the events on that planet."

"What...?"

"It is about time you started to communicate. You need to understand I am not your enemy."

"Alright, I'll talk to you, but first tell me about what happened to Koll on *Corros*."

"Ah, how odd you humans are. He was in charge of a scientific team based there. Their research concerned something rather dangerous, so Military Command insisted on placing it somewhere isolated. One day a support mission arrived to find the whole base destroyed; nothing remained of it. The official report says the contraption they were working on exploded, and wiped out everything around it for a vast distance. The event apparently occurred only hours before the ship arrived.

"They checked a nearby airfield and found Koll laying unconscious on the ground with a broken leg and other significant injuries. Two damaged scout vehicles destroyed from within by mines were also retrieved, and a dead Tollean soldier. Koll was required to account for those anomalies when he regained consciousness, and he reported the planet had been attacked by an overwhelming human force that triggered the device by accident."

"That's a lie!"

"Really? His superiors did not believe it either. Coordinators who lose their entire command are not looked upon favorably. There was no real evidence to refute his story, but he was demoted, sent to minor postings and then here. So tell me, human, what actually happened. I am guessing you were there?"

The knowledge Koll was the one who had occupied her father's mine site, and from whom she hid for over a year, flooded her mind. He it was who captured Ben's ship, and chased Echo and Ben after they destroyed the camp and fled in the scout car. Now she knew why he was so engrossed in her and the crossbow. He had seen both before, and the sight of them triggered memories.

She was still not sure she should be talking to this alien, but she needed to know more. If Koll commanded on *Corros*, she had a score to settle with him.

"I was a survivor of the original attack. I lived alone there for three years, and when Koll and his scientists arrived, I hid in the jungle and watched them. I destroyed the base using mines from the naval station at the next town, and blew up their device. That's what caused all the destruction, not an attack force. Two little humans—me, and an escaped prisoner Koll let get away."

"Ah … interesting." The tone of Kemmin's voice showed surprise. Echo could have sworn if he had had eyebrows, they would have arched. "You survived the initial assault?"

"Yes. I wasn't in my town when it was attacked."

"In that case it serves the fool right, doesn't it? He was also the leader of the flight that led that incursion, and you are proof he failed to do the job properly."

An electric jolt lanced through Echo like a lightning bolt, going straight to her heart; a tide of red surged into her brain, laced with a hatred she thought long buried. From deep in her subconscious an image resurfaced, a tall alien shooting down her father in the mine compound. Koll, the same miserable individual who sat for hours staring at her through the bars of her cell, was the one responsible for the death of her father, her family and every person she had known in her childhood.

Her planned strategy took a sudden about-face. She needed to get out of this cage and go after Koll no matter what the cost, with any ally she could find even if he was the enemy.

"You don't like him, do you?"

"I neither like nor dislike him. He and others of his ilk give the Tollean people a bad name, and he represents everything I find reprehensible about our species. I am sure you have similar individuals in your Federation. Sad to say, I am in no position to do anything about him at the moment." The alien lifted his nose high and sniffed in a disdainful manner.

"I thought he was afraid of you?"

"True, but he is also my jailer; I am a political prisoner here. In my past life, I was a powerful member of Tollean society, and I still have considerable influence. It is why he fears me. He knows one word from me and he will end up the target of an assassination, or worse, in the slave markets. I can do little to him as long as he remains here in this base, but if he should ever leave…"

At that moment, the door burst open and Koll stormed into the room. He strode across to the table and grabbed the mechanism Kemmin used to cancel out the spy devices.

"How dare you," he screamed. "This is my prisoner. You may not talk to her without my consent!"

"I will do so whenever and however I please, Koll. You really do need to be more careful how you speak to me; it could have a profound effect on your future prospects. Consider the safety of your estranged wife and children before you interfere with me again." Kemmin stood, gave a deep sigh to indicate he did not care about any concerns Koll may have, and strolled out of the room.

Koll stared after him for a few seconds, then also strode from the room, completely oblivious to the raw hatred fomenting in the cage behind him.

# Chapter Sixteen

BEN LOOKED DOWN ON the alien base, this time from a safer, more distant position. The beachhead operation had been a success, and several hundred ships ranging from the colossal battle-carrier *Pellargo* to small one-man planetary attack craft now approached the principal target in a widely spread formation.

The Tollean complex sprawled across a barren, heavily cratered and airless satellite of one of *Cardoon's* gas giants, unsuitable for any normal purpose except mining, but ideal for military use due to a low gravity of one-sixth Federation standard and a complete lack of atmosphere that made the task of landing and launching spacecraft much simpler.

Ben's first reconnoiter of the moon revealed a significant number of enemy craft, but now only a handful remained. Despite the best efforts of the fleet, the sentries guarding the wormhole had succeeded in sending an alert message before their destruction. Almost all Tollean ships in the system diverted to intercept, and most of them had already been destroyed. Positioned between the gateway and the base, they had extracted a heavy toll before succumbing to the sheer numbers of the invasion force.

Now the ships of humanity turned their attention to the primary objective, which even allowing for the absence of support ships was still a force to be feared. The installation bristled with powerful ground based weapons installations, everything from plasma pulse cannons to rail guns, all pointing straight at the approaching threat.

Other than *Persephone* there was nothing in this system of much interest to anyone, but the Tolleani valued the gateways that made *Cardoon* a crossroad to multiple other stars. They would not give it up without a fight.

The incentive for the human incursion related more closely to the research station, its mysterious chief scientist and the virus believed to have originated there, but there was no doubt the gates would be of as much value to humanity as to the aliens. Admiral Lord Baquir did not intend, however, to waste more good men on a mere ground installation, no matter how powerful it might be.

Several dozen smaller fighting craft were absent from the body of the attack force, but Ben knew exactly where they were. Beyond enemy detection, they had deployed to the far side of the moon to make their approach to the base unseen, and their arrival at the scene of battle was only seconds away.

Called 'mud skippers', these small machines were part of the contingent of the carrier itself. Each little more than a pilot sitting astride a gigantic plasma cannon, they could fly at almost zero altitude and were exceptionally maneuverable.

Their mission was to sweep in and attack the target at ground level, flying well below the elevation of the major weapons. Given a few seconds of clear approach, the highly effective little fighters would decimate the primary defenses, and then retire to let the fleet complete the job.

"There's some movement down there," Jerry commented. "Looks like the remaining ships are about to make a run for it. Typical."

Suddenly the skippers appeared, streaking in meters above the surface and approaching from all points. From Ben's position in space, it was clear each ship was targeting a particular weapon, as each installation exploded in a ball of incandescence. Their primary mission achieved, the little vessels continued to harass any other point of resistance available, a swarm of tiny specs whirling over the complex like flies over a corpse. It took only seconds for the bases best defenses to fall, allowing the fleet to approach unopposed.

Three ships Ben had observed earlier lifted off and shot away, shields on full, attempting to put as much distance as possible between themselves and the human attack.

"FS391, Captain Teague. *Pellargo* Command here. Come back?"

"Teague here."

"Five enemy vessels in all have escaped. Two of them are heading for the number 3 gateway."

"Yes, sir. Rat's deserting a sinking ship, I expect."

"Quite so. Our destroyers are in pursuit. The three that just lifted are surface strike craft, and they are on course for *Persephone*. We are sending ships to intercept. You will follow them and attempt to pick up your ground squad. "

"Yes, sir. On my way. Out."

Ben swung his ship off station and set a course for the moon, driving the engines to maximum speed. He doubted he could catch the enemy before they reached the research dome, but he was not overly concerned. If Echo and her team had been successful, they should be well away from the critical zone by now, on their way to the pickup point.

When the crunch came, his priority would instinctively be the welfare of his lady, ahead of the scientists or the mission. In his mind, her safety far outweighed the other members of her team, or the individual they went to rescue.

His understanding of the incursion was sketchy at best. The assignment had been to drop the squad at the top of the atmosphere of the little world, and pick them up again later from a high ridge several days march from the base. He knew only that it was a rescue and retrieval, and had a lot to do with the pandemic spreading throughout the Federation worlds, but the lack of detailed explanation in the briefing annoyed him.

Nothing he had read or been told about the moon warranted what was happening now. The enemy, it seemed, specifically intended to demolish the dome; why else would they send ground attack ships rather than a transport? Their mindset did not include rescuing their own men at any cost, especially when an overwhelming invasion force made escape the most important consideration. Ben could not help wondering what was so crucial about the place that the Tolleani would seek to destroy it before allowing it to fall back into human hands. Or perhaps that should be *who?*

He hoped Echo's mission had been successful, and she was clear. He prayed she would remember to turn on the emergency locator he gave her, should anything happen to their pickup signal device.

\* \* \*

The diminutive alien called Torrick eased his head through the partly opened doorway, took a quick look around, and entered, another food tray in his hands.

"I was looking to see if Koll was in here," he mumbled, placing the tray on the floor against the bars of the cage. "I don't much like him, and he treats me like I am some sort of animal. My Lord said you speak our language. Can you, Sir?"

"You're rather short for a Tolleani."

The little alien drew himself up to his maximum height and puffed out his chest. "I am not Tollean, thank you, and I am a perfectly normal height for my kind."

"Which is?"

"I am a Tolleasin. I come from a world colonized by the Tolleani many, many hundreds of years in the past. The colonists changed over time because of the higher gravity and radiation, and after many generations became a hybrid of the original line. We are related to them, but shorter and stronger, and equally as capable and intelligent. About a century ago the Emperor re-absorbed us into the expanding empire, and reduced us to second-class citizens, virtually slaves."

"So you are Kemmin's slave."

The small alien stood bolt upright, shaking his head vigorously. "No, not at all. I am my Lord's aid and assistant. He is a great Tolleani, and does not treat me as a slave. When he was exiled here, I chose to come voluntarily. My life is devoted to his service."

Torrick looked down at the plate. "I've bought four of those in here since they caught you. You haven't touched anything. You must be starved by now."

Echo stared at the food. True, she was famished, but she did not intend to touch any food given her by an alien.

"Kemmin said he was my friend. Can I believe him?" *Can I believe you?*

"Oh, yes, he…"

"Then I need you to do something for me then. See the gear over there. There is a small packet in one of the pockets of the harness. That's what I eat. Will you get it for me … please?" The pack she referred to contained her high potency ration pills.

The little alien turned his head towards the table. Like his bigger cousins, he lacked the muscles for facial expressions, but it was clear from his hesitation he was reluctant to carry out the request.

"Are you worried Koll is watching?" Echo asked.

"No. Surveillance devices no longer work in this building. My Lord asked me to fix it, so I installed a device in the electrical system. Koll's cameras and microphones will record only static, and the fool will never manage to figure out where I hid the jammer. It's driving him to despair." The little alien waddled across and fumbled through Echo's field harness until he found the item she requested. Reaching out, he passed it through the bars.

"That is not poison, I hope, Sir?"

"No. Don't worry; I have a debt to repay before I die."

An hour after Torrick departed, the door opened and Kemmin entered, taking the seat by the door once again.

"You might be interested to hear your companions somehow managed to survive out in the jungle. At least five of them are still alive."

Echo did not respond, but it was good to know most of the remaining squad members still lived. Assuming, of course, that this alien could be believed. It could easily be a trap to put her at ease.

"I am sad to say the old human scientist you rescued has died. Koll has half his men out chasing them, and they found the body abandoned beside an animal track."

*Damn!* Echo's shoulders slumped. Mendoza was the whole point of the incursion. Regardless of whether some of the team made it to the pickup, the principle objective of the mission had failed. Then again, there was still the phial case.

"You made quite a mess of it, did you not? First you rescue the wrong person, and then you lose the one you did take."

Echo looked up, a deep furrow creasing her brow. "What do you mean the wrong person?"

"My dear human, you rescued the wrong one, as I just said."

"We came to get the chief scientist. We did that."

"No, you did not. *I* am the head scientific officer on this base, and its administrator. Your mission here was to rescue me!"

So unexpected were the words, they did not at first register in Echo's mind. She shook her head, unsure she heard correctly. "No, that's not possible."

"Allow me to clarify for you. Your superiors intercepted a communication drone telling you several human scientists were still alive, the virus infecting your worlds came from here, and that an anti-viral agent had been developed here. The message requested rescue, am I correct."

"How could you know *any* of that? Did you torture it out of one of your prisoners?"

"Absolutely not! They are Koll's prisoners, not mine. I know because *I* was the messenger. *I* advised your authorities of the situation, and that *I* wanted to defect. Your mission here was to rescue me, and my aid Torrick. This was undoubtedly known to your commander, but I am guessing he has not survived."

"Why would Fleet waste resources in an attempt to recover an enemy defector?"

"Ah, but you see, I am not your enemy. I am perhaps the best, the only chance you have to end this war without endless ongoing violence. Perhaps if I explain?"

For the next few minutes, Kemmin expounded upon why he considered himself such a valuable prize. The Tolleani were, according to him, once a peaceful race expanding into an at that time human-free galaxy at a slow but steady pace. The emperors in older times had been men of relative peace and wisdom, and the growing empire flourished.

Three hundred years ago, the first humans were encountered by a Tollean military craft, in a region under Empire control. The ship was a colonization vessel, and the Tollean captain fired upon it without warning or authority. After a forced crash landing on a high mass, high gravity world, it was forgotten by the politicians, but not by the military.

The ship's course was backtracked and exploration ships sent out until the nearest human worlds were discovered. When reports reached the Emperor, he chose to pursue a tactic of separation until proximity required measures more specific. The Empire watched, studied and waited.

At the time of his death, his son took the throne and enjoyed a long and healthy reign, in which he strengthened and reinforced the policy of his father. Unsure of their new galactic neighbors and more militaristic by nature, he built a respectable space force; insurance against the possibility humans would prove a threat to the peaceful Tollean people.

He too died, leaving two sons and a daughter. The oldest son, the legitimate heir, refused the crown. An academic, he was dedicated to his research, having no interest in politics or royalty. It was the gravest of mistakes. In his stead, the younger son assumed control.

The new Emperor, Pentus Al Tambr, was a monster, a psychopathic individual who sought only personal strength and aggrandizement. Prior to becoming ruler he commanded the navy, and with their force to back him became a monarch with absolute power. At first, there had been resistance and several worlds died, blasted clean as a warning to others. Naval commanders who resisted the emperor's directives disappeared and those who supported him became stronger, and wealthier.

Less than six months after the coronation the sister vanished without trace, and the older brother was placed under house arrest.

"A few years ago," Kemmin explained, "Al Tambr declared war on the human race. I suspect you know the rest."

"Where do you come into all this?"

"I was exiled here because I represent an enormous threat to the Emperor. He is a seriously unpopular ruler, and the groundswell to remove him grows by the day. At this time there are a number of worlds preparing to rebel against him and negotiate a peace with humans, using the war as a cover for their preparations."

"And you?"

"I am what you would call a figurehead. To the rebelling worlds, I am a focal point around which they can unite. My noble bloodline gives legitimacy to the rebellion without raising the ire of the general populace. That is why I am here. Pentus fears me above any other, but dares not assassinate me for fear it would cause immediate and irreversible insurrection. So instead, he sent me against my will to this little moon, at the rear end of the empire and ruled by a megalomaniac."

"Who the emperor hopes will eventually kill you."

"I expect so. Should I die in this place, Pentus would have someone else to blame. I doubt it will happen, however. Even here, I have power. Some of the senior personnel at the naval base back me, or at least acknowledge my standing and power, and through them, I am able to maintain contact with my supporters. There are many millions of them on dozens of worlds, and that is why Koll fears me. One word from me and he will become a target, as would his family. He is too terrified to touch me without a direct order from his superiors. Even that would not save him afterwards, as he is well aware."

"Why would your Emperor place you in the care of someone so incompetent if you're so important? Doesn't being here carry a risk of your escaping?"

"No, it would not be so easy. Koll is only my jailer, and the Emperor has probably never heard of him. My real guards are the military, and only a handful of the personnel on the base support me. With a major presence in this system, it would be difficult for me to get away. If I *could* get a ship, they would apprehend me before I reached a gateway. A rescue attempt by my own people is impossible because of the guard drones on the gateways. It was the best I could do to get a messenger through the gate to your fleet, and even that was a stretch; without the help of loyal followers at the base, I would not have succeeded."

"You didn't. The drone was retrieved in…"

Kemmin lifted his head and gazed at her with emotionless eyes. She guessed the Tolleani did not yet know about the dispersion field that allowed human ships to sneak around unseen. Perhaps she should keep her mouth shut.

"So, why do you want to defect?"

"My intention is to carry an offer to your Federation from those members of the Tollean navy who privately support peace. The message requested my removal from the reach of the Emperor so I could act as a mediator and intermediary for negotiations with the rebel worlds."

Echo remained seated at the center of her cage, peering out at Kemmin's inscrutable face. A suspicion crept into her mind. Was this arrogant alien more important than she could ever imagine?

"Who *exactly* are you?"

"You need only know I am the leader of the revolutionary movement. The faction is already significant in size, and growing. With his military forces away fighting the war, Al

Tambr fears us and knows he is vulnerable. So, now it is up to you to help me get away from here, yes?"

# Chapter Seventeen

KOLL HUNCHED OVER THE desk in his private surveillance room, his emotionless eyes staring at the monitor. This was proving to be a most disagreeable day.

Lord Almighty Kemmin spent considerable time, far too much, with the female human prisoner, but there was nothing to be done about it. Kemmin had the power to do everything he threatened. As a regular routine Koll intercepted and examined every communiqué leaving the station, but never managed to find anything subversive. The Tollean noble used a code system of some kind he found impossible to unravel.

He knew he was powerless to stop the leakage. Strict orders from Command permitted all communication between Kemmin and the system base, and someone there was ensuring his messages went wherever intended. He had friends in the military.

All links with that base had now ceased, most likely due to a major failing in the communications system. It did not help to improve Koll's temper. He focused his attention on his monitor, his anger boiling as he realized Kemmin once again had the better of him. The screen showed nothing but snow, and only static blared from the speakers on the desk.

That damned aristocrat had somehow managed to block all surveillance in the building; not with the simple device Koll removed the first time, but a more sophisticated one hidden somewhere he could not discover. Hours searching for the source of the interference had failed. Koll suspected Torrick was responsible; despite the little toad's bumbling behavior, he was a genius with anything electronic.

Worse, the lock on the cage had been changed, and either one of Koll's own guards or that little slave was responsible. Security coordinator, be damned—he had no control over his own prisoner, and at least one of his men was helping Kemmin. Of course, nobody admitted to the crime. Koll considered the whole business an unforgivable insult. He could trust no one.

Early the previous day a signal had arrived from the pursuit team Koll sent out after the invaders. The old scientist was dead, his body abandoned. One Tollean guard had been killed and three humans had vanished, while the remaining two were heading for a nearby ridge, no doubt their pick up point. No other explanation explained their retreat further into the jungle, away from the only safe place on this moon.

Where the missing three were was a mystery. With luck, they would die out there with the old professor, denied the ability to re-enter the safety of the dome. With only a handful of guards left Koll swore the enemy, on the off chance they might return, would not get inside. All entrances were locked, his men under orders to keep them so unless ordered otherwise. The door to the power and air plants, the most likely way the infiltrators got in, was also sealed, with detectors in the ductwork.

He cursed beneath his breath, the entire galaxy the object of his resentment, and began flicking between the surveillance cameras installed throughout the complex. Nothing inside the accommodation or laboratory buildings worked, but those targeting the exterior airlocks still functioned. Should anyone try anything, he would know.

Still muttering to himself, he flicked from one camera to the next and stopped at the one in the landing platform ready room. The crew of the assault craft were climbing into their flight gear. Once suited, they ran from the room, to be picked up seconds later by a monitor overlooking the main exit.

Leaving the outer door open, they sprinted across the platform and climbed the boarding ladder to the ship. Koll fumed as he watched it lift off and vanished into the cloud cover.

He pushed back from the desk, black clouds swirling in his mind. Pac had abandoned him. *How dare he?*

Koll knew he should have reported the incursion, but he had wanted the credit for stopping it. Now he had only four men, and everything seemed to be collapsing around him.

As he sat back and struggled to control his mounting fury, he noticed several lines of text appearing on one of the monitors—it was a warning message from the base. They were under heavy attack from an unknown force, presumed to be Federation.

*Damn*, Koll thought. There was only one explanation for the attack and the sudden departure of Pac. *Humans are invading the system.* He doubted their ability to defeat the forces of the Emperor, but the possibility existed.

He possessed standing orders for such an eventuality. In case of invasion, he was to dispose of Kemmin and Torrick, then deal with any remaining human scientists. He breathed a deep, gratifying sigh. At last, he could legally eliminate those fools, and while he was at it, the old woman who troubled him for reasons he had not yet fathomed. Koll rose from his seat with such force the chair slammed against the wall, then removed his pistol from its holster and strode from the room.

*   *   *

The door to Echo's prison crashed open and Kemmin stormed in, moving straight to the door of the cage. In his hand, he carried a laser pistol. Echo wondered where a prisoner would get such a thing, and concluded it must be from those of Koll's guards who supported him.

"We must be going, now! Your forces invade the system, and Koll is behaving like a maniac." Producing a key, he turned the lock and wrenched the door open. "Your equipment, quickly."

Without hesitation, Echo rushed across to the table and began climbing into her battle harness. She was out of the cage, and did not care who had opened the door. Her gear appeared to be undamaged, other than a few items from the pockets scattered across the bench.

The sheath of crossbow bolts she usually carried strapped to a thigh was still there, but her bow was gone, along with her laser weapons. The harness pouch containing explosive mines was also empty. Everything Koll considered a lethal weapon had been removed accepting only her knife, with scant attention paid to the rest. Drawing the long, thin poniard from its sheath, she verified its condition then strapped it to her calf.

"That arsehole took all my weapons."

"Torrick is working on that. They are in Koll's office."

The little alien burst through the door as Kemmin spoke, a bundle in his arms. "The Coordinator is not there," he spoke in Tollean. "So I sneaked in and found these." He turned towards Echo. "Do not shoot me or my lord, please, Sir." He stepped forward, presenting the rifle, pistol, and crossbow. There were no mines.

Once again in her battle harness, and armed, Echo sensed the adrenaline rising within. She was free, and did not intend to waste the opportunity. The chance of escape was still marginal, but there were other matters to deal with.

"Much better. Now tell me where I can find Koll."

"No, no. We must move, now! At this minute, he gathers what guards he still has. We may not succeed in killing them all, so go we must. I am your first priority."

"I'll be the judge of that. Where is he?"

"I did not release you to pursue a personal vendetta. You are here to rescue me, not to kill that mad idiot."

For a few seconds Echo let herself dwell on her hatred, then tried to regain focus and pull back to her mission objectives. *Calm down girl.* "Where are the other prisoners?"

"This is not the time. It is essential for us to go now. Do you wish us all to die?"

"Where do you suggest we go?"

"The greenhouse. Once we lock ourselves inside, we should be able to keep the guards out long enough for your ships to arrive. The Albandier woman knows me. She tells me there is safety there."

"Lead me to the other scientists. We go nowhere without them. If you won't help, I'll find them myself; you're welcome to come along if you wish."

The tall alien stared at her with the blank expression so ubiquitous in his race. He shook his head with frustration, and then nodded affirmation. "Follow me."

* * *

The few remaining members of the pre-invasion scientific staff were in the general quarters, the area sealed to serve as a prison. Under normal circumstances at least one guard always remained at the entrance, but now it was unguarded. Koll had moved his strength elsewhere, presumably to the exits from the complex.

Echo fired on the lock and broke through to a lounge-style common room. Four individuals, three men and a woman, peered up at her in varied states of surprise.

"How many of you are here?" Echo asked. "Where is everyone else?"

One of the men, a young, pasty looking individual dressed in a tracksuit, stood and peered at the imposing alien figure, his body trembling visibly. "F … five of us. Libby is in th … the kitchen. The rest are dead, murdered … by *them*." He raised a shaky finger towards Kemmin and Torrick.

"No, not these two. They're friends." *Maybe*. "Call your companion in here; we're leaving. Now!"

Within a minute, the small group of refugees was on its way to the sub-basement elevator and stairwell; now responsible for the scientists, Echo wasted no time in getting them to safety.

If the aliens should find themselves in an untenable position due to the invasion, they would send a ship to destroy this base; so much had been made clear in the briefings, and now she understood why. If Kemmin spoke the truth, he was too important a person to have him fall into human hands.

Echo cared nothing for either the alien lord or his little sidekick, her concern focused entirely on the scientific staff, and she would not allow the few who had survived to die in a conflagration of fire. How to avoid that scenario she had no firm idea, but one was beginning to form in her mind.

The short journey passed without incident. Wherever Koll had his men posted, it was not there. He may have gathered his forces to find Kemmin, or gone to the cage room. Only four guards remained in the dome, but where they were, Echo could only guess. If Kemmin's advice about Koll's movements was true, at least some of them would be with him in the complex, looking for her and her new charges. She thought she understood Koll enough to know she and the alien lord would be his first priority.

The elevator, repaired since the rescue squad's initial departure, was ascending; at least one alien was on his way up. She watched the indicator lights, and considered waiting in the hope the occupant was Koll himself. With an effort, she forced herself to re-focus on the task at hand.

"The stairs," she ordered. "Everybody down to the lower basement, now." The scientists, worn down by months of starvation and deprivation, staggered into the stairwell under the guidance of Torrick. The looks on their faces showed some of them still believed they were being led to their deaths.

Kemmin stayed behind, his pistol leveled at the elevator. Whether or not he was trustworthy was still a debatable issue. Echo had difficulty accepting him as an ally; to her all Tolleani were enemies, a belief bolstered by the knowledge the one she hated most was somewhere in this complex. This one claimed to be a friend, and his actions so far supported that. Now he stood by her to protect the other humans. Without him, her odds were five to one, with him, considerably better. It was a sobering thought.

Once the others were gone, Kemmin turned and followed, with Echo close behind. She was determined to keep him in her sights until sure of his trustworthiness. His actions made sense if he was telling the truth, and meant he *was* ally rather than enemy, but she did not intend to rush to any conclusion without due consideration.

Two storage levels sat beneath the dome, the first immediately below the plaza and the second, the spacious, tank-filled sub-basement, deeper within the base of the cliff. Echo exited the stairwell, using the tanks as cover to sneak across to the elevator door. The floor indicator was set at the top level. With luck, nobody would come down for a while.

Her rag-tag party waited at the passage leading to the exit. With a raised hand, she ordered them to hold their position, fitted a bolt to her bow and crept onward to the tunnel leading to the lower exits.

The lower airlocks were the obvious place to escape. One or more of the remaining guards would be posted there. Easing herself forward, Echo stopped at a bend in the passage, ten meters short of the point where it divided, and snuck a look around the corner.

At the junction stood a ragged pile of storage modules forming a part-built wall about a meter high and placed to provide cover while commanding all three passages. No guard was in sight, but within seconds, one appeared from the side tunnel carrying another crate that he dropped on top of the construction before stepping out of sight. Left to defend the tunnels alone, he was building himself a fortress, blocking access from all directions.

Watching him leave again, Echo knelt on the floor, bringing her crossbow to bear on the structure ahead. Adrenaline coursed through her body, pushing her awareness higher. Every sight, each sound, even the metallic odor of the Tollean air in the underground passage, seemed sharper to her senses. Exposed, she would not give the guard a chance to fire at her first.

The alien reappeared, carrying yet another crate and intent on his task. He dropped it onto his wall, and then glanced up, just as a crossbow bolt slammed into his forehead.

Echo launched herself forward and pushed through the fragile barrier, stopped to make sure the guard was dead, and turned into the external airlock passage. Her charges would need environment suits to escape into the jungle, and according to Albandier, those hung in a storeroom to one side of the lock bay.

They were gone. The room was empty, the contents presumably removed as a precaution. Echo cursed beneath her breath as she ran back to the junction. Looking towards the basement, she spotted Kemmin bringing the scientists. His suggestion to head for the greenhouse airlock now looked like the only option.

She did not seriously expect to find anything there either; according to Margritte Albandier, the anteroom at that exit now served as a guardroom, with all the station equipment removed long ago. However, the airlock led to a covered and sealed walkway. Escape was still possible; Albandier kept suits and masks in her shed.

Kemmin crept up and peered along the tunnel. With only a brief glance at the body of his fellow Tolleani, he crouched down beside Echo.

"You are quite skilled with that weapon, are you not?"

"I've had a bit of experience. One less alien, one less problem … sorry."

"Do not concern yourself. The guard is one of Koll's, not mine. I mourn not his passing. With four of them outside, the ones your people killed earlier, and this one, there are three remaining, one of whom will not fire on Torrick or me. I cannot guarantee the same for you, I am sorry."

"And I can't promise I won't shoot him if I see him."

"Accepted. We must be wary of Koll as well. An incompetent cripple he may be, but he is a crack shot. Also a … your word would be 'coward', which works in our favor."

"Wait here." Echo stepped over the body and entered the corridor to the greenhouse airlock bay, from where a side exit opened to the guardroom. It was empty, as expected.

Beyond the airlock the covered walkway extended several hundred meters to the dirty, green-streaked glasshouse structure. The way was exposed; anybody in the tunnel was easily visible to a guard outside the transparent walls, and the thin panels offered no protection against serious weapons fire.

An armed Tolleani could sit in the dense surrounding vegetation and pick off each of her group in turn. Echo felt certain that wherever those guards were, they would not be outside the dome, and it was highly unlikely those Koll sent out in pursuit of her team would be anywhere near.

The first chamber of the greenhouse presented the next hurdle. With the retrieval of her battle harness Echo now had her helmet, complete with air filters, and both Kemmin and Torrick could tolerate the atmosphere long enough to reach the outer area. The problem of the civilian scientists remained.

Echo turned to the alien lord as he came up behind her. "I want you to wait here and protect everyone while I go ahead. I'll try to get masks from Albandier if she's still there, and come back for you."

"Perhaps you should stay here. I will go; the old woman knows me."

"No," Echo barked. "You're the one who asked for our assistance, so now you can help by working with me." Kemmin had to understand she was in charge; she felt bound by circumstance to accept him as an ally but still found it difficult to overcome an instinctive reticence in trusting him. Despite his assurance not all Tolleani wanted war, she hated them all nonetheless, and one in particular. That itch needed dealing with, and soon.

The inner section of the greenhouse was hot, humid and uninviting. Native plants, in most instances less than friendly, crowded the avenues between the beds. This was deliberate; many of the more interesting specimens were exceptionally aggressive, and Albandier encouraged them to invade the paths as an extra incentive for the Tolleani to stay out and leave her alone. A single clear path wound through the tangle, but it was not obvious to anyone unaware of its existence, and unwise to travel without protection.

The alien guards and Koll thought Albandier to be a harmless old woman, but Echo considered Margritte to be far from such. The elderly scientist had created a virtual stronghold, one that could only be breached through the inner chamber or from the outside, both of which avenues she controlled to a degree the enemy either ignored, or did not realize.

Echo eased her way to the center divider, avoiding the strange plants as best possible and thanking the gods for her combat suit. She paused, squinting through the filthy glass walls in hope of seeing the old woman. The door was locked, and secured on the other side with a chain. She rapped on the door with the butt of her pistol.

Seconds later Albandier appeared. Echo took a deep breath and lifted the visor on her helmet to let the woman see her face more clearly. Margritte peered at her for a moment, then fumbled to clear the door and allow entrance.

"You're supposed to be dead!" A broad grin spread across her face.

"Not yet. I'm hard to kill. I need your help."

"Of course, Dear. I have someone here who will be happy to see you."

Echo's attention lifted, a ray of hope lighting up her mind. The only 'someone' she could think of was one or more of her squad members. At least one of them had survived; Echo prayed it was Katch or Sarra—if Cooney or his toady

Petrovsky, then there would be problems. Margritte was smiling, so it was unlikely to be one of them.

"Fine, but I need help first. I have five of your fellow scientists behind me, and I need environment suits."

Albandier's face lit up. "Certainly, yes. Wait." Dashing away through the surrounding crops she returned a minute later with a box. "These will do. I will come with you."

"No, you stay here and let us back in when I return. Keep your door locked." Echo grabbed the container and dashed back towards the airlock.

# Chapter Eighteen

KATCH'S HANDS WERE STEADY as he leveled his pistol at Kemmin. His reaction had been instinctive when the Tolleani emerged from the tangle of vegetation and entered the outer chamber behind Echo's refugee group. His finger was poised to fire when Echo stepped between him and his target.

"No, stop!" Echo shouted. "He's a friend. He helped us escape; he's on our side."

"I find that hard to believe. You can't trust any of these bastards."

Behind him, Sarra also raised her rifle, this time toward Torrick. Upon seeing Echo and the scientists, she lowered the weapon and waited to see what would develop. Unlike Kemmin, the little Tolleasin was unarmed.

Margritte Albandier stepped forward and placed a hand on Katch's arm. "She's telling the truth. This one has been helping us. He's a prisoner here as much as we are."

Kemmin froze for a moment, and then ever so slowly lowered his own pistol. "I am sorry, my friend. I did not intend to startle you." He replaced the gun in its holster and turned his attention to closing and locking the door to the inner chamber.

After a moment's pause, Katch lowered his weapon and wrapped his massive arms around Echo. "You can't believe how happy I am to see you, baby girl. We thought you were dead. What happened?"

Echo eased herself away and took a deep breath; at times, the man did not know his own strength.

Minutes later, the group stood in the cleared area Albandier referred to as her camp. For the first time since leaving her prison, Echo felt it safe to breathe.

"They hit me with a stun device; gave me a hell of a shock and knocked me out. I woke up in a cage. I think Tandie is dead. I saw her body before I went down."

"She is. I watched her fall, and we found her outside the greenhouse a few hours ago. The bastards took her through the airlock and dumped her. The jungle has almost grown over the body and we couldn't get her back—makes for an efficient disposal system." Katch shook his head and looked away.

For a moment, silence reigned as the small group contemplated the loss of their team member. Echo studied her friends. A warmth spread within her at seeing the two who have become so close to her in the last year.

Both were equally overjoyed to see her, but both were exhausted. It showed in their eyes, glazed with the resignation of those who had battled without rest for a long, long time. Streaks of unknown things from the local vegetation covered their combat suits, evidence their journey out and back had been difficult and fraught with danger.

Sarra Corian dropped to squat on her haunches, her face strained and worn. Katch lay down on his back and closed his eyes. Not far away, Bernie Greer huddled with his five fellow scientists. Kemmin and Torrick sat together, apart from the group.

"What happened to you?" Echo asked, squatting beside Katch.

The big man lifted his head and peered at her through tired and bloodshot eyes. "We headed towards the pickup point. Sarra and I tried to come back for you but Cooney vetoed it. A bunch of Tollean guards pursued us, and they were only minutes behind us most of the way. We came back because there was no point going on. We lost Mendoza."

"Tell me."

"The old guy was ill and weak. Cooney ignored that and pushed him too hard. He collapsed from exhaustion and died. That's when we decided to abandon the mission plan and come back for you. We didn't know if you survived or not, but without Mendoza we decided to find out. We had no reason not to."

Echo smiled, shaking her head. "I'm not so sure. Mendoza was not our primary target. Cooney was wrong." Katch peered back at her, frowning. He opened his mouth as if to speak, then stopped.

"We were sent here to rescue the administrator," Echo continued. "Cooney assumed that meant Mendoza, but this base is under Tollean control and they put their own people in to supervise. The current base administrator is Kemmin; he's an academic, not a soldier."

"That can't be right. What value is he to Fleet?"

"I'm not sure yet. The little one, Torrick, is some kind of electronic whiz kid I think, and he was responsible for the drone that brought us here. He tells me he remotely hacked the mainframes at the naval base, re-programmed an automatic messenger drone and sent it away. He was trying to smuggle a message through when Ben picked it up. Kemmin wants to defect."

Katch shook his head. "Again, why would Command give a toss?"

"Kemmin is a very important person by his own account. He's a member of Tollean nobility, I think, and a significant figurehead for a rebel movement in the Empire. He and the rebels want peace and are prepared to negotiate with us if we help them. The Emperor is too afraid to have him eliminated and turned into a martyr, so he sent him here, to Coventry. I gather that for public consumption he's the commander of the base, but in reality even though he's in charge, he's as much a prisoner as our people. He's the one we came here for."

"If you believe that then I will accept it, but I don't trust him." Katch rolled on his side and closed his eyes again.

Greer stared at the ground, chewing over Echo's words in his mind. He walked over and sat beside her. "I agree Kemmin is a friend, just for the record. There's something else I should tell you. I have little faith in Cooney's getting those phials home." His face split in a knowing grin. "The minute I met the fool I pegged him as incompetent. When he grabbed them from me I took measures."

Reaching inside his environment suit, he removed the second case, identical to the first. "Besides, he doesn't have the research to go with them."

"You had a backup?" Echo asked.

"Of course, and more. I have a digital copy of our notes. The thing is not a virus in the truest sense of the word, but something that behaves like one. Knowing it was deadly to our alien biology, we studied it looking for medical applications, and developed the antiviral agent and vaccine."

"Yes, I remember," Echo said. "Red for the base strain, green for the antidote and blue for the vaccine."

"Correct. The Federation wants the original strain to develop an antidote. We've already done all that, and with it, the pandemic can be stopped quickly. Surely, that's the most important consideration."

Greer's finger moved to rest on the fourth phial. For a moment he paused, unsure of whether to speak further. Deep in contemplation he glanced at Kemmin, then tapped the fourth, orange phial, closed the case and placed it back inside his suit.

"We have to leave here," Echo said. "By now, our invasion force will be attacking the enemy base, and if they succeed, Tollean ships will come to destroy this station, and Kemmin. We have to move to a safe place, if such a thing exists on this moon."

"The landing pad," Greer said. "We can steal the ship up on the platform and fly out of here."

"That left some time ago," Katch mumbled, his eyes remaining closed. "We heard it lift off. They must have got word of the invasion and gone to join the fight."

"No, no. The supply ship."

Echo turned her attention to the scientist again. "What?"

"There's a shuttle up there, parked over at the back against the cliff face. You can't see it from here because of the storage containers Koll stacked in front of it. He insists on keeping it here; I think he's outfitting it as his personal escape pod should worse come to worse. It stays fueled and ready but he never uses it."

"It never occurred to him Kemmin might try to escape in it?"

"As far as I know Kemmin can't fly. He's a scientist and academic, not a warrior. Can you fly it?"

Echo stared at the ground for a moment. She, Katch and Sarra all received training in spacecraft operation, but only in human craft. With luck, they could interpret the controls of a Tollean vessel, but nothing was certain. Conversely, it might well be their only option.

"I don't know. What sort is it?"

"I'm sorry, no idea. I've only ever seen it from a distance, and from the dome you can only just see the nose."

The strange pseudo-night fell once again. Beyond the glasshouse walls the plants moved ghost-like in the half-light. Echo sat guarding the divider door, as she had done for the last few hours in case the enemy decided to break through. Part of her wanted it to happen. She ached for a chance at Koll; every time she thought of him, her rage mounted. Shuffling to ease the pressure on her behind, she peered through the glass into the darker inner chamber.

If the hatch to the tunnel opened, the lights beyond would be visible through Albandier's blockade of alien vegetation. The other entrance, the exterior door to the glasshouse, was also in the inner chamber. The only other way in was to cut through the glass walls, and that would take minutes, enough to warn Echo and her companions.

Katch pushed through the vines and stood beside her. "I'm here to relieve you. Anything happening, Baby Girl?"

"Thanks. All quiet here; nothing from the walkway entrance, and no sign of movement at the outer door."

"You expect Koll to try to get in that way?"

"No. He has no reason to do so. As far as he's concerned, we're trapped in here with nowhere to go, and he has only a handful of guards left up there. I'm guessing the ones he sent out after you will return eventually, and then he'll attack."

"Yeah, I wouldn't worry too much about that." Katch sat cross-legged on the ground beside Echo. "We killed one of them when they caught us out in the valley and managed to lose the rest, but they re-acquired our tracks and kept following. When Sarra and I decided to come back, we lay 'doggo' and let them pass. I'm guessing they'll continue chasing Cooney until they catch him. I don't like their chances; he may be an arsehole and an incompetent, but he's a dangerous killer."

"If they survive they'll have to come back. I don't think their environment gear is as effective as ours in the long term."

"Ah, well, that's it, isn't it," Katch said. "From what I've seen their suits aren't intended for long sorties, but that's what they're doing. They stand an excellent chance of dying if they stay out too long. I live in hope."

"Yes, I guess so. Thanks for relieving me. I better get some sleep."

Echo rose and pushed through the vines towards the back of the chamber. She settled next to the sleeping form of Sarra at one side of the clearing, well away from where the scientists huddled and where Kemmin and Torrick kept each other company. Almost asleep, she sensed a gentle hand shaking her arm. Margritte Albandier crouched beside her.

"I need you to see something, my dear," the elderly scientist said. "Come, and put your helmet on." Echo groaned, scrambled to her feet and followed Albandier to the tool shed, where the old woman unlocked the door and entered.

The inside was almost empty. At one end tools and boxes lay in a heap, and at the other a block and tackle hung from the wall just below the roof panel. The floor of the structure consisted of several alloy plates, from one of which a metal loop extended a few centimeters.

Margritte closed the door and locked it from the inside, then fetched a lantern. She pulled a face mask from her overalls and strapped it over her face. "You might like to adjust your filters for outside air."

Reaching for the block and tackle, she slipped the hook through the loop and pulled on the rope. A floor panel hinged up and back, revealing a deep hole dug into the ground beneath the glasshouse. An alloy ladder rested against one side.

"What's this?"

"This, my dear, is the way to the true secret of this moon. Shall I go first?" The old woman's eyes glittered, excitement welling within. Echo nodded and waited as Margritte climbed down into the darkness, lighting the way with her lamp. Echo followed until she stood in a dug passage about four meters down.

"The Kylax made this. They live underground and have extensive tunnels running all through here."

"How did you find your way down?"

"I didn't. They came to me. I was working in the garden one day when the ground caved in and one of them climbed out. Frightened the bejesus out of me, I can tell you. Of course

I'd seen them before, and now I've learned to understand them…"

"And the tool shed?"

"We, the other scientists and I, dragged it across to cover the hole. We decided we needed to keep them secret, even from humanity, until we understood more about them. The shed helps keep the entrance safe, and keeps their atmosphere out of my greenhouse."

Echo looked along the tunnel. It was around two meters in diameter, carved from the solid sandstone of the basin floor. The walls showed clear score marks, indicating the use of hand tools.

Margritte moved away, holding the lantern higher. Echo tried to work out where they were going, estimating the passage went back under the cliff face a short distance along from the ledge on which the dome sat.

A few hundred meters on, the path widened and Echo swore there was light ahead. Margritte turned the lamp off. A carpet of glowing, moss-like growth covered every surface, and lit the way forward.

"It's a form of bio-luminescence," she explained. "We believe the vegetation here uses symbiotic micro-organisms to produce the illumination, the same way plants on our worlds do. We still don't understand the exact relationship but the glow is strong enough to see by." Moving on, she led Echo into an enormous cavern, also lit by the native growth.

Echo's jaw dropped as she stepped out and took in the surroundings. Several hundred meters across in every direction, the high-domed chamber had a flat floor. Primitive, close-packed, roofless buildings stood everywhere, strange mud and timber structures reminiscent of ancient Indian cliff dwellings of *Old Earth* Echo once saw in a book. Kylax moved between them, engaged in activities the nature of which she could only guess.

Margritte stepped over beside her, leaning in to speak. "I told you these creatures were intelligent. They have a primitive technology, about equal to our earliest agrarian civilizations. They are the third such species, after those Tollean bastards and us. Come and sit with me over here; we have to wait for them to approach."

They sat down on the rock floor and waited. All around, the strange, crab-like creatures stopped whatever they were doing. Several approached, at first moving towards Albandier, but then diverting their attention to Echo.

"They've been watching your people out in the jungle, and they know we are the enemy of the Tolleani," Margritte said. "Open the visor on your helmet, Dear, but make sure your filters are still in."

Within minutes, dozens of the creatures filled the surrounding space, the largest one approaching until only a meter away. Slowly it extended its long, flexible stalk towards her face, causing her to draw back instinctively.

"Let it, my dear. You've done this before, so you know it won't hurt you. They asked me to bring you here."

"You can understand them? It's nothing but emotions … vague impressions."

"I have a deal more experience at interpreting than you do. Try your best; this is important."

Echo saw several of the creatures gather around the first, their stalks touching its carapace. Beyond them more joined in, and others in turn behind them, until all were linked.

The pad on the end of the first creature's stalk rested on Echo's forehead and her perception flooded with images, vague, fleeting, laced with emotion. In time, the visions cleared, as if the Kylax had managed to adjust to her lack of experience.

At first, scenes of the creatures and their world played across her mind like a movie. Her sense of awareness heightened with a feeling of joy at the beauty of this world, not the hellish place seen by her but the paradise of those who evolved here. They loved this moon, their home, as did all the place of their creation.

The story began to change. Echo received vague impressions of humans and the Kylax together. She realized she was receiving a history lesson of sorts, the mood still positive. The native inhabitants of *Persephone* had discovered the arrival of sister intelligence from above the clouds, and in their insatiable curiosity they found joy in the interaction. The humans, Echo realized, were Margritte and her people, the first to discover this amazing race.

Again, the vision changed, and now showed the Tolleani, colossal ships screaming overhead and soldiers hunting through the jungle, shooting down the helpless creatures without mercy. The sensations darkened, from exuberance at being alive to curiosity, then to fear. Echo sensed a call for help born of desperation, and then resignation.

Suddenly, she understood what the Kylax were trying to say. An intelligent, peaceful species in the early stages of technological development, they feared for their existence.

Against the power of the Tolleani they were defenseless, and saw the inevitable outcome of the occupation of their moon as the extinction of their own kind. Echo and her squad, the first armed beings capable of resisting their persecutors, gave them hope. They were asking for assistance from another alien species, one they saw as a potential ally as technologically advanced as their enemy.

Margritte's voice filtered through the flood of sensations. "Give them hope."

Understanding what the woman required of her, she began to visualize within her own mind, attempting to create a message she hoped her new friends would understand.

She imagined a fleet of vessels attacking other ships to show her people were fighting the Tolleani, then herself shooting Tollean guards, and humans and Kylax standing together. She struggled to make herself understood; forming clear pictures in her mind did not come easily. She was unsure they understood the concept of spaceships, or even space, something unknown to their species until the arrival of humanity. She prayed her efforts were enough.

A wave of joy, brief but distinct, filled her mind. The stalk withdrew from her forehead, and the creatures backed away. Dropping their bodies on the rock floor they huddled, legs pulled in to their sides, as if entering a state of dormancy.

"They are expressing contentment," Margritte explained. "Gratitude. We must go now."

"I made them a promise, I think. How can I ever keep it?"

Margritte reached out a hand to Echo's helmet and turned to face her. "You made the promise; it is for others to keep it. The only people who know about the Kylax, that they are intelligent, technological, loving and thinking beings, are those of us on this moon. If we fail to escape this place—if *you* fail—the knowledge dies with us. The rest of the galaxy sees this world as the deepest pit of all the hells, and may never take the trouble to look further again."

"You said an invasion is under way. This species will not survive those Tollean bastards, and if we win they might still die if the truth of their nature remains a secret. My colleagues and I chose to keep quiet because we feared for them. We were wrong. We should have told everyone, and now our failure places them in jeopardy. I trust you to help us make good our failing."

*Make good their failing.* The words repeated in Echo's mind. She did not come here for that and it was not her responsibility, but how could she ignore it?

# Chapter Nineteen

THE GROUP GATHERED IN the glasshouse clearing, shielded from view by the makeshift walls of green. Echo mused about the massive quantity of food grown here, far more than needed by the small contingent of human prisoners that had survived under Koll's cruel care.

"I didn't intend to do that at first," Margritte admitted when questioned. "When they first put me down here a guard always stayed with me. Gave me the willies, I can tell you. Each chamber has separate environmental controls, so I convinced them their air was killing the vegetables, and demanded they let me modify this end to Terrestrial normal. After a few days, my minder moved out to the room in the exit passage.

"Then I started planting things to keep myself amused. We had a huge range of seeds gathered over the years to see what would grow here, so I experimented. I planted everything that climbed around this spot for some privacy, and in this heat and humidity … well, it all just took off. The guards gave up coming in here months ago once they realized I would not try to escape."

"Why did you keep the environment suits stored in the shed?" Echo asked.

"It was a bit pointless; if we leave here, there's nowhere to go outside. Still, one can never know…"

Echo realized she liked Albandier. The elderly scientist was a force to be reckoned with, one of which the Tolleani were unaware.

The group sat in a huddle around a makeshift meal of produce from the gardens. Echo, Katch and Sarra refrained, sticking to their supplements. The field-ration pills required weaning off after a mission, and sudden changes back to normal food involved problems they did not need for now.

Not far away Kemmin and Torrick sat on their own, picking away at a small pile of fruits they were able to eat without discomfort. Katch had refused their inclusion in the group and ordered them away. He did not trust them at all, and wanted to discuss strategy without them present.

"The guards that chased us into the jungle haven't come back yet," he said. "They must have stuck to Cooney, so if any survive it will be a while before they return here."

"That gives us some time," Echo said. "We need to work out what to do next."

"What do *you* think?" Sarra asked. It had become obvious since their reunion that in Cooney's absence both she and Katch saw Echo as the new team leader, rank notwithstanding.

"We need to pick our priorities. I expect the attack on the Tollean base is well and truly over by now so if the enemy sent ships to destroy this place and kill Kemmin, they're on route now and will be here anytime."

"Our rescue will also be on its way if we won," Katch said. "It'll go to the pickup point but there's no way we can get there in time. Cooney will report us dead if he and Petrovsky make it out alive, and that'll be that."

"Fine, so we're on our own." Echo stared into the distance, trying to piece together the different avenues available into one coherent course of action. The original plan to reach a high, rocky ridge several days away at the far end of the valley, where a large ship might easily land to retrieve the team, seemed impossible now. With her fingertips, Echo touched the small bump where Ben's locator beacon hid beneath her suit. "Or not. I think we have to get up to the platform."

Katch stared up in the general direction of the landing pad. "Every remaining Tolleani will be between us and there."

"I agree, but only a handful are left and we can deal with them. The pad is our only option as far as I can see. We have to get these guys,"—she waved a hand at the seven civilians seated around them—"away from here, and in particular Greer. Then there's Kemmin."

"Who should be your primary concern," a deep voice spoke from across the clearing. "You still do not understand your entire purpose in being here is the rescue of me."

Echo turned her attention to the alien. Friend or enemy, he still exhibited the unbelievable arrogance she concluded must be a trademark of his species. "You can hear us from there?"

"Of course. My race has far better senses than do humans. Better eyesight, hearing and smell. Even our taste is superior."

*How can you possibly know that?* "If you say so. I'm still not convinced we can trust you."

"I find that unfortunate. I have done all I can to show my friendship, including the rescue of you from your cage. Only through my efforts are your scientific friends still alive, and has the old woman been able to stay unmolested down here. Koll would have killed them all, as he did most of their colleagues. I suspect your hatred of him taints your ability to trust me."

Echo's thoughts fixed on Kemmin's remarks. He was right; since escaping from the cage her focus had centered on the security chief. The need to keep Kemmin alive, to rescue the scientists and their research, and to get word of the Kylax to those who mattered, all took second place to her primary goal. One way or another, that monster would die before she left this planet, so her father, family and the other colonists of *Corros* could rest peacefully.

Kemmin rose and strode across to the group, followed by his diminutive shadow. Seating himself, he considered each of the science team survivors in turn. A loud snort came from Katch.

"You should advise your aggressive colleague to accept the fact I want to help, and keep his own council."

For a moment Echo thought Katch would explode, his muscles tensing as he prepared to launch himself at the alien. A war between him and the arrogant lord was the last thing she needed.

"No, Katch! He's right. He's acted only as a friend. For now at least, we have to believe him. We can't afford to be fighting among ourselves."

After a second her friend gave an abrupt nod and resumed his seat, but his eyes remained fixed on the Tolleani.

"Alright," Echo continued. "What do you suggest, Kemmin?"

Kemmin turned his attention again to the scientists. "Do any among you not acknowledge my assistance in keeping you all alive in the past?" Greer and Albandier nodded. Several of the others looked puzzled and kept quiet; Echo suspected they had no idea of what the alien Lord may have done on their behalf.

Kemmin turned back to Echo. "It is clear you will not reach your retrieval in time, as you have acknowledged. It is also true the Emperor will not condone my escape or capture and the authorities will have orders to prevent that. If your invasion succeeded, a Tollean destroyer *is* on its way here to crush this base. Even if your forces pursue, ours will arrive first."

"Yes, and…?"

"We must go back inside as you planned, and make our way to the landing platform before an attack ship gets here. Koll's shuttle is the only way off this moon."

"We don't know what kind of ship it is. If it's Tollean, I can't guarantee we can fly it. I know you can't, and none of us have flown any of your ships."

A small voice spoke up. "Excuse me, sir, but I can," Half-hidden behind his enormous master, Torrick raised his hand.

Kemmin smiled. "Once again, you see I have thought this through. Before choosing to accompany me here, Torrick served as my personal pilot. He can fly a Tollean shuttle. We will wait in space until your ships retrieve us. Otherwise we are dead, especially if we stay here."

"This greenhouse is the safest place," Margritte suggested forcefully. "They have no reason to bomb here."

"My people do not need an excuse. We do not usually destroy without cause, but when something is marked for destruction, it is done completely. Besides, all the air maintenance machinery is located in the station. Koll can turn it off, and you will run out of breathable air. I will, of course, survive."

"How do you suggest we reach Koll's ship?" Echo asked before Kemmin's arrogance could start another fight.

"There is only one way. There are no paths up the cliff face, and you can't expect your old woman to climb. Nor half of you others, for that matter."

"I'm not going," Margritte interjected. "I'm too decrepit. I would hold everyone up."

"Of course you're going," Echo countered.

"No."

"Not even to save your precious Kylax cities?" Kemmin asked.

Albandier's face blanched, her jaw dropping. "You know about them?"

"I am a scientist, and like you I study what is around me. Koll uses those creatures for sport—I acknowledge their importance."

"Fine," Echo interrupted. "So, how do you suggest we do it?"

"We return to the basement and walk up the stairs. How else?"

"We can't…" Sarra began.

"No, wait," Katch cut her off, raising his hand. "As much as I hate to admit it, he's right. The space crew is gone, and the pursuit squad hasn't returned yet. Three guards and their mad chief can't defend the station. The three of us are armed and ready, and more than enough—four if you include him." He waived a hand at Kemmin. "As Echo said earlier, we should have a fighting chance of getting through. We reach the platform by the main exit, grab the ship and leave."

"How long can we last before we are picked up?" Greer asked from the back of the group. "A short-run shuttle can't have much in the way of supplies."

"This one does," Kemmin replied. "The guards tell me Koll set it up as his personal emergency-escape module, and it is stocked to keep him alive for months."

"We can't eat your food."

"Yes you can. It will unsettle you a little, but you will survive. We are not much different, you and I, and our space rations are rather bland—nothing you cannot handle if need be."

Echo considered the plan, ignoring the conversation as it deteriorated to trivial 'what if' bantering. Kemmin was correct. The only easy way to access the landing platform, the only possible way for the older and more infirm members of the scientific team, was through the dome.

Despite Albandier's insistence she was too old to go, Echo did not intend the elderly scientist should remain. She admired the woman for her resourcefulness, and wanted to let her make her own reparation for so called 'failings', by carrying word of the galaxy's third known technological beings to the outside worlds. Margritte Albandier was, by Echo's assessment, a hero, and she deserved recognition as such.

The idea of escaping through the station appealed to Echo. She had previously refrained from suggesting it as a means for the others, having already decided to give control of the group to Katch, and re-enter the station alone. Her score with Koll remained to be settled, and the current plan of action suited her perfectly.

"I lost my mines when I was captured. Do you or Sarra still have yours?"

Katch nodded, grinning back at Echo in the dim light.

\* \* \*

Damned humans!

Koll strode from the stairwell towards the landing pad airlock. This was not going well, and now Kemmin had escaped. The arrogant fool had actually fired a laser pistol at him. Where he had obtained such a thing was unknown, but it had forced Koll to seek out his remaining guards to have them carry out the executions he should have been able to deal with himself. Of course, he was well aware of the aristocrat's location somewhere in the greenhouse, but getting at him was not going to be easy.

The team sent after the enemy infiltrators were out of the equation. The last report received indicated they had lost one of their number and since then the radio had remained silent.

No help would come from that direction. The lead group of humans, now down to two individuals, was heading for a pick-up point and the guards continued the pursuit, sticking to the task appointed them.

A recent attempt to call them back had failed, indicating their communications were down. It was an annoyance; they would have been more use here. Koll now knew the location of the missing humans. His surveillance had detected their approach not long ago, so they were certainly with the escaped female, down in the greenhouse.

The human soldiers now numbered three, all armed and, judging from their performance so far, excellent at their job. With no way to contact his away-team, his remaining forces were inadequate to guard the station, deal with the insurgents, kill the damned lord and his sidekick, and more importantly, protect himself.

Two of the remaining guards were at the point where the tunnel branched to the lower exits, and could command ingress from either. They had reconstructed the barrier half built at the junction by the previous and now dead guard, and this time Koll hoped they would not be so stupid as to get themselves shot. The airlocks were sealed, so with the guards in position he could do no more.

The third of his men sat by the airlock to the landing pad. Koll had counted on the assistance of Pac and his crew, and when they scrambled and flew their ship away to join the battle it was clear he had once again been let down by his inferiors.

For now, Kemmin would have to stay where he was, effectively trapped. The best option available was to prevent the humans from getting back inside, and Koll still had some tricks up his sleeve. The main ventilation plant at the rear of the station controlled the air supply to both parts of the greenhouse, so as soon as the opportunity arose he would cut the air off and use lasers to punch a few holes in the damned place. It would be interesting to see how they coped with nothing to breathe but the native atmosphere of this moon, regardless of filters.

The invasion exacerbated the problem; no doubt it was the reason he had received no reply to his request for assistance. The penetration of the station could be a part of the larger incursion. With only a handful of second-rate guards and his requests for additional forces ignored, command could not blame him for the escape of their prize exile.

Of course there was no way, in Koll's mind, that the enemy could defeat a full Tollean regional base. The ground-based weapons had the power to blow the biggest battleship to dust. One might never be too careful however, and he had taken certain precautions against a worst-case scenario.

Scowling at the solitary guard as he stormed through the airlock, Koll pulled a filter mask over his face and hobbled across to the back of the landing field. The shuttle sat alone behind a wall of stacked containers. A human vessel, it had been here at the time of the original Tollean acquisition of the moon, and he had insisted on keeping it. In the preceding months, considerable care had gone into fitting it out to suit his personal needs.

The little ship had all the basics, including a wormhole generator and additional pod tanks to increase the range for the small but efficient engine. The markings on the exterior were now Tollean. It took him ages to figure out how everything worked, so different were its controls to anything he had flown before, but in the end, he had succeeded. The ship had several sleep pods—he would need only one—and enough supplies to stay in space indefinitely.

The contingency plan was simple: if by some unlikely chance the enemy won the system back, Koll would escape and make his way to a wormhole, the sole survivor of an overwhelming attack on his command by a vast human fleet. Abandoned by the navy he would have fought valiantly to hold the station, but finally escaped with no other option. Of course, Kemmin would be reported dead.

Koll took care to check the shuttle, making sure the tanks were full and ready to go. Like all emergency vehicles it was intended to operate at a moment's notice, and he had taken every precaution to ensure that it did.

Giving himself a mental congratulation for a job well done, he closed the hatch and returned to the airlock, intent on cutting off the air supply to the greenhouse.

\* \* \*

Behind a waist high wall of metal storage boxes the two Tollean guards tasked with preventing ingress contemplated their situation. They had no option but to carry out the orders given by their officious overlord, but deep within the mind of each lurked the same, nagging doubts.

The Coordinator gave no idea of how many humans were outside, or where they were likely to attack. His order was simply to prevent anyone from coming in by either entrance. After giving it, he had disappeared back to the upper levels and no word had come from him since.

Thanks to stories told by the space crews who came and went, Koll's demotion and exile to this place was well known. All had heard the rumors about how he lost his last command in its entirety. He now seemed to be doing his best to repeat the events of the past. Of the original contingent of twelve guards only three remained, and the ancestors alone knew what the future held for them.

The flight crew that left earlier had warned of an invasion before leaving. Koll did not care; he had his shuttle, and every guard knew he would abandon them without a thought. Each understood this well. Marooned on this moon the chances of seeing their homes or loved ones again were poor if the enemy took control of this planetary system.

No word had come from the four ordered to chase the insurgents. None had ever been outside before except to accompany the commander on his morbid hunting expeditions. What a waste those were: the damned creatures on this moon were inedible. Beyond that, nobody ever went out without good reason.

Both guards wondered if their friends were alive. Should any return they would be locked outside as much as the humans, and stood every chance of being cut down before getting back in. The enemy insurgents were capable soldiers; even the captured one had escaped easily despite Koll's precautions.

One guard had an additional concern. He did not wish to find himself firing on Kemmin. The noble lord's standing was well known to him and he had helped him in the past, in many secret, little ways. He prayed it would not come to a standoff between them.

A thunderclap echoed along the corridor from the direction of the greenhouse exit, sending a shock wave towards the barricade. Moments later a second explosion followed, from the jungle airlock.

# Chapter Twenty

RISING FROM THE WALKWAY floor, Echo rushed forward to survey the damage. As hoped, the hinges to the outer door lay in shreds of torn metal, the door now hanging askew, held only by the twisted lock mechanism. All around, the glass walls of the walkway had been shattered and blown out by the force of the blast, letting the outside air flow into the tunnel and through to the airlock.

Echo wrenched the door open sufficient to squeeze through, just as the sound of another detonation reached her ears, echoing down from the junction.

The inner door had also suffered damage, but had been open at the time of the blast. Behind her, Kemmin's face appeared through the gap. "You have been successful, yes?"

"I don't know yet. We're only guessing the guards are there, so we bring the others to this point, and wait for a signal."

Katch and Sarra emerged from the dense vegetation and rushed across to the airlock. The outer door now lay twisted on the path outside the entrance. Several donut mine secured to the lock and hinges had dislodged the door with devastating effect.

Again, the inner door was open, and the outside air flowed unhindered to the interior. Katch dashed through, scoped the passage and took a crouched position, his rifle aimed forward. Behind him, Sarra forced the inner door shut and used her laser to weld it in position; a small chance remained of the alien pursuit contingent returning and attacking them from the rear.

The bay inside was unguarded and empty. Sarra took a knee beside Katch, weapon at the ready. "I'm guessing we were right," she said. "With so few guards they must be at the junction. Getting past them is *not* going to be easy." She stretched to look around her companion. "With two explosions at once, they may not know exactly where we are coming at them from. That should help."

"So might this." Reaching into a pocket Katch removed a small, cylindrical object. "One smoke screen, coming up." Bomb in hand he crept to where the corridor led out of the airlock bay. His back flat against the wall, he shuffled forward until he could see inside. Ahead, a barrier of crates, rubble and assorted equipment blocked the way. Barely had he eased his head around for a better view when a blast from a laser licked past within centimeters of his helmet visor and impacted the opposite wall.

*These boys are good*, Katch thought, *and this is bloody dangerous!* The aliens would allow only one chance at success, and it could come at a considerable risk.

Crouching, Katch took a donut mine from his harness and placed it on the ground beside the smoker, then with a second thought retrieved another and set the timers of both to five seconds. Sarra moved up, then stepped back again in anticipation of what she knew was about to occur. Easing forward again, Katch hurled the smoke bomb as far possible without exposing himself. The enemy reciprocated instantly, with another barrage of fire.

Mines in hand, he crouched, ready to go. The smoker discharged, blocking out all vision and most of the light with dense, blue-black fumes. Unable to see a clear target, the Tolleani shot wildly, the dazzling red beams of their lasers lancing through the smoke, turning the narrow corridor into a death trap.

Katch could not see any better than the Tollean guards, but did not need to. He waited for the laser fire to stop, then launched himself around the corner, took as many strides as he dared, and prayed he would not be hit as he pressed the activator buttons on the mines and hurled them as hard and high as possible.

The expectation was they would ricochet off the ceiling and over the barrier. If not, the explosive force should be sufficient to stun the guards long enough for him and Sarra to reach them. He dropped flat to the floor as the explosives left his hands. A sharp dagger of pain lashed into his flesh as he fell.

In the confines of the corridor, the explosion was enough to deafen the gods. It came with a shock wave like a hammer blow to the top of Katch's head. The helmet served its purpose well; the explosion shook him badly, but caused no permanent harm. Pain from a laser wound burned fiercely, driving a lightning bolt of agony deep into his brain. Everything was deathly quiet, his hearing deadened by the ear-splitting noise. He lay motionless, stunned, waiting for his mind to clear.

Most of the smoke blew out with the force of the explosions. Visible as a dark shadow through the haze, the makeshift wall now resembled a disordered pile of scattered refuse. The mines did not go over as Katch hoped, but the double blast had been devastating none the less.

From behind her prone companion Sarra rushed forward, leaping over the rubble to reach the enemy position. Without waiting to see if they were dead or alive, she fired at the inert alien figures, and then assumed a defensive posture, facing along the corridor in the direction of the basements. Satisfied the immediate threat had passed, she yelled along the tunnel towards the greenhouse.

"Clear! You can bring them in now."

At the walkway airlock bay, shrouded in dense smoke blown down from the junction, Echo heard Sarra's call and moved forward, the rescued scientists following in a small huddle urged on by Torrick with Kemmin bringing up the rear.

A scene of chaos greeted them. With her back to Echo, Sarra still faced towards the basements, ready for any attack. Sitting on a crate and propped against the wall, Katch applied a sealant to what appeared to be a wound on his side. Part of his suit hung in a loose flap where he had cut it away, and a dark gash, a laser burn, slashed across his rib cage. Hearing Echo approach, he grinned, his face twisted with pain.

"Almost blacked out for a minute. Just a scratch."

"More than, by the look of it. Will you be okay?"

Katch took a small injector from a pocket on his webbing and held it up. "Will be now. This stuff lets you fly without wings." He pressed the injector to his skin and sat back, waiting for the drug to work its magic.

Echo nodded acknowledgement. The field medication served one purpose only: to keep a soldier on his or her feet, and fighting. In a few hours, Katch would have to take another dose or lapse into unconsciousness.

"We can't stop here," she said. "Assuming our guess is right, only two of them are left including Koll, and we should have a good chance of getting through to the landing pad. Trouble is we don't know where they are or what they will do. We'll need to be extra careful."

"I'll help Katch," Sarra said without turning her head.

"No. The civilians can help him if necessary. He should be all right as long as he stays dosed up. You stay with me and help get us out of here." Slapping her friend on the shoulder, Echo led the way forward.

The enormous chamber of the lower basement hummed with the sound of machinery. Echo eased her way towards the stairwell, using the bulk of the huge tanks to cover her from any waiting welcome party.

Close behind, Sarra and Kemmin watched her back. With all remaining threats ahead of them, the alien noble had decided he did not need to protect the scientists any more, leaving Torrick to bring them along while he joined Echo and Sarra at the point. Sarra's forehead creased in a deep frown; like Katch, she still did not trust him.

Echo remained apprehensive about having an armed Tolleani behind her, but could do little about it under the circumstances. So far, Kemmin had given her no cause to doubt him, and he even helped wherever possible. If he actually sent the message to Fleet and was the true focus of the mission, then she did not have a choice. She trusted Sarra and knew any unwarranted move from the alien, and the girl would cut him down without a second's thought.

The stairs to the upper levels were only meters away, and the only practical way up. The elevator control panel had been repaired yet again, most likely because of Koll's reticence to use the stairs because of his limp. The elevator was faster but also the most dangerous, and Koll would certainly be waiting for them. Above, the stairwell exited close by the lift doors, and no doubt the last-remaining guard would be hidden there to watch them both. The odds of safely sneaking up via the stair well were better, but not by much.

Kemmin crept up beside her. "Might I a suggestion make?" he asked.

"Go ahead. I can't stop you."

"I recommend the three of us go up and wait below the top step. After five minutes, Torrick will send the elevator up empty. If a guard is there, it will distract him long enough for one of us to take a clean shot."

Echo turned towards the alien. "You don't have many qualms about shooting your own kind, do you?"

"Koll is not my *kind*, as you say. He represents everything bad about my race, and I would not hesitate to remove him if necessary. The remaining guard will be … unfortunate, but I have a greater destiny."

"Oh, really?"

"Of course. I want peace for both my people and yours. I have a sufficiently large following among my people to bring it about, with help. A single sacrifice to save millions, perhaps billions of lives is not such a travesty."

"Fair enough," Echo turned her attention back to the stairs. Humans had followed the same philosophy often throughout their history. Kemmin's justification was valid, but she found it hard to accept altruism from anyone of his race. "I go first. You stay behind me, Sarra behind you."

Kemmin nodded, then waved for Torrick to come forward and explained the plan to him. Echo checked her gear in preparation, and felt once again the small lump under her suit, the transmission beacon Ben gave her. It remained in place despite her having been captured; whoever disarmed her while she was unconscious had done a poor job. Reaching in, she squeezed the device to activate it as Ben had instructed. It was doubtful the signal would reach far enough for detection, but not using every possible advantage was pointless.

Satisfied no immediate threat awaited them at the stair well, she stepped forward, while farther back in the basement, the scientists huddled in a small group awaiting the command to move.


Margritte Albandier stared blankly at a circuit box on the nearby wall. Like most of the original personnel in this base she understood how everything worked, and knew that the unit was the control for the surrounding tanks.

Amongst them were massive stores of compressed oxygen and hydrogen, for making water for the labs and for drinking as a safer alternative to filtering the deadly water of this world. Both gasses were dangerously flammable.

Somewhere deep within Margritte's mind, something snapped. After months alone with only the Kylax for company, her major priority had long ago become the preservation of those strange, intelligent creatures at any cost. Having the young soldier carry word back to the right people was necessary, but in her mind the old scientist believed it would never be enough. She did not consider the possibility she herself might get home alive with the girl's help. More was needed, something to stop people coming here again. The dome had to be destroyed.

As she stared at the box, all she saw was an enormous store of highly combustible gases. It did not occur to her the action she contemplated would not produce the desired outcome of itself, or that it would only delay the inevitable. Gas did not explode without ignition and scientists would want to return here, perhaps not until long after she was gone, but eventually.

Each tank connected to a main pressure-bleed pipe leading to the outside. Quickly she looked around to see if anyone was watching. Her thoughts were not quite clear as she punched at the screen to close the outer vents, opened the internal bleed valves on selected tanks, and allowed those tanks to vent to the basement.

In time, the hydrogen would float up through the stairwell and pool in the highest point of the dome. The oxygen would also fill the station, raising the concentration until the place became a highly combustible firetrap ready to be triggered by the smallest spark. The possibility she might still be there when that happened eluded Albandier's troubled mind.

At the top of the stairwell, Echo lay flat against the steps and surveyed the plaza. Twenty meters away a maintenance platform faced the elevator and behind it, unseen beyond a foot and part of a calf, the last guard crouched.

It was a well-chosen position, from where he could observe both the lift doors and stairs, and fire on anyone ascending either way. *As expected*, Echo thought. She wondered if the alien realized he was the last of his number. He *must* know he was alone with a mad commander who did not care whether he lived or died, and Echo could imagine the fear running through his mind.

Koll was forty meters further back, seated on a raised garden bed wall and seemingly unconcerned. Echo watched; he seemed preoccupied with a hand held screen device. In his current position he presented a clear target although over a long distance, and a gnawing voice in the back of her mind urged her to attempt the shot.

She wanted—needed badly—to kill him, to avenge everyone lost on *Corros*. With the other guard so much closer, she could not shoot Koll without giving away her presence in the stairwell. She thought of her charges. *Patience*.

On the steps beside her Sarra lay prone, her rifle aimed at a point at the top of the maintenance platform directly above the visible foot of the guard. She was the finest sniper in the squad; if anyone could take a killing shot, it was she.

Echo moved her position on the stairs, careful not to alert the alien guard, and carefully brought her rifle to bear on the distant figure of Koll. Without warning, the bell on the lift sounded and the doors slid back.

It took only a second. Alerted by the chime the alien raised his upper body and fired at the opening doors of the elevator. A bright blue beam lashed out from Sarra's rifle, and a body collapsed behind the platform.

Less than a second after Sarra's shot, a blast from Echo's rifle lanced out towards the security chief, barely missing as he dipped down to retrieve something. The distance had been too great, and Echo readily acknowledged that she was not as good a marksman as was her companion.

Looking across the courtyard Echo saw Koll jump to his feet and head for the building at the rear of the plaza. The body of the last remaining guard had not moved. The mad security commander was alone now, and Echo intended to take full advantage of the situation.

"Think you got him?" Echo asked.

Sarra rolled on her back and grinned. "Course I got him!"

"Take everyone across to the landing platform. Shouldn't be any guards left to give you trouble."

"What are you planning to do? As if I don't know."

Echo had not attempted to disguise her need to deal with the troublesome chief of security. "I'm going after Koll. He's gone into the admin block, and he'll hole up there. If I can't get him, I'll blow the place apart." She patted the harness pocket containing donut mines given to her by Katch.

\* \* \*

Barbus Koll rifled through the shelves inside his office safe. Minutes earlier he had seen his last guard downed by enemy fire and knew he was in serious trouble. All thought of defending his post vanished and instinctive self-preservation took control. The only courses left open to him were to escape in his private shuttle and reach the naval base, or head through the nearest wormhole to a safe Tollean system and disappear into the vastness of the Empire.

In view of Kemmin's friends and the orders he claimed to have given them, the second option might prove safer. The case on the desk contained numerous documents and cards. They were the soul means to accessing a fortune hidden in a myriad places, squirreled away by him over many decades. Never leaving anything to chance, he had begun compiling his personal insurance the day he joined the forces.

In a stroke of luck he had left the documents in a secure bank when assigned to *Corros*, otherwise they and the wealth they represented would be long gone. Since that catastrophic event, aware his future prospects were limited, he now kept everything always by his side and did not intend to leave anything behind.

The last documents retrieved, he slammed the case shut and hobbled from the office, turning towards the rear of the building. The humans would be in the plaza by now, so crossing that way to the landing pad airlock would be impossible.

The best alternative was to sneak out by the rear door, for which he had the only key, and thence via the air-conditioning plant to the gap between the rear of the dome and the cliff face.

By the time his attackers discovered his escape, he would be on his way around the back of the dome to the shuttle. He could breathe the native air for a while, and it would hinder his enemy more than him.

He wondered if the guards sent after the human insurgents still survived, but dismissed it without a moment's thought. He did not care. They had failed him. They were not important.

# Chapter Twenty-One

THE DOOR TO THE administration block beckoned. Echo peered into a long, empty corridor. No sound or movement betrayed Koll's location, but according to Kemmin the coordinator's office was a windowless room at the rear of the building, so she entered and crept towards the back, her pistol held ready.

Half way along, a door to a stairwell opened to the left. It led, Echo guessed, up to the perimeter walkway. Checking nobody was inside, she continued on to the end of the corridor.

A single door stood ajar. Inside was a small room with a massive desk and a number of cabinets. Several computer monitors filled the desktop, behind which lay an office chair pulled back in such haste it had crashed and toppled against the wall. The room was empty and a second, open door led out to the rear of the building.

Cabinet drawers lay upturned on the floor, the aftermath of someone searching for something in a hurry. No doubt Koll came straight here after the stairwell attack. By now he could be anywhere, possibly on his way to his escape shuttle. Echo did not like his chances; Sarra and Katch would reach the platform airlock first.

Echo did not see him on the way in, so it was probable he had ascended to the walkway and escaped that way, or else was still inside the building. No time remained to waste looking for him. With a deep sigh of regret, she switched her attention back to the scientists, returned to the plaza and headed for the exit. If Koll was attempting to escape, she would more likely catch him there.

Everyone was at the airlock. To one side, Katch leaned against a wall, a proud defiance in his eyes. A dark stain covered his side but with the help of the field medications, he stood upright and ready to go. Echo understood her friend well; a physically powerful man, it would take more than a laser burn to keep him down.

The rescued scientists waited against the inner wall with Kemmin and Torrick. They trusted Echo to lead, having remained silent during the passage through the station. She prayed to the gods that she would not let them down. From here, their future depended on several tenuous assumptions: that the shuttle was still there and they could reach it before Koll, that they would be able to operate it and that a friendly ship would find them in space.

Nobody knew if the attack on the system had been successful, and although Ben assured her overwhelming numbers of ships made victory a certainty, Echo knew nothing was ever so clean cut.

Koll was still around somewhere. He was on his own, no doubt driven to desperation by that knowledge. A terrified individual was the most dangerous one. His fatal mistake had been to send half his men out into the jungle in pursuit of Cooney. None of them returned, and all could be dead in the biological hell that covered every square kilometer of land on this moon.

It was possible Koll had a private way out of the dome. It had only four exits, but that did not allow for anything he might have done without the knowledge of anyone else. Echo hoped he was not ahead of them, in which case the shuttle might be gone before they arrived.

"Everyone ready?" she asked. "Everyone got their face mask on?"

*　*　*

The barren ridge rose high above the jungle-choked valley floor at the point where the river exited to a narrow coastal plain and ran down to the dark sea. Almost sixty kilometers from the station, the rugged but stable location was chosen in preference to the unstable, swampy ground of the clearing the mission team used on their arrival. The rocky summit of the ridge was sufficiently free of vegetation to allow a large spacecraft to land.

Ben circled his ship, sweeping in from the seaward side until he had a clear view of the area. There was no sign of human life and no locator signals. He shook his head, studying the terrain as Jerry moved them in closer.

The idea Echo might not have succeeded in her mission was something he did not want to contemplate, but it was hard not to imagine the worst-case scenario. After everything they had been through in the last few years and despite the fact that, both being serving members of Fleet, they saw little of each other these days, he dreaded the idea of her not being there anymore.

"This can't be right," he grumbled. "I can't believe none of them made it. It's not…"

"I wouldn't give up on that girl of yours so quickly," Jerry said, concentrating his eyes on the screens. "She's not likely to let those furry-assed clowns beat her without a real fight."

"I would never do that; she never did with me. Take us around again."

The flight from the Tollean naval base had been uneventful, the *Infiltrator* boring at maximum speed direct to *Persephone*. They encountered no enemy vessels on the way, although Ben knew several were in the general vicinity. Ships had been sent to destroy the station, but they were not his problem; other Fleet vessels were in pursuit, and would have intercepted somewhere in interplanetary space. Radio communications were silenced, so he did not know if the enemy had been destroyed or not.

"What now, Cap?"

"I don't know. The dome is a scientific station, not a military base. Unless a whole division of Tollean marines is holed up in there, I find it hard to believe not one of our guys managed to reach the rendezvous, successful mission or not."

"What about the contact we detected after we dropped them off?"

"Most likely a spacecraft. A routine supply-ship or something like it? They should have been down into the atmosphere before it reached them. "

Ben stared at the screen for a moment. Echo would be somewhere between the research station and the ridge below, assuming she was still alive and mobile.

"Wait," Jerry said. "The scanners have picked up something. A signal … very weak."

Ben turned towards his second in command, a faint hope creeping back into his mind. "You think…?"

"A personnel locator, type 'PR49', coming from the direction of the station."

Ben's heart leapt into his throat. PR49 was the model he gave Echo before her departure for the mission. "Head for the dome. And pray."

"Done, and done."

\* \* \*

The landing platform was a tarmac area perched on the cliff-side ledge, empty but for a fuel station, assorted servicing modules and a double height row of massive shipping containers left over from the original construction. The area was deserted.

Echo sprinted across to the end of the container stack and snatched a quick glimpse behind. The emergency vehicle stood perched like a giant, grey, metal bug, its hatch shut, the boarding steps withdrawn.

"Doesn't look like your favorite alien is here yet," Sarra said, drawing up beside her. "I'll bring Torrick across so he can fire it up."

"The shuttle door—it's closed."

"It's an emergency vehicle. They're never locked, are they?"

"No, but this one is. See the metal latch on the outside? We'll have to break it off first; should be easy enough with a blaster. I'll do it while you fetch the others. Keep an eye out for Koll. He'll be around here somewhere."

Echo ran at a crouch to the vessel and examined the makeshift lock. The device was primitive in the extreme for a spacecraft, a bog-standard hasp welded to the outer edge of the door and frame to secure them.

*This is Koll's personal insurance*, she thought. *He must have secured it using whatever resources available, to keep anyone else out.*

With the human prisoners under strict security, it said a lot about how far the security chief trusted his own men. Perhaps he considered it necessary because of Kemmin, but considering the Tollean lord managed to obtain a pistol from somewhere, an old hasp lock would not have stopped him.

Echo studied the setup. It looked human, even to the typical padlock. Another quick examination and the truth hit her: this craft was of Federation manufacture. No doubt Koll acquired it after the initial invasion of this base and worked out how to operate it. The fact of its origin and that it was unwanted was probably the only reason his superiors permitted him to keep it here.

As she pulled her pistol from its holster, she remembered the time she first encountered the alien on her home world of *Corros*. According to Ben Teague, Koll tried to force him to open the ship on which he arrived. Later they discovered the dispatch vessel secured by Koll's orders at the nearby space base. Koll was—had been—a pilot, and apparently found human ships irresistible.

It served Echo's purpose well. She could fly this one without Torrick or Kemmin's help, placing a little more control of the situation back into her hands. Careful not to damage the door she set the pistol and began burning through the lock.

Behind her, Sarra bought everyone across towards the shuttle. The small knot of masked humans crouched by the container barrier, Kemmin's tall figure, incongruously without a mask, standing beside them.

Without warning, a beam lashed out and hit the hull shell above Echo's head. She ducked and turned in a single, smooth motion, then flattened herself on the tarmac as more blasts blazed from the corner of the dome base. Behind her, the group by the containers scattered and dropped to the ground as shots slammed in over their heads.

The attacker remained hidden, but she knew from where the shots originated. Determined to put him on the defensive, Echo fired in the direction of the incoming assault. Koll had another way out of the dome, having approached through the narrow gap between the structure and the rear cliff face. It was pure luck she and her party reached the shuttle first, if only by a minute.

From behind a stack of pallets, Koll emerged and hobbled towards the airlock. With his access blocked, he had no option but to head back inside, but to return the way he came would expose him to Echo's fire. He dashed from one cover to the next, clutching his case to his chest. His cane was missing, but the loss did not appear to hinder him at all; nothing slowed a desperate individual.

Echo aimed towards the point where she expected he would emerge. A dark, crouching form broke for the hatch, and she fired. The blast missed its target and splashed against the wall.

A red indicator light flashed on the side of her pistol, signaling that the energy source was drained. She reached over her shoulder for her laser rifle, but instinctively grabbed something else, the crossbow carried in its harness throughout the entire mission, and that had miraculously survived her stay in Koll's animal cage. Without pause, she snatched a bolt from the quiver on her calf and loaded the bow. As she ran across the tarmac, she spotted her quarry by the entrance. He would have trouble there; on the way out, Kemmin had fused the lock with his blaster.

For a few short seconds Koll fought to activate a door that was beyond opening, then stood back and used his pistol to blast the mechanism, allowing the outer door to swing free. Echo raised her crossbow, took aim and fired as he made a dive for safety. Driven by his own momentum he tumbled through the opening as the bolt hit him cleanly between the shoulder blades, just below his neck, the case he carried dropping from his hand as the arrow struck.

Echo stopped in her tracks. Her first inclination was to pursue him, but the voice in the back of her mind told her it was not a smart idea. The first bolt had been a kill shot, the shaft no doubt burying itself in Koll's spine. He was almost certainly dead, or almost so.

If by some miracle he survived he would be waiting for her inside, and was still armed. The crossbow would be useless in such close quarters, and besides, she had a group of civilians and a pompous, Tollean ass to get to safety.

A loud whine filled the air and she saw a sleek gray shape swoop in over the ridge at the head of the valley and turn towards the dome. With a flattened, broad hull, it was unlike any ship she was familiar with, and it did not appear to be making a landing approach.

"Down!" she yelled, sending her companions diving for cover behind the containers. Leaping across the tarmac, she dropped to the ground behind a tow-tractor.

Echo felt a hot blast of air as a blue-white plasma ball leapt from the nose of the approaching vessel and slammed into the shuttle. A second blast hit the side of the dome wall. The attacking ship pulled up and skimmed over the top of the massive structure, and something small detached from the underside of the hull and dropped towards the roof. The spacecraft, Tollean in origin, was here to destroy the base, indicating the Fleet invasion had been successful. This ship was after Kemmin!

For the space of a breath nothing happened, and then the dome erupted in a searing ball of incandescent flame. The research station was a bomb waiting for a trigger. The flame blew outward, forced up and over the heads of the refugees by the low but solid skirting wall that formed the base of the structure.

When the device dropped by the alien ship speared down through the roof and exploded, it triggered a hydrogen and oxygen fueled fireball, raising the temperature inside instantly. The panes of armor glass shattered under the pressure of the explosion, shards spearing in every direction driven by the force of the blast. Echo kept her head down, hoping the tractor would protect her from being flayed alive. She prayed her companions were safe, sheltered by the storage containers.

The attacking craft, its mission accomplished, climbed up to the cloud cover. Seconds later another ship, a Fleet destroyer, screamed overhead and pursued the attacker.

Of the once-imposing dome little remained but a twisted metal skeleton collapsed on a plascrete rim. Broken fragments of the panes lay everywhere, and fires burned fiercely within the blackened and crumbled remains of the accommodation, lab and administration blocks.

The roar of hot air shooting skyward blanketed the landing pad, and popping noises came from the fires within the ruin. The sounds of Echo's companions gathering themselves together was drowned by the rush of air streaming in across the platform to feed the conflagration. Echo rose to one knee and gave herself a quick once over. Apart from a severe scorching, minimized by the amazingly resilient sortie-suit she wore, there appeared to be no damage.

She looked across at the airlock to see the entire station reduced to a disordered pile of burning rubble. To one side, Koll's escape shuttle also burned, a half melted mound of metal and plastic slag.

Koll was under the remaining tangle of wreckage of the dome, and most likely dead, crushed as the framework collapsed. *Good riddance,* Echo thought. If alive, he could not survive. With an arrow in his back, no shuttle to escape, no dome to take refuge inside, and no survival gear, he could not last for long on this hostile moon despite his being able to tolerate the air for short periods.

*That's for my Dad*, she thought, rising to her feet. *And everyone else on Corros!*

Echo approached her companions as they emerged from the containers.

"Anyone hurt?" she asked as Sarra acknowledged her with a nod.

"Albandier got hit by a lump of glass. She's injured, but alive ... just. Katch is trying to patch her up, but I don't like her chances. Otherwise, a few bad burns are all."

As she spoke, another roar sounded along the valley, and yet another warship appeared above, descending rapidly. As Echo watched, it settled at the outer edge of the platform. Within seconds, the hatch opened.

It was an *Infiltrator*, and the face that peered at her from the open entry was one she thought never to see again. This was Ben's ship, and the man with whom she had suffered through so much in the past, the one soul who meant more to her than anyone else in her life, beckoned from the hatchway, a wide grin visible below his breathing filters.

It was over!

# Chapter Twenty-Two

ECHO SLUMPED ON A fold down seat. In the empty metal belly of the ship the scream of the engines made conversation impossible as they strained to lift the weight of the vessel off the landing platform and back into space. For the moment, she did not much feel like talking.

The mission was complete, and despite the loss of all squad members but Sarra, Katch and herself, looked increasingly like a success. They had rescued all surviving scientists except Arthur Mendoza, and the critical base strain of the 'virus' with them. In addition, there was the antiviral agent material, prepared in secret by those forced to remain at work by the Tolleani.

Those small, colored phials carried by Bernie Greer were a blessing. With the help of Mendoza's notes, they would allow the rapid synthesis of both antivirus and vaccine en-mass, for almost immediate distribution to the worlds so far infected.

Because of the long incubation period of the organism that allowed it to spread planet wide before the first victims became apparent, the virus would be a problem for years to come, but with constant vigilance the danger would end in time.

Then there was Kemmin. When Ben landed and the group crossed the tarmac to board, he had an almost apoplectic fit as the tall, imposing alien strode towards him, pistol in hand. Only

Echo's quick reflexes stopped him as he drew his own weapon and took aim at what he saw only as an enemy. She spotted his reaction and stepped in front of Kemmin, her hands raised.

Once on board Echo explained to Ben the primary directive for the mission, as she now understood it, to rescue the base administrator. It was not Mendoza, the man in command prior to the Tollean takeover, as all assumed. It was the alien lord, the enigmatic, arrogant scientist placed in charge of the research station by the emperor himself as a form of exile.

Lifting her eyes from the floor she saw Kemmin and Torrick seated opposite. Each sat with hands in shackles, the only condition under which Ben would allow them onboard.

Despite Echo's assurance the Tollean lord sent the message drone, Ben refused to accept him as a friend, muttering something about leopards never changing their spots. Echo had no idea what a 'leopard' might be, but suspected it was some kind of wild animal similar to those she once encountered on *Kerac* 5.

She could not help being perplexed by Kemmin. Assuming all he told her was true—and that was yet to be established—why was he so crucial that Fleet risked an entire squad to retrieve him?

By his own admission a Tolleani of high standing and a member of Tollean nobility, his manner was of someone used to being obeyed, in the habit of giving orders and not asking favor.

There was no doubt in Echo's mind the station attack had the specific aim of destroying Kemmin. But who was he? Why was the Emperor so afraid of him as to impose exile under military guard and yet not have him killed. He was an individual who could not be executed for fear of public backlash, or allowed to run unchecked.

Nor could Emperor Al Tambr allow him to escape, or worse, be taken prisoner by Fleet. His presumed death at this time would give the Tollean ruler cause to blame it on humanity, rather than have the responsibility fall upon himself.

Kemmin's eyes stared back at Echo without trace of emotion. Not at all happy about the manacles he was nonetheless unharmed, and safe. An intelligent individual, he accepted the situation with a stolid patience. If his story proved true, he would soon be free and working with humanity to bring piece. If not...

The ship rose above the clouds and into space. Echo released her seat belt and floated to the front of the hold. She settled beside the stretcher where securing straps restrained Margritte Albandier as Katch tried to seal the severe wound she had suffered. The old scientist appeared to be in shock. She lay unresponsive as Echo's friend rushed to finish despite his own weakened state, driven on by the drugs in his system.

"So, you're still with us?"

Albandier's eyes opened and stared up at Echo. They were dull, and almost lifeless. After a few seconds, she closed them again and lay still. Katch leaned over and studied the readout on the med-unit on the bulkhead above her. He glanced at the transfusion pump, and then shook his head.

"The glass cut a major artery. Too much blood loss. This is going to be close."

Albandier opened her eyes again and smiled weakly. "It takes more than some alien assholes to put me down, my dear."

Echo placed a hand on her arm. "The captain of this ship tells me we have this system back again, and a fleet flagship has come through the gateway, so you'll be safe in a proper medical facility soon. You and your handsome nurse here. Anything I can do?"

"Remember your promise, Dear. In case I don't make it home tell everyone about the Kylax. The federation needs to know about them. It must protect them. The research station will be re-opened I suppose, and we need to study and nurture them. *Persephone* is their world, not ours."

"The dome is destroyed. Strange, that. The Tollean missile must have been a beauty."

"Yes, perhaps so." A glazed look spread across Margritte's face as she reflected back on something. She opened her mouth to speak, then stopped and closed her eyes.

Once Katch was finished with his patient, he collapsed into the corner. Sarra hovered over him, checking his vital signs. The drugs taken in the tunnel would still be in his system, but danger would come when they wore off. Designed for field use only, they left the taker worse off afterwards, unless the next port of call was a hospital bed. According to Ben, the flagship was only eighteen hours away, so help would come for him in time. The future for Albandier was not so certain.

Nearby, the rescued scientists whispered among themselves, all apparently unharmed. Bernie Greer sat alone, his hand wrapped across the front of his now torn and grimy lab clothes, protecting the inner pocket where he carried the phial-filled container.

Echo secured herself against the bulkhead beside Katch. This was the same hold from where the mission had commenced, now empty of the sleds used to descend to the moon. For the first time since the operation began, Echo felt at ease. At last able to reflect back, she realized she had done something worthwhile.

Assuming Kemmin was indeed the true objective, her actions had been for the best. Cooney was wrong, and jumped to far *too* many conclusions. She had achieved all their objectives, including the rescue of a significant enemy defector and potential ambassador for peace. Perhaps most important of all, the antiviral material would save millions of lives, and for their safe retrieval she knew she was responsible, with help from Sarra and Katch.

She felt better about the two medals sitting in her locker on the flagship, having never before accepted she either deserved or earned them. The first resulted more from Ben's actions than hers, the second the result of cooperation between many people, both civilian and military. This time, it had been largely her efforts. She had made a difference, at last.

\* \* \*

Jackson Cooney hauled himself up the almost sheer outcrop. His sortie-suit leg blackened and burned from a blaster strike, he struggled on boosted by field medication. The objective, the flat, open space designated as the pick-up point, was only meters away.

The injury occurred several hours earlier, when the pursuing Tollean guards caught up with him at the base of the ridge. Three of them had made it that far, dogging him relentlessly since Khamisi, Corrian and Greer abandoned him and headed back. No doubt those traitors were dead now, swept up by the pursuit.

Only Petrovsky stuck by him, as was to be expected; he knew enough about the man's past to ensure loyalty. It did not matter now; Petrovsky's corpse lay in the vegetation below, cut down by blaster fire at the start of the climb.

His death was fortunate; the fall warned Cooney, giving him time to dive for cover. Hidden behind a rocky outcrop, he set his own ambush for the pursuers. A good if not excellent sniper, he took out the first of the three aliens as they emerged from the jungle boundary. The second fell as they attempted to circle around him, a difficult task on the open rock outcropping.

The third proved more elusive. Alone, the remaining alien fought with a fury born of fear, unleashing a constant barrage of fire at the place where Cooney hid. One shot drilled through Cooney's left thigh, but did no fatal damage.

Then the attacker made a critical mistake, taking position behind a boulder at the base of a scree slope above which leaned an overhanging buttress. Cooney fired on the overhang, cutting away enough of the rock to destabilize the rubble below. The resulting avalanche overwhelmed the Tollean in a river of moving boulders, wiping away the last of Cooney's problems.

He stood alone on the top of the ridge. The sole survivor, he would return victorious to Fleet, bearing with him the means of salvation for the stricken worlds of humankind.

True, the part of the mission concerning the retrieval of Mendoza failed, but it was not his fault. The rescue of that old fool went without a problem—even better considering the death of his biggest nemesis, Bourke. He was not responsible for the old scientist's weak heart or his collapse on the way to the pickup point. Besides, it could always be blamed on the mutiny by Bourke's fellow conspirators.

The phials were now the crucial thing. Protected in their tiny case, they remained safe in his harness, and they would be his salvation. They would make him a hero.

Time had run out. While approaching the ridge through the last remnant of jungle, he had heard the roar of a spacecraft. The retrieval ship may have gone, but the fact it came at all meant the invasion was a success, so Fleet would be active in the system for a long time to come. Reaching into a pocket, he activated a distress beacon secreted before the mission as a backup measure.

* * *

Flight Leader Pac peered at the image on his screen. Far below only a blasted ruin remained of the research station. That at least was a success, and Kemmin was dead without any doubt. More gratifying still, so was that arsehole Koll. Nobody could have survived the blast.

During the attack on the military base three ships, including his own, escaped and flew to *Persephone* to carry out the Emperor's command, to destroy the station and its prisoner before retreating. The enemy caught them en-route, downing the other two Tollean craft. Two Fleet ships were destroyed in return. Pac survived, chased by the last human destroyer.

Desperate to complete his mission he raced for the moon, the enemy close behind. On arrival he did not hesitate to carry out the assigned task, knowing from his time stationed there what needed to be done. The destruction of the only ship on the landing platform, Koll's 'escape clause', came first. A flyover of the structure then sent a ground penetration bomb through the weakest point, the broad flat expanse of glass at the top.

The scale of the explosion staggered him. The power of the explosive charge was sufficient to destroy any living thing within, but the reality went much further. It penetrated as expected, but the entire dome blew in an unexpected fireball, shattering every pane in unison and incinerating everything inside in an instant. Pac wondered what he had hit to have such an effect.

After the attack, he turned on the remaining human pursuit craft, which now lay somewhere beneath one of the moon's seas. The survivors of the Tollean occupation forces had fled to rendezvous with a mother ship in the next system. He would follow, and intended to escape alive. Free of his attackers, he had first wanted to make sure of his success before making for a safe gateway.

The communications officer gave a soft bark, and announced a weak signal from a point nearby. Pac groaned; Kemmin did not survive, he was positive, and he was sure Koll did not either. That left a question as to who was calling for help. He breathed a sigh of frustration and ordered his pilot to head for the signal source.

* * *

Cooney's vision was blurred, blood running down his forehead from a deep gash on his scalp. Too exhausted to stand he sat on the bare rock, no longer possessing the energy to move further, and prayed a rescue ship would trace the locator to find him.

Reaching into his webbing, he retrieved the phial case. His future depended on the small, black box, so the contents had better be still intact. Opening the flap, he examined the phials.

Red, yes, the actual virus strain if he remembered Greer's comments. It was undamaged, as were the green and blue tubes. Cooney withdrew the last and turned it over in his fingers. Greer never mentioned that one, but it didn't matter. The scientists would work it out.

Like the others, the fourth tube was sealed with a waxed stopper; it contained a bright, orange liquid, clear and viscous. He held it closer, aware of a slight stickiness on his hands. A hairline crack, only just visible, curled around the glass below the cap.

"Damn," He muttered. Whatever was in there was probably important, so he would have to be careful. Taking the greatest of care, he slid the tube into the case and eased it back into a pocket.

A faint roar sounded across the valley. Looking up, he spotted a small object high in the sky, flying below the bottom of the ever-present cloud cover.

*That didn't take long,* he thought. *Good!*

Through blurred vision the new arrival was indistinct, but it could only be his rescue. It was most likely the same vessel he had heard from the jungle, the retrieval ship sent to extract him. Its presence earlier meant it unlikely any alien ships remained in the vicinity, so all was well.

Exhausted, he lay back on the rock and waited, his head spinning. He was only half-aware as a grey hull hovered above, and vague figures descended on cables towards him.

# Chapter Twenty-Three

ON BOARD THE FLAGSHIP, the carrier *Pellargo*, Echo strode along the corridor towards the office of Admiral Lord Salazar Baquir.

She and her companions had returned to the mother ship several days ago. Upon their return, Katch went to the medical wing with Margritte Albandier. Echo and Sarra were ushered into the debriefing room and grilled on the details of their mission, then allowed to retire to quarters, clean up, and eat their first proper meal in many days.

Of the rescued scientists Echo had seen and heard nothing. By now, Greer and his precious cargo were no doubt on their way to one of the primary worlds, most likely *Cymbel 3*, the governing planet of this region of human occupied space.

Nor had she seen anything of Kemmin or Torrick. Still cuffed, they were led away under heavy guard almost as soon as Ben's ship settled into a dock. *Pity*, she thought. Two years ago, she would have shot either of them on sight. Now she almost liked the strange little Tolleasin, but doubted she would ever accept the arrogant Tolleani.

A uniformed adjutant raised her head from the monitor on her desk in the Admiral's outer office. She gave Echo a head-to-toe once-over, gave a slight nod of approval and a smile, hit a switch and announced the arrival.

Echo was not concerned; she had been given warning and was now clean and groomed, and wore a washed and pressed uniform. Appearance did not concern her; what puzzled her most was why the Admiral wanted to see her.

On a signal from the aid, she stepped into Baquir's office. The old commander of the *Pellargo* Fleet sat behind an enormous desk of genuine wood, his dark eyes studying her from beneath dense, grey eyebrows.

Much to Echo's surprise, Ben, Bernie Greer, and the always-imposing figure of Ronus Kemmin were also present. The alien no longer wore restraints, and seemed at home if not quite comfortable, in a human chair much too small for his frame. Both of the men stood, both bearing broad smiles. That was promising, she thought. She was not in trouble.

"Sub-Lieutenant Cinta Bourke reporting as requested," she announced, standing to attention.

"At ease, please, Lieutenant," the old admiral said.

"Sub-Lieutenant, Sir."

"Do not correct me, young lady. You can report to commissary for your new insignia after you leave. You are no doubt wondering why I called you here."

Echo nodded, a little taken aback.

"You can thank our friend, Lord Kemmin, for that. He asked for your presence. Please take a seat." He fumbled with some papers for a moment before continuing. "We have a solid record of the mission, from the reports of yourself and your surviving squad members. Damned unfortunate bit of bad luck being detected by an enemy ship on arrival. It shows our dispersion field is not perfect yet."

Echo nodded again.

"Still, best laid plans and so on. Doctor Greer has also given us his version of events after your team escaped from the base, including the problems caused by Lieutenant Cooney. Under the circumstances, you've done well."

"Thank you, sir."

"His Lordship has told us what happened to you after you were separated from the others and imprisoned. It seems we owe the rescue of both him and our scientists to you. Not to mention the viral material and Mendoza's notes. You will be pleased to know they are now on their way to where they can be of some use. Doctor Greer's associates are also en-route, and he will join them soon. Now, your reason for being here."

"Yes, sir?"

"Are you aware of whom Lord Kemmin is?"

"No, sir. I've guessed he's from Tollean nobility. He told me himself he's highly regarded by many of his people, that he's defecting, and wants peace between our races. That's all I know."

"And yet you chose to trust him enough to help him escape?" The admiral's eyebrows arched as he spoke.

"I think it was more the other way around, sir. It seemed the right decision at the time."

"Very well. For your information, Lieutenant, he is *indeed* a powerful member of Tollean aristocracy. He is the oldest son of the last emperor, and Pentus Al Tambr's older brother."

At first, the words did not register in Echo's mind. Then her jaw dropped. The arrogant alien she had rescued was a prince of the Tolleani, brother to the individual so determined to destroy humanity.

"The names ... they're different."

"My brother changed his name when he ascended ... took ... the throne," Kemmin interjected. "Quite common in our royal line."

"Lord Kemmin should have replaced his father," the Admiral continued, "but he's a peace lover, and his father was anything but. His younger and more vitriolic brother placed him under house arrest immediately upon taking the throne for himself, then exiled him. Fortunately, many within the military support His Lordship, and we can use this to our advantage.

"Lord Kemmin will help us establish back-channel dialogue with these rebels, and with care, we can aid them in overthrowing the Emperor. If we succeed, His Lordship will become monarch in his brother's place and peace will be established."

"Yes, sir," Echo responded. *Kemmin, ruler of the largest empire in known history—human or Tollean history, at least.*

"Yes, indeed. However, it will take considerable time. Meanwhile, we'll take him to the safest place possible. He will leave soon for *Tantallus*, and you will be going with him."

"Me, sir?" Echo was stunned, and certain she had heard the Admiral incorrectly. The Tolleani said nothing, allowing Baquir to continue talking.

"Most personnel in Fleet will have trouble accepting an enemy as an ally, and we have a problem with finding someone reliable to accompany him to our prime world. Lord Kemmin was most impressed with the way you handled yourself during his rescue, and he trusts you. He finds you capable, reliable and

271

dedicated, and wishes you to accompany him as his personal bodyguard. You will do so on Captain Teague's ship, leaving at commencement of the next duty period. Sergeant Sarra Corian and Sub-Lieutenant Akachi Khamisi will join you.

*Sergeant! Sub-Lieutenant!* Echo smiled; her friends would be happy to learn that.

"After delivering our guest, you will return to this fleet for re-assignment. We will find you a new squad, together … perhaps something special. Wouldn't want to break up a winning team, would we?"

"No, sir." Echo felt her heart swell with the knowledge that she and her friends would not be separated.

"We will be directing most of our special squads to the task of carrying the antivirus to those of our colonies in systems close to or under threat by the Tolleani, where the potential danger is too great to send in civilian teams. Perhaps that might suit you for a change?" The Admiral smiled, and before Echo could reply, turned towards Kemmin. "That's about it," I think. You might like to prepare for the voyage, Your Lordship."

Kemmin rose, his face as expressionless as ever. Echo wondered if he was happy about the situation, difficult as it was to read emotions from their unchanging facial expressions. He nodded to the admiral, Ben and Doctor Greer, then turned towards Echo and bowed deeply, oh-so-slowly, from the waist. Without another word, he strode to the door and left the room.

"Most disconcerting individual," Baquir muttered, turning his attention back to Echo. "Both Captain Teague and the good doctor have recommended you be filled in on a few background details, should you so wish. You made some serious calls on this mission, and placed yourself in extreme jeopardy doing so. More importantly, they were the right choices, so you have I think, a right to know for what you staked your life and future. Feel free to ask me anything you like. I will answer if I am able."

"Thank you, sir. I guessed a lot about Lord Kemmin, but not that he was the Emperor's brother."

"Not that alone. You rescued seven of our finest scientists, and their work. We are indebted to you. You must have some questions."

Echo thought about it for moment. Some things still puzzled her, but she was uncertain she had the authority to dig too deep.

"May I ask why we were not all told the real objective of our mission? It would have made it simpler if we had known, once we lost Commander Brenner and Doctor Dewhurst."

"Ah, yes, well, my fault. Once we deciphered Lord Kemmin's message we realized the mission was urgent and we had no team available to send in. We had no choice but to send you in straight from the Academy, our best graduates led by our most experienced available commander. Brenner knew you were more than up to it, but had some concerns about certain other members of the team. He felt that if told they were going to rescue a Tolleani nobleman, they might have caused problems. Better they did not find out until they had no choice. My call, I'm afraid, and not my best."

Echo nodded in acceptance. It was not hard to work out whom the problems might have come from.

"Margritte Albandier. Is she alright?"

"She's still in the medical bay, dear woman. Still critical, but we are hoping she'll be fine. Quite a daunting old lady, I think."

"She deserves a medal for bravery, sir. Has she told you about the Kylax?"

"Indeed," Baquir leaned back in his chair and smiled. "A new, intelligent, tool using species. How about that! The Doctor here will be taking a full report back to *Cymbel* and we will do what we can to protect them. Oh, and we are sending a team to retrieve what remains we can find of your squad members. Excepting those we lost before entry into the atmosphere, we should be able to pick up their harness locators."

"May I, Admiral?" Greer interrupted. "Echo, I want to personally thank you for everything you've done for me and my colleagues. We are forever in your debt. The research station will be rebuilt, and we'll be placing an emphasis on the study and protection of the Kylax. That's all down to you: they would not have survived, except for you. "

"Thank you. I do have one other question?"

The admiral nodded his consent.

"Doctor Greer, about the four phials in the case you brought with you. You told us what most of them contained. May I ask about the orange phial?"

Greer glanced apprehensively across to the Admiral, who gave a barely perceptible nod of the head. "I think we can trust the Lieutenant to keep her mouth shut."

The doctor nodded. "I did not want to mention this, but now Lord Kemmin is gone, it should be alright. The fourth phial contains a new strain of the 'virus'. You see, the Tolleani are biologically similar to ourselves, but lack the cell receptors that allow the original organism to invade us. It attacks human cells and causes death, but cannot infect our enemy."

"Yes, so I understand."

"The first Tollean commander of the base chose to keep Doctor Mendoza and myself working in the labs during our imprisonment. I suspect he hoped we would find something else useful to them. We didn't waste our time. We were able to obtain Tollean DNA from our captors—it's not very different to our own—and develop a second strain. It works much like the original, but attacks the enemy, and not humans. Once we had the DNA, it was quite easy even under duress.

Echo's heart skipped a beat and she took a deep breath, tears welling inside as she realized the full meaning of those words. Finally, she had achieved something she could be proud of, only to find herself instrumental in unleashing yet another weapon of mass destruction.

"You can't use that…" Echo cut herself short, aware of the presence of the Admiral.

"No, not now," Greer said. "When we developed it, we had no idea what was going to happen in the future. After Kemmin told me what he was up to I had second thoughts, and the Admiral agrees with me. There are only two phials; the first is now secure, and the other is lost somewhere in the swamps of *Persephone*. It's a hybrid, and Tolleani specific, so it won't survive on the moon if it ever gets loose. Our sample will be kept under security against the small chance it does, and a vaccine will be developed."

At that point, the admiral interjected. "Commander Teague has informed me of your concerns about some of the things the two of you have done in the past, and you have my word this agent will not be used, and will never be attributed to you in any way. We want peace, and we can learn much from the Tolleani. We do not wish to wipe them out, now or ever."

Echo breathed a sigh of relief. "Thank you, sir."

"Be aware Lieutenant, neither Lord Kemmin nor his assistant must ever hear a word of this. If peace is at all possible, they must never know we have a way to destroy them, as they tried to do us. You will be in constant contact with both of them during the delivery to *Tantallus*, and you will not speak of this. You have been told only because I think you have a right to know what you brought back, and because I am prepared to trust you. Do *not* prove me wrong."

Minutes later, Echo walked towards her barracks to prepare for the journey to *Tantallus*. The voyage would take many months, most of it asleep, but she would have a chance to see the major administrative world of the Federation, something she thought would never happen, and to spend time with Ben.

Her mind now more at ease, she at last felt satisfied she had made a difference. The future represented by Kemmin was a massive unknown, but thanks to her, the antivirus was an immediate blessing for humankind. All acknowledged that without her efforts the mission might never have succeeded.

More importantly, a follow up mission to *Persephone* had found no traces of life in the ruins of the dome. The alien responsible for the slaughter of her father, her family and her entire community on *Corros*, was dead by her hand.

"One for you, Dad," she mumbled, walking along the corridor with a vague smile on her lips, and her head held high.

\* \* \*

Fleet Overlord Stanis Nai Pesca stood behind the desk in his palatial cabin, on the primary ring of one of the largest warships in the Tollean space forces, and glared at the pathetic figure before him.

The recent loss of a major regional facility was disastrous and not a thing he could overlook. Only three vessels escaped, one carrying the lord commander of the base, and two of the smaller attack craft. The third ship, under the command of a flight leader named Pac, came through the gateway only minutes before a squad of human ships blocked it permanently. It was a disaster.

Pac came bearing gifts, or so he thought. Somewhere in the course of the battle, instead of doing what he should have done in fighting to the death, he captured an enemy prisoner and now presented the pitiful creature to justify his own cowardice.

The human in question, an injured, barely alive excuse for a soldier, stood supported by two Tollean guards. It was doubtful he would be of any use to anyone, his face a picture of madness driven by the sheer terror of capture. His body shook visibly and so far, the translators had not been able to discern a single coherent word from him beyond a constant muttering about some medication or other.

Still, Nai Pesca's own orders required any human captives be bought straight to him. One could never tell if any of them might be useful. The last lot had been very much so. Captured from a research station in a nearby system before its destruction, they were inoculated with the nasty disease discovered in the labs of the moon the enemy called *Persephone*, and allowed to escape during transport. Nobody was sure of the results, but rumor indicated the plague was spreading, with the potential to overwhelm the entire human domain.

He was not sure how he felt about that. The order to release the disease came direct from the Emperor, but Nai Pesca had carried out the orders grudgingly. He was a fighter, not a murderer, and the whole affair seemed a dishonor to him.

He was not a particular fan of the Emperor—a power hungry maniac, in his opinion—and believed having such an individual in control could only spell disaster in the long term. The revolutionary movement was gaining momentum, something he and several of his top ranking associates secretly supported. In his position, however, he could not openly reveal this until the right time.

Waving his hand dismissively he turned his back as the guards dragged the captive away; it seemed unlikely the miserable creature would live much longer. He wondered about his friend, Kemmin, a Tolleani for whom he held deep respect. The survivors of the attack had reported his death, officially from enemy fire demolishing the base of which he was the administrator. *Such a great loss!*

Nai Pesca began an examination of the items before him, things found on the captive at the time of apprehension. They were predictable: a laser pistol without power, various packages appearing to be food and medical supplements, and so on. Only one thing aroused his curiosity.

Amongst the items was a small, black case, closed with a flap and a clasp. Picking it up, he opened it and examined the contents. It contained four glass phials, each a different color. He removed them and placed them on the desk.

They were innocuous enough, small tubes of colored liquid sealed with waxed stoppers. Nai Pesca was not an academic or scientist, and the idea they might be something important or dangerous did not occur to him. After all, what would something controversial be doing in the pocket of a half-dead soldier, in the jungle of a hostile moon? Everything of value was taken from the station there long ago.

Picking up one of the phials, an orange one, he noted stickiness. Carefully he wiped a finger across the glass and held its tip to his nose. *Musky smell?* With a twist, he broke the wax seal, removed the stopper, and raised it for another sniff.

One!

Resealing the phial, he flipped the intercom and called his adjutant, ordering him to remove the items from the desk and to have the phials incinerated, in case. The assistant snapped to attention, swept them into a container and retreated to the outer office, where he looked more closely at the pile of trash.

There was a pistol; one never knew when that could be useful. Realizing it was a human weapon he placed it in his desk drawer as a souvenir. Next, he examined the box containing four glass tubes. Sniffing each in turn, he decided they could not be important, otherwise his boss would not have ordered them disposed of.

Two!

Annoyed his lord and master thought him suitable for such trivial tasks, he threw everything into the trash disposal.

An hour later, a base rating cleaned the bin at the end of the chute and discovered the phials. Having no idea what they contained, but sure they did not belong in his recycling, he removed the stoppers and poured all four into a waste drain, in the process smearing smelly liquid all over his hands from one which was cracked, and shattered while he was holding it.

Three!

Tired and frustrated at the end of a long and hard shift, he went to the locker rooms to clean up and change back to his normal fatigues. Several of his friends were present, and the group exchanged pleasantries, catching up on new gossip. High on the agenda was the rumor a new enemy prisoner was on board, and locked in the ship's brig. Eager for his end-of-shift meal, the rating clasped the hands of his crewmates and left the room on route to the mess hall.

This particular mess served the midsection of the vast star ship. He gripped hands with fellow workmates and spoke with many others as he retrieved his rations and headed for a table. They in turn moved away to different parts of the cavernous chamber to join their own teammates.

The rating looked up from his tray at the gathering crowd. It was change of shift, and workers streamed in from every entrance.

Soon, over five hundred would fill the hall.

The End

**Echo's adventures are far from over. Watch for upcoming adventures in the series 'ECHO'S WAY'**

# Author's Note

## DID YOU ENJOY 'ENEMY ALLY'?
## IF SO, YOU CAN MAKE A BIG DIFFERENCE.

Dear Reader:

Reviews are the most powerful tool I have when it comes to getting attention for my books, and help bring them to the attention of other readers. They also increase the chances of the better review and promotion sights picking the book up, and increase a book's visibility on major book sights.

If you've enjoyed 'Enemy Ally' and have five minutes to spare, I would be eternally grateful if you would leave a review (an honest one, and as short as you like) on the book's review page at your **favorite bookstore or on BookBub or Goodreads**

Thank you
Mike Waller

EXCERPT – FALCON'S CALL

# Chapter 01

NO LARGER THAN A baseball, it moved at a pace several times that of a high-velocity bullet. Spawned of a cataclysmic conflict between three larger asteroids, it streaked mindlessly through space, oblivious to either destination or destiny.

Far ahead, a swarm of small, sand-grain-sized meteoroids, the result of a freak impact between two of the adversaries, heralded its coming. An even more unlikely second collision, a glancing blow between the third contender and rubble from the first two, sent the rock in the swarm's wake, on the exact identical course despite odds in the trillions to one.

Contrary to popular belief, objects in the asteroid belt are not densely packed. They are in reality far apart and collisions are rare. The region of space through which this wanderer and its precursors now passed was almost empty.

But not quite!

\* \* \*

A hot, tropical sun beat down on brilliant, white sand. Salt spray swirled along the waterline as a warm, murmuring breeze drifted in from the vastness of the South Pacific Ocean. The sounds of children's laughter drifted up from the water's edge, mixed with the raucous skirl of seagulls.

Joe Falcon half-opened his eyes. A young woman clad in a brief, suggestive, white bikini strolled across the beach towards him.

A glance in his direction.

A warm, friendly smile.

Helen, his beautiful wife of just a week, with her soft, gentle voice and the look of an angel.

A week? It seemed like a day.

He watched her approach. Life was satisfying, becoming better by the minute.

A split-second blink.

When his eyes opened again she was gone, the sand where she walked smooth and undisturbed. From somewhere nearby the rat-tat-tat, staccato rattle of an automatic weapon shattered the harmony, followed by the shrill, piercing whine of a siren.

Something smashed hard onto his head.

"What the f…?"

Joe's forehead struck the solid, unforgiving bulkhead of the captain's cabin. Weightless, he struggled to regain equilibrium. His eyes blind in the pitch-dark, his ears rang to the noise of the ship's breach alarm. He reached out wildly in the darkness, his hand falling on the latch of the bathroom door.

Seconds earlier, he'd been reclining in the hot Australian sun, luxuriating in the soothing, caressing breeze of a time long gone but still cherished; a moment of bliss, a hard bang and a rude awakening.

The beach dimmed in memory as, with eyelids squeezed tight, Joe battled to silence the persistent gremlin breaking rocks behind his temples. Every few seconds a sharp, machine-gun rattle echoed through the structure around him.

Something was not right.

The dim emergency lights flickered on and Joe's brain tumbled back to reality. The faint, ever-present vibration was absent, the accommodation wheel motionless. When rotation ceased Joe's body had continued, inertia launching him from his bunk. Deprived of the small but crucial centrifugal gravity he had drifted without waking across the tiny room and into the opposite wall.

With a gentle push against the bathroom door, he floated across to the crisis locker and his emergency suit and then dragged the stiff fabric over his limbs as best possible in the zero-g.

Satisfied at last—he had not done this for a long time—he clipped the bubble helmet to his belt, planted his feet on the near wall and tapped the com-patch.

"Sarah? What in God's name…?"

"Meteor shower, Boss." The voice belonged not to his first officer but to Terry Caldwell, the second engineer. "We been hit! Micro-m's"

"You're joking, right?"

"Wouldn't do that, Boss."

Joe whistled through his teeth. The source of gunfire in his dream now made sense; the irregular pings sounding through the toughened alloy structure of the ship were minute, sand-grain-sized meteoroids hitting the outside of the accommodation wheels.

Chances of being in the path of a meteoroid swarm were billions to one, a once in a lifetime event if at all. Unlikely, Joe thought, to happen again before he died.

"What's our status?"

"Not too bad, Boss. Sizes less than two millimeters, mostly. We got maybe three hundred hits overall but the old girl can handle it. Only a few bad ones: three on the reactor module, four on fusion-drive two, three more on the tanks, and six on the spine. No damage to the crew areas."

"The accommodation wheels aren't turning. What happened to the power?"

"We lost the feed from the reactor," Terry replied. "I got us on backup now."

"Good man. Engines?"

"Unit two's got a few hits. It can be repaired, I reckon, but we might need a dock."

"Anyone outside?"

"Yeah. The guys are out on the rock, 'round the back. They should be safe. External links are down, so Sarah's going out after them. She's in the lock now."

Joe grunted acknowledgment. The vessel was tethered to the surface of an irregular shaped asteroid approximately three hundred meters across, the latest target in their never-ending treasure hunt through the Asteroid Belt. The 'guys', Carl Geddes and Peter Stanley, had been out taking core samples and soundings for analysis in the lab.

A rock like this was not generally worth the effort but Carl had requested more time to check it over, muttering something about it being part of a planetary body, probably Mars, which somehow ended up here in the Belt. Unlike the typical metallic or carbonaceous asteroids in the area, this one was igneous rock.

Chunks of Mars thrown off by meteor impact often turned up on Earth, but how such a massive piece found its way out here Joe could not imagine—hardly surprising since it was not his field. He was navy, or had been once.

"Are you alright, Sarah?"

"Yes, Captain," the voice of his first officer replied over the intercom. "Almost ready to go out now."

"Sounds like the shower's over."

"I wouldn't be going otherwise. Oh, hang on, I may not need to. The boys are coming around the rock now."

Joe smiled—his first officer was younger than every one of the 'boys' on the ship by several years. "Good. Be careful. Terry, I'm on my way up. Are all the crew in suits?"

"You bet, Boss."

Joe berated himself for leaving his com-patch off, stared at it for a moment, tapped it off again and then pulled himself through the doorway into the corridor.

Dim emergency lights illuminated the interior of accommodation wheel number one, throwing dark, surrealistic shadows on the curved walls. Near-silence haunted the motionless structure, the constant drone of the ventilation replaced by an almost indiscernible shush from the backup system.

Joe's nose wrinkled at the faint, 'canned' odor of the air. It felt cold. He shivered and then decided it was his imagination. The temperature was normal but the cool, bluish, secondary lights cast an unnatural pall that fooled the senses.

Opposite the door, a window looked towards the bridge and forward docking module. All was motionless beyond the polycarbonate pane, confirming the lack of wheel rotation. Joe launched himself at the exit ladder and floated up to the central spine, ignoring the rungs—without gravity, they were superfluous.

An open hatch in the hub led up to the corridor within the spine of the ship. Joe glanced aft; a few meters away another rotating sleeve, also motionless, marked the ship's secondary wheel. The cargo-zone access hatch beyond was shut. Joe guessed Sarah had secured it on her way to the service bays.

Nothing else appeared compromised other than the lights, suggesting damage was limited to the electrics, tanks and engine. A lucky escape; the situation could have been far worse.

As Joe entered the bridge Terry turned, his battered, scar-covered face showing obvious concern. That face always intrigued Joe. At some point in the past, it had undergone considerable involuntary re-arrangement. Joe did not ask; it was not his business. That's how it was in the Belt.

"Any hull breaches?"

"The engine module, tanks and upper work bays," Terry replied. "The shower hit mostly aft of the wheels. Bit of luck, hey Boss?"

"Engineering?"

"We lost … oh, hang on … got a faint pressure drop in wheel two." Terry peered briefly at a read-out above his head. "A pinhole breach—easy fixed."

"Fine. Engineering?"

"Oh, right. One engine out. Reactor's okay. One of the bigger buggers tore straight through the casing on the primary power loom forward of the radiation shield. A broken piece of the case must've taken out the power cables. Mari and Sam are getting ready to go now."

Joe nodded. Marius Pine and Sam Bright, the ship's chief and electrical engineers, would sort the mess soon enough. Joe took a great deal of pride in *Butterball's* crew. They did their jobs expertly, neither needing nor expecting orders. Joe pulled himself into the command chair.

The mineral prospecting ship *Butterball* began life as a long-haul supply freighter built for the Earth to Mars cargo run before the Resources War. Little more than a long, spinal gantry connecting the bridge and docking module to the aft engineering units, she resembled a giant stick insect in space. The backbone contained an access corridor and formed the conduit through which ran high-voltage lines delivering electricity from the reactor to all other parts of the ship. Those cables now lay in shreds.

The view on the command screen currently looked aft towards the radiation shadow-shield. Behind the bridge module, two counter-rotating habitat wheels contained the living and working quarters for the crew. With the loss of power, the vessel now functioned on batteries alone, and rotation of both wheels had stopped.

Further aft, removable work and cargo flats sat around the spine. From there, the business of mineral surveying and prospecting took place. In the bottom, forward work bay Marius and Sam were getting ready to begin emergency repairs.

Long streamers of liquid spewed into space from two of the many tanks lining either side of the gantry between the upper and lower flats, diffusing into rainbow clouds of crystallized, frozen vapor. *Butterball's* lifeblood boiled away in a cloud of glittering diamonds.

"Xenon numbers three and seven," Terry confirmed. "There's still enough to get home once we carry out repairs, but only just. We still got one fusion engine, so we should be solid, Boss."

Joe's heart sank. The ship's main engine was a xenon-ion drive that provided low but constant thrust and used little fuel. This allowed her to accelerate at a slow, steady rate, ideal for her original intended purpose of freighting between Earth and Mars but useless for working the asteroids.

Above and below the primary engine were twin deuterium-tritium fusion boosters, fitted during the refit for faster maneuvering near targets in the Belt. One was now out of action, so *Butterball* would have to rely more on the ion drive, making close-quarters work more difficult.

Joe cringed as the proximity alarm let out a loud, chilling wail.

Something unseen slammed into the still functional number-one booster. At enormous velocity, the baseball-sized meteoroid punched through the unit, reducing it to a twisted mass of scrap metal as the impact wrenched it from its mountings. Alarms screeched as the ship automatically cut the wrecked unit off from the reactor.

Joe slumped back into his seat, took a deep breath and waited for his heart to stop pounding. If the rock had struck a meter or two lower, it would have hit the ion drive. A few meters further forward and it would have taken out the reactor and killed them all.

It was a frighteningly close call.

"Shit," he murmured. "Trip's over."

\*     \*     \*

Allan 'Waldo' Pearce peered through the fogged windscreen as he maneuvered his brand new Porsche into the darkened parking lot. Hoarfrost-covered gravel crunched beneath the tires as he turned into what he considered his personal parking space and killed the ignition.

Easing ample legs sideways, he struggled to extricate himself from the seat—the direct result of a large, overweight man in a sleek, underweight car. He peered up towards the ridge. In the darkness ahead, the massive, ghostly domes of the Franklin Telescope Complex loomed in the crisp night sky.

The facility perched far back on the western edge of the Mount Wellington plateau, over a thousand meters closer to the stars in the clear, southern skies of Tasmania. From here, the resident scientists enjoyed an unequaled view of the galaxy, but still with the nearby comforts of the cozy metropolis of Hobart. Little more than an hour away, the small capital city of

Australia's island state sprawled along the lower, eastern slopes of the mountain and the beautiful Derwent River Estuary.

With the full bulk of the flat-topped mountain between, the city lights did not interfere with the telescopes, and the closeness of civilization compensated for the long hours of solitude with which Allan chose to fill his life.

"God, it's bloody freezing up here," he cursed. He hated the cold but accepted it for the sake of his work. Eager to escape the late autumn chill he reached in to retrieve his briefcase and bag, and then locked the door of the vehicle. For a man of his size the sports car was absurd, but he drove it regardless to remind everyone a man of his status could afford the better things in life. Without doubt one of the preeminent members of his profession, he found getting respect from his fellow workers the hardest part of the job.

He shivered, and crunched his way along the gravel walkway between the lot and the entrance to the observatory. With every labored step his breath streamed in curling whorls of frozen white drifting away into the night. A battered, old, leather jacket did little to warm him as he pulled it tight around his girth and pressed on.

Low, shielded footlights lit the way. The management permitted an absolute minimum of exterior lighting around this complex, to avoid interference with the array of giant optical telescopes. At the front entrance, Allan pushed his way through the swinging doors into the comparative warmth of the foyer.

"Evening, Allan," the security guard greeted, his eyes remaining glued to his newspaper and the steaming coffee in his hand. Allan ignored him, turning towards the reception center. The man annoyed him, and persisted in addressing him by his first name. He shuffled across to the reception desk and the svelte, young woman with the misfortune to be tonight's shift manager.

He flashed his best, winning smile. "Good evening, Sophia. How are you tonight?"

"None the better for being here," she replied, casting a disapproving glare at the astronomer's yellow-toothed leer.

"You can always cheer things up a bit by agreeing to dine with me sometime."

"In your dreams, Allan." She returned the sweetest smile she could muster.

The University fawned over Pearce, one of the most prominent astrophysicists in his field, and considered itself privileged to have him at all. Sophia did not share that opinion. Only his unshakable belief she would one day succumb to his charms allowed her to be so blunt without suffering the wrath of her superiors.

"Ah well, I live in hope." Wiping away a pretend tear, he lowered his head in feigned misery and shuffled in the direction of the control room.

On most nights, other scientists shared the complex, but tonight Allan worked solo. Of all the observatories he had worked in, he preferred this one. Possessing the latest in optical and computer systems, the lab had a small office in which he could work apart from the telescope's operational personnel.

He liked the solitude. Accepted, company through the long night hours could occasionally be pleasant, but he preferred working alone. Grateful for a chance to work undisturbed, he threw his bags to the floor and logged into the workstation.

With the system functioning properly, he waited as the telescope sought out the region containing his current object of interest. He had scanned the area several times in the past year but his latest, still unexplained discovery stemmed from a spontaneous decision to take a last look a few weeks ago.

An increasingly popular scientific endeavor in recent decades, hunting for asteroids, meteoroids and comets reflected an increasing awareness of the fact something enormous and soulless was inevitably destined to plow through humanity's peaceful and ignorant bliss in the near future.

First begun in the twentieth century, the field lost favor soon after, overshadowed by the more glamorous objective of finding exoplanets, particularly Earth-type ones. Forty years ago the search for near-space objects once again reached prominence due to a rock the size of a small bus slamming into the slums on the outskirts of the Indian city of Mumbai. Thousands died and a jaded branch of astronomy again became fashionable. Everyone suddenly realized there was an endless supply of cosmic bullets out there.

The trick lay not in finding anything new but rather, something changed. At regular intervals, scanners recorded a patch of sky and within minutes computers carried out a comparative analysis against previous records of the same area. Any variation triggered a report, flagging the anomaly for closer inspection. Any change in position indicated a body, a comet or asteroid, moving through near space.

The operations manager already had the schedule for the night, so while the hired help got the scope ready Allan shuffled over to the kitchen to brew a fresh batch of coffee.

In his mind, astronomy rode on caffeine. He intended to consume far more than considered healthy in the course of the night, sufficient to keep him tossing in his bed all the next day. With the first of many cups in hand, he returned to the desk and checked the screen.

"Ah, there you are my little beauty."

A dozen observatories were tracking this new target but Allan had found it first. In the last few years, using either Earth based observatories or orbiting satellite telescopes, he had discovered numerous comets and other significant objects, a score placing him comfortably in the ranks of his field, he thought.

He always insisted his discoveries be in some way named after him; he never succeeded. It was against current convention to have an astronomical body named after the discoverer.

The target tentatively designated *NE372BJ4* first appeared fifteen days ago, an uncatalogued object barreling in from the far reaches of the Solar System. A bright blue flare on a single image first drew Allan's attention to this specific region of space. The phenomena did not re-occur, but the scan identified an unusual target moving near the coordinates of the original event.

Something about this one did not gel. Object *NE372BJ4* appeared slightly elongated by the vapor tail typical of all comets, but it was still well beyond the orbit of the planet Jupiter, much too far from the Sun for a tail to be developing. In addition, the light curve was wrong. Uniform and unvaryingly bright, it differed from other objects in deep space, which tended to fluctuate in brightness as they rotated or tumbled.

A week earlier, Allan had contacted a friend at the Outer System Exploration Laboratory. By sheer coincidence, *OSEL's* latest mission was close to the target, so the university had lodged a formal request for the probe to take a photograph. The unmanned *Cox 24* spacecraft would pass *NE372BJ4* at a distance of less than five-hundred-thousand kilometers, a hop and a step in astronomical terms.

Intrigued by Allan's discovery, OSEL agreed to power up its systems as the two travelers shot past each other at breakneck speed. The encounter had come and gone hours earlier, and tonight Allan expected to see the results.

By the time the call came, he was well into his third game of computer chess and fourth packet of potato chips, the crumbled remains of which lay scattered everywhere around his chair. The monitor to his left flickered and Davis Clarke, a close friend and member of the *Cox 24* team, peered out from beneath long and untamed hair. Behind him a small group of fellow workers milled about, drinks in hand, as they smiled and waved in the direction of the camera.

"That you, Waldo?"

"Hey, Dave. What's with the crowd? You guys having a party or something?"

"Yeah man. Got bad news for you. You don't get to name another comet after yourself. Hard cheese, old buddy."

"Shit!" Allan shoved his keyboard aside and turned to face Clarke, more than a little annoyed at his associate's lack of tact. "Why the hell not?"

"Check your data feed."

Allan turned his attention back to his workstation as a series of images began to scroll across the screen. As the first came up, he took his closest look yet at object *NE372BJ4*.

"You're going to be famous, buddy," Clarke said.

"I'm already..." For a few short moments, he stared at the fuzzy, elongated image. His jaw dropped. "Holy snappin' duck sh..."

"You're a rock star Allan." Clark's voice faded into the distance. "We're *all* going to be famous, man!"

If you would like to continue reading "**FALCON'S CALL**" you can check it out at:

http://www.mikewallerauthor.com

# ABOUT THE AUTHOR

Mike Waller is a writer of Science Fiction and Space Opera adventures, including the 'Echo's Way' stories and other stand-alone works. He currently lives in Queensland, Australia.

Mike's online home is at:
https://www.mikewallerauthor.com/

You can connect with him on Facebook at:
https://www.facebook.com/AuthorMikeWaller/

You should email him at
mike.waller@mikewallerauthor.com
Mike answers every email received.

# GET A FREE BOOK from Mike Waller

Join my reader's group, and receive a free copy of one of my books

Building a relationship with my readers is the very best thing about writing. I occasionally send non-spamming newsletters to members of my Readers Group, with details on new releases, special offers and other bits of news relating to my and other authors' books. You can unsubscribe from the group at any time.

http://www.mikewallerauthor.com

# Books by Mike Waller

## The 'ECHO'S WAY Series
Solitude's End – An Echo's Way Adventure
Dark World – An Echo's Way Adventure
Enemy Ally – An Echo's Way Adventure

## The FALCON Trilogy
Falcon's Call
Falcon's Ghost
Falcon's Bane

## Other
Hawk: Hellfire
Brothers Of Mind

Check them all out at:
http://www.mikewallerauthor.com

MIKE WALLER

www.ingramcontent.com/pod-product-compliance
Lightning Source LLC
Chambersburg PA
CBHW050141120726
47903CB00002B/444